Deemed 'the father of the ~~scientific detective story~~ , ~~R.~~
Austin Freeman had a long and distinguished career, not least as
a writer of detective fiction. He was born in London, the son of a
tailor who went on to train as a pharmacist. After graduating as
a surgeon at the Middlesex Hospital Medical College, Freeman
taught for a while and joined the colonial service, offering his skills
as an assistant surgeon along the Gold Coast of Africa. He became
embroiled in a diplomatic mission when a British expeditionary
party was sent to investigate the activities of the French. Through
his tact and formidable intelligence, a massacre was narrowly
avoided. His future was assured in the colonial service. However,
after becoming ill with blackwater fever, Freeman was sent back to
England to recover and, finding his finances precarious, embarked
on a career as acting physician in Holloway Prison. In desperation,
he turned to writing and went on to dominate the world of
British detective fiction, taking pride in testing different criminal
techniques. So keen were his powers as a writer that part of one of
his best novels was written in a bomb shelter.

The Puzzle Lock

R Austin Freeman

HOUSE OF
STRATUS

This edition published in 2001 by House of Stratus, an imprint of
Stratus Books Ltd., 21 Beeching Park, Kelly Bray,
Cornwall, PL17 8QS, UK.

www.houseofstratus.com

Typeset, printed and bound by House of Stratus.

A catalogue record for this book is available from the British Library
and the Library of Congress.

ISBN 0-7551-0373-4

TO
VINCENT STARRET

CONTENTS

CHAPTER ONE

The Puzzle Lock

I do not remember what was the occasion of my dining with Thorndyke at Giamborini's on the particular evening that is now in my mind. Doubtless, some piece of work completed had seemed to justify the modest festival. At any rate, there we were, seated at a somewhat retired table, selected by Thorndyke, with our backs to the large window through which the late June sunlight streamed. We had made our preliminary arrangements, including a bottle of Barsac, and were inspecting dubiously a collection of semi-edible *hors d'oeuvres*, when a man entered and took possession of a table just in front of ours, which had apparently been reserved for him, since he walked directly to it and drew away the single chair that had been set aslant against it.

I watched with amused interest his methodical procedure, for he was clearly a man who took his dinner seriously. A regular customer, too, I judged by the waiter's manner and the reserved table with its single chair. But the man himself interested me. He was out of the common and there was a suggestion of character, with perhaps a spice of oddity, in his appearance. He appeared to be about sixty years of age, small and spare, with a much wrinkled, mobile and rather whimsical face, surmounted by a crop of white, upstanding hair. From his waistcoat pocket protruded the ends of a fountain-pen, a pencil and a miniature electric torch such as surgeons use; a silver-mounted Coddington lens hung from his watch-guard and the middle finger of his left hand bore the largest seal ring that I have ever seen.

"Well," said Thorndyke, who had been following my glance, "what do you make of him?"

"I don't quite know," I replied. "The Coddington suggests a naturalist or a scientist of some kind, but that blatant ring doesn't. Perhaps he is an antiquary or a numismatist or even a philatelist. He deals with small objects of some kind."

At this moment a man who had just entered strode up to our friend's table and held out his hand, which the other shook, with no great enthusiasm, as I thought. Then the newcomer fetched a chair, and setting it by the table, seated himself and picked up the menu card, while the other observed him with a shade of disapproval. I judged that he would rather have dined alone, and that the personality of the new arrival – a flashy, bustling, obtrusive type of man – did not commend him.

From this couple my eye was attracted to a tall man who had halted near the door and stood looking about the room as if seeking someone. Suddenly he spied an empty, single table, and, bearing down on it, seated himself and began anxiously to study the menu under the supervision of a waiter. I glanced at him with slight disfavour. One makes allowances for the exuberance of youth, but when a middle-aged man presents the combination of heavily-greased hair parted in the middle, a waxed moustache of a suspiciously intense black, a pointed imperial and a single eye-glass, evidently ornamental in function, one views him with less tolerance. However, his get-up was not my concern, whereas my dinner was, and I had given this my undivided attention for some minutes when I heard Thorndyke emit a soft chuckle.

"Not bad," he remarked, setting down his glass.

"Not at all," I agreed, "for a restaurant wine."

"I was not alluding to the wine," said he, "but to our friend Badger."

"The inspector!" I exclaimed. "He isn't here, is he? I don't see him."

"I am glad to hear you say that, Jervis," said he. "It is a better effort than I thought. Still, he might manage his properties a little better. That is the second time his eye-glass has been in the soup."

Following the direction of his glance, I observed the man with the waxed moustache furtively wiping his eye-glass; and the temporary absence of the monocular grimace enabled me to note a resemblance to the familiar features of the detective officer.

"If you say that is Badger, I suppose it is," said I. "He is certainly a little like our friend. But I shouldn't have recognised him."

"I don't know that I should," said Thorndyke, "but for the little unconscious tricks of movement. You know the habit he has of stroking the back of his head and of opening his mouth and scratching the side of his chin. I saw him do it just now. He had forgotten his imperial until he touched it, and then the sudden arrest of movement was very striking. It doesn't do to forget a false beard."

"I wonder what his game is," said I. "The disguise suggest that he is on the look-out for somebody who might know him; but apparently that somebody has not turned up yet. At any rate, he doesn't seem to be watching anybody in particular."

"No," said Thorndyke. "But there is somebody whom he seems rather to avoid watching. Those two men at the table in front of ours are in his direct line of vision, but he hasn't looked at them once since he sat down, though I noticed that he gave them one quick glance before he selected his table. I wonder if he has observed us. Probably not, as we have the strong light of the window behind us and his attention is otherwise occupied."

I looked at the two men and from them to the detective, and I judged that my friend was right. On the inspector's table was a good-sized fern in an ornamental pot, and this he had moved so that it was directly between him and the two strangers to whom he must have been practically invisible; and now I could see that he did, in fact, steal an occasional glance at them over the edge of the menu card. Moreover, as their meal drew to an end, he hastily finished his own and beckoned to the waiter to bring the bill.

"We may as well wait and see them off," said Thorndyke, who had already settled our account. "Badger always interests me. He is so ingenious and he has such shockingly bad luck."

We had not long to wait. The two men rose from the table and walked slowly to the door, where they paused to light their cigars before going out. Then Badger rose, with his back towards them and his eyes on the mirror opposite; and as they went out, he snatched up his hat and stick and followed. Thorndyke looked at me inquiringly.

"Do we indulge in the pleasure of the chase?" he asked, and as I replied in the affirmative, we, too, made our way out and started in the wake of the inspector.

As we followed Badger at a discreet distance, we caught an occasional glimpse of the quarry ahead, whose proceedings evidently caused the inspector some embarrassment, for they had a way of stopping suddenly to elaborate some point that they were discussing, whereby it became necessary for the detective to drop farther in the rear than was quite safe, in view of the rather crowded state of the pavement. On one of these occasions, when the older man was apparently delivering himself of some excruciating joke, they both turned suddenly and looked back, the joker pointing to some object on the opposite side of the road. Several people turned to see what was being pointed at, and, of course, the inspector had to turn, too, to avoid being recognised. At this moment the two men popped into an entry, and when the inspector once more turned they were gone.

As soon as he missed them, Badger started forward almost at a run, and presently halted at the large entry of the Celestial Bank Chambers, into which he peered eagerly. Then, apparently sighting his quarry, he darted in, and we quickened our pace and followed. Halfway down the long hall we saw him standing at the door of a lift, frantically pressing the call-button.

"Poor Badger!" chuckled Thorndyke, as we walked past him unobserved. "His usual luck! He will hardly run them to earth

4

now in this enormous building. We may as well go through to the Blenheim Street entrance."

We pursued our way along the winding corridor and were close to the entrance when I noticed two men coming down the staircase that led to the hall.

"By Jingo! Here they are!" I exclaimed. "Shall we run and give Badger the tip?"

Thorndyke hesitated. But it was too late. A taxi had just driven up and was discharging its fare. The younger man, catching the driver's eye, ran out and seized the door-handle; and when his companion had entered the cab, he gave an address to the driver, and, stepping in quickly, slammed the door. As the cab moved off, Thorndyke pulled out his note-book and pencil and jotted down the number of the vehicle. Then we turned and retraced our steps; but when we reached the lift-door, the inspector had disappeared. Presumably, like the incomparable Tom Bowling, he had gone aloft.

"We must give it up, Jervis," said Thorndyke. "I will send him – anonymously – the number of the cab, and that is all we can do. But I am sorry for Badger."

With this we dismissed the incident from our minds – at least, I did; assuming that I had seen the last of the two strangers. Little did I suspect how soon and under what strange and tragic circumstances I should meet with them again!

It was about a week later that we received a visit from our old friend, Superintendent Miller of the Criminal Investigation Department. The passing years had put us on a footing of mutual trust and esteem, and the capable, straightforward detective officer was always a welcome visitor.

"I've just dropped in," said Miller, cutting off the end of the inevitable cigar, "to tell you about a rather queer case that we've got in hand. I know you are always interested in queer cases."

Thorndyke smiled blandly. He had heard that kind of preamble before, and he knew, as did I, that when Miller became communicative we could safely infer that the Millerian bark was in shoal water.

"It is a case," the superintendent continued, "of a very special brand of crook. Actually there is a gang, but it is the managing director that we have particularly got our eye on."

"Is he a regular 'habitual,' then?" asked Thorndyke.

"Well," replied Miller, "as to that, I can't positively say. The fact is that we haven't actually seen the man to be sure of him."

"I see," said Thorndyke, with a grim smile. "You mean to say that you have got your eye on the place where he isn't."

"At the present moment," Miller admitted, "that is the literal fact. We have lost sight of the man we suspected, but we hope to pick him up again presently. We want him badly, and his pals too. It is probably quite a small gang, but they are mighty fly; a lot too smart to be at large. And they'll take some catching, for there is someone running the concern with a good deal more brains than crooks usually have."

"What is their lay?" I asked.

"Burglary," he replied. "Jewels and plate, but principally jewels; and the special feature of their work is that the swag disappears completely every time. None of the stuff has ever been traced. That is what drew our attention to them. After each robbery we made a round of all the fences, but there was not a sign. The stuff seemed to have vanished into smoke. Now that is very awkward. If you never see the men and you can't trace the stuff, where are you? You've got nothing to go on."

"But you seem to have got a clue of some kind," I said.

"Yes. There isn't a lot in it; but it seemed worth following up. One of our men happened to travel down to Colchester with a certain man, and when he came back two days later, he noticed this same man on the platform at Colchester and saw him get out at Liverpool Street. In the interval there had been a jewel robbery at Colchester. Then there was a robbery at Southampton, and our man went at once to Waterloo and saw all the trains in. On the second day, behold! The Colchester sportsman turns up at the barrier, so our man, who had a special taxi waiting, managed to track him home and afterwards got some particulars about him. He is a chap named Shemmonds; belongs to a firm of outside brokers. But nobody seems to know much about him and he doesn't put in much time at the office.

"Well, then, Badger took him over and shadowed him for a day or two, but just as things were looking interesting, he slipped off the hook. Badger followed him to a restaurant, and, through the glass door, saw him go up to an elderly man at a table and shake hands with him. Then he took a chair at the table himself, so Badger popped in and took a seat neat them where he could keep them in view. They went out together and Badger followed them, but he lost them in the Celestial Bank Chambers. They went up in the lift just before he could get to the door and that was the last he saw of them. But we have ascertained that they left the building in a taxi and that the taxi set them down at Great Turnstile."

"It was rather smart of you to trace the cab," Thorndyke remarked.

"You've got to keep your eyes skinned in our line of business," said Miller. "But now we come to the real twister. From the time those two men went down Great Turnstile, nobody has set eyes on either of them. They seem to have vanished into thin air."

"You found out who the other man was, then?" said I.

"Yes. The restaurant manager knew him; an old chap named Luttrell. And we knew him, too, because he has a thumping burglary insurance, and when he goes out of town he notifies his company, they make arrangements with us to have the premises watched."

"What is Luttrell?" I asked.

"Well, he is a bit of a mug, I should say, at least that's his character in the trade. Goes in for being a dealer in jewels and antiques, but he'll buy anything – furniture, pictures, plate, any blooming thing. Does it for a hobby, the regular dealers say. Likes the sport of bidding at the sales. But the knock-out men hate him; never know what he's going to do. Must have private means, for though he doesn't often drop money, he can't make much. He's no salesman. It is the buying that he seems to like. But he is a regular character, full of cranks and oddities. His rooms in Thavie Inn look like the British Museum gone mad. He has got electric alarms from all the doors up to his bedroom and the strong-room in his office is fitted with a puzzle lock instead of keys."

"That doesn't seem very safe," I remarked.

"It is," said Miller. "This one has fifteen alphabets. One of our men has calculated that it has about forty million changes. No one is going to work that out, and there are no keys to get lost. But it is that strong-room that is worrying us, as well as the old joker himself. The Lord knows how much valuable stuff there is in it. What we are afraid of is that Shemmonds may have made away with the old chap and be lying low, waiting to swoop down on that strong-room."

"But you said that Luttrell goes away sometimes," said I.

"Yes; but then he always notifies his insurance company and he seals up his strong-room with a tape round the door-handle and a great seal on the door-post. This time he hasn't notified the company and the door isn't sealed. There's a seal on the door-post – left from last time, I expect – but only the cut ends of tape. I got the caretaker to let me see the place this morning; and, by the way, Doctor, I have taken a leaf out of your book. I always carry a bit of squeezing wax in my pocket now and a little box of French chalk. Very handy they are, too. As I had 'em with me this morning, I took a squeeze of the seal. May want it presently for identification."

He brought out of his pocket a small tin box from which he carefully extracted an object wrapped in tissue paper. When the paper had been tenderly removed there was revealed a lump of moulding wax, one side of which was flattened and bore a sunk design.

"It's quite a good squeeze," said Miller, handing it to Thorndyke. "I dusted the seal with French chalk so that the wax shouldn't stick to it."

My colleague examined the "squeeze" through his lens, and passing it and the lens to me, asked: "Has this been photographed, Miller?"

"No," was the reply, "but it ought to be before it gets damaged."

"It ought, certainly," said Thorndyke, "if you value it. Shall I get Polton to do it now?"

The superintendent accepted the offer gratefully and Thorndyke accordingly took the squeeze up to the laboratory, where he left it for our assistant to deal with. When he returned, Miller remarked:

"It is a baffling case, this. Now that Shemmonds has dropped out of sight, there is nothing to go on and nothing to do but wait for something else to happen; another burglary or an attempt on the strong-room."

"Is it clear that the strong-room has not been opened?" asked Thorndyke.

"No, it isn't," replied Miller. "That's part of the trouble. Luttrell has disappeared and he may be dead. If he is, Shemmonds will probably have been through his pockets. Of course there is no strong-room key. That is one of the advantages of a puzzle lock. But it is quite possible that Luttrell may have kept a note of the combination and carried it about him. It would have been risky to trust entirely to memory. And he would have had the keys of the office about him. Any one who had those could have slipped in during business hours without much difficulty. Luttrell's premises are empty, but there are people in and out all day going to the other office. Our man can't follow them all in. I suppose you can't make any suggestion, Doctor?"

"I am afraid I can't," answered Thorndyke. "The case is so very much in the air. There is nothing against Shemmonds but bare suspicion. He has disappeared only in the sense that you have lost sight of him, and the same is true of Luttrell – though there is an abnormal element in his case. Still, you could hardly get a search-warrant on the facts that are known at present."

"No," Miller agreed, "they certainly would not authorise us to break open the strong-room, and nothing short of that would be much use."

Here Polton made his appearance with the wax squeeze in a neat little box such as jewellers use.

"I've got two enlarged negatives," said he; "nice clear ones. How many prints shall I make for Mr Miller?"

"Oh, one will do, Mr Polton," said the superintendent. "If I want any more I'll ask you." He took up the little box, and, slipping it in his pocket, rose to depart. "I'll let you know, Doctor, how the case goes on, and perhaps you wouldn't mind turning it over a bit in the interval. Something might occur to you."

Thorndyke promised to think over the case, and when we had seen the superintendent launched down the stairs, we followed Polton up to the laboratory, where we each picked up one of the negatives and examined it against the light. I had already identified the seal by its shape – *vesica piscis* or boat-shape – with the one that I had seen on Mr Luttrell's finger. Now, in the photograph, enlarged three diameters, I could clearly make out the details. The design was distinctive and curious rather than elegant. The two triangular spaces at the ends were occupied respectively by a *memento mori* and a winged hour-glass and the central portion was filled by a long inscription in Roman capitals, of which I could at first make nothing.

"Do you suppose this is some kind of cryptogram?" I asked.

"No," Thorndyke replied. "I imagine the words were run together merely to economise space. This is what I make of it."

He held the negative in his left hand, and with his right wrote down in pencil on a slip of paper the following four lines of doggerel verse:

> "Eheu alas how fast the dam fugaces
> Labuntur anni especially in the cases
> Of poor old blokes like you and me Posthumus
> Who only wait for vermes to consume us."

"Well," I exclaimed, "it is a choice specimen; one of old Luttrell's merry conceited jests, I take it. But the joke was hardly worth the labour of engraving on a seal."

"It is certainly a rather mild jest," Thorndyke admitted. "But there may be something more in it than meets the eye."

He looked at the inscription reflectively and appeared to read it through once or twice. Then he replaced the negative in the drying rack, and, picking up the paper, slipped it into his pocketbook.

"I don't quite see," said I, "why Miller brought this case to us or what he wants you to think over. In fact, I don't see that there is a case at all."

"It is a very shadowy case," Thorndyke admitted. "Miller had done a good deal of guessing, and so has Badger; and it may easily turn out that they have found a mare's nest. Nevertheless there is something to think about."

"As, for instance – ?"

"Well, Jervis, you saw the men; you saw how they behaved; you have heard Miller's story and you have seen Mr Luttrell's seal. Put all those data together and you have the material for some very interesting speculation, to say the least. You might even carry it beyond speculation."

I did not pursue the subject, for I knew that when Thorndyke used the word "speculation," nothing would induce him to commit himself to an opinion. But later, bearing in mind the attention that he had seemed to bestow on Mr Luttrell's schoolboy verses, I got a print from the negative and studied the foolish inscription exhaustively. But if it had any hidden meaning – and I could imagine no reason for supposing that it had – that meaning remained hidden; and the only conclusion at which I could arrive was that a man of Luttrell's age might have know better than to write such nonsense.

The superintendent did not leave the matter long in suspense. Three days later he paid us another visit and half-apologetically reopened the subject.

"I am ashamed to come badgering you like this," he said, "but I can't get this case out of my head. I've a feeling that we ought to get a move of some kind on. And, by the way – though that is nothing to do with it – I've copied out the stuff on that seal and I can't make any sense of it. What the deuce are fugaces? I suppose 'vermes' are worms, though I don't see why he spelt it that way."

"The verses," said Thorndyke, "are apparently a travesty of a Latin poem; one of the odes of Horace which begins;

> 'Eheu! fugaces, Postume, Postume,
> Labuntur anni,'

which means, in effect, 'Alas! Postume, the flying years slip by.' "

"Well," said Miller, "any fool knows that – any middle-aged fool, at any rate. No need to put it into Latin. However, it's of no consequence. To return to this case; I've got an authority to look over Luttrell's premises – not to pull anything about, you know, just to look round. I called in on my way here to let the caretaker know that I should be coming in later. I thought that perhaps you might like to come with me. I wish you would Doctor. You've got such a knack of spotting things that other people overlook."

He looked wistfully at Thorndyke, and as the latter was considering the proposal, he added:

"The caretaker mentioned a rather odd circumstance. It seems that he keeps an eye on the electric meters in the building and that he has noticed a leakage of current in Mr Luttrell's. It is only a small leak; about thirty watts an hour. But he can't account for it in any way. He has been right through the premises to see if any lamp has been left on in any rooms. But all the switches are off everywhere, and it can't be a short circuit. Funny, isn't it?"

It was certainly odd, but there seemed to me nothing in it to account for the expression of suddenly awakened interest that I detected in Thorndyke's face. However, it evidently had some special significance for him, for he asked almost eagerly:

"When are you making your inspection?"

"I am going there now," replied Miller, and he added coaxingly: "Couldn't you manage to run round with me?"

Thorndyke stood up. "Very well," said he. "Let us go together. You may as well come too, Jervis, if you can spare an hour."

I agreed readily, for my colleague's hardly disguised interest in the inspection suggested a definite problem in his mind; and we at once issued forth and made our way by Mitre Court and Fetter Lane to the abode of the missing dealer, an old-fashioned house near the end of Thavies Inn.

"I've been over the premises once," said Miller, as the caretaker appeared with the keys, "and I think we had better begin the regular inspection with the offices. We can examine the stores and living-rooms afterwards."

We accordingly entered the outer office, and as this was little more than a waiting-room, we passed through into the private office, which had the appearance of having been used also as a sitting-room or study. It was furnished with an easy chair, a range of bookshelves and a handsome bureau bookcase, while in the end wall was the massive iron door of the strong-room. On this, as the chief object of interest, we all bore down, and the superintendent expounded its peculiarities.

"It is quite a good idea," said he, "this letter lock. There's no keyhole – though a safe-lock is pretty hopeless to pick even if there was a keyhole – and no keys to get lost. As to guessing what the 'open sesame' may be – well, just look at it. You could spend a lifetime on it and be no forrader."

The puzzle lock was contained in the solid iron door-post, through a slot in which a row of fifteen A's seemed to grin defiance on the would-be safe-robber. I put my finger on the milled edges of one or two of the letters and rotated the discs, noticing how easily and smoothly they turned.

"Well," said Miller, "it's no use fumbling with that. I'm just going to have a look through his ledger and see who his customers were. The bookcase is unlocked. I tried it last time. And we'd better leave this as we found it."

He put back the letters that I had moved, and turned away to explore the bookcase; and as the letter-lock appeared to present nothing but an insoluble riddle, I followed him, leaving Thorndyke earnestly gazing at the meaningless row of letters.

The superintendent glanced back at him with an indulgent smile.

"The doctor is going to work out the combination," he chuckled. "Well, well. There are only forty million changes and he's a young man for his age."

With this encouraging comment, he opened the glass door of the bookcase, and reaching down for the ledger, laid it on the desk-like slope of the bureau.

"It is poor chance," said he, opening the ledger at the index, "but some of these people may be able to give us a hint where to look for Mr Luttrell, and it is worth while to know what sort of business he did."

He ran his finger down the list of names and had just turned to the account of one of the customers when we were started by a loud click from the direction of the strong-room. We both turned sharply and beheld Thorndyke grasping the handle of the strong-room door, and I saw with amazement that the door was now slightly ajar.

"God!" exclaimed Miller, shutting the ledger and starting forward, "he's got it open!" He strode over to the door and, directing an eager look at the indicator of the lock, burst into a laugh. "Well, I'm hanged!" he exclaimed. "Why, it was unlocked all the time! To think that none of us had the sense to tug the handle! But isn't it just like old Luttrell to have a fool's answer like that to the blessed puzzle!"

I looked at the indicator, not a little astonished to observe the row of fifteen A's, which apparently formed the key combination. It may have been a very amusing joke on Mr Luttrell's part, but it did not look very secure. Thorndyke regarded us with an inscrutable glance and still grasped the handle, holding the door a bare half-inch open.

"There is something pushing against the door," said he. "Shall I open it?"

"May as well have a look at the inside," replied Miller. Thereupon Thorndyke released the handle and quickly stepped aside. The door swung slowly open and the dead body of a man fell out into the room and rolled over on to its back.

"Mercy on us!" gasped Miller, springing back hastily and staring with horror and amazement at the grim apparition. "That is not Luttrell." Then, suddenly starting forward and stooping over the dead man, he exclaimed: "Why, it is Shemmonds. So that is where he disappeared to. I wonder what became of Luttrell."

"There is somebody else in the strong-room," said Thorndyke; and now, peering in through the doorway, I perceived a dim light, which seemed to come from a hidden recess, and by which I could see a pair of feet projecting round the corner. In a moment Miller had sprung in, and I followed. The strong-room was L-shaped in plan, the arm of the L formed by a narrow passage at right angles to the main room. At the end of this a single small electric bulb was burning, the light of which showed the body of an elderly man stretched on the floor of the passage. I recognised him instantly in spite of the dimness of the light and the disfigurement caused by a ragged wound on the forehead.

"We had better get him out of this," said Miller, speaking in a flurried tone, partly due to the shock of the horrible discovery and partly to the accompanying physical unpleasantness, "and then we will have a look around. This wasn't just a mere robbery. We are going to find things out."

With my help he lifted Luttrell's corpse and together we carried it out, laying it on the floor of the room at the farther end, to which we also dragged the body of Shemmonds.

"There is no mystery as to how it happened," I said, after a brief inspection of the two corpses. "Shemmonds evidently shot the old man from behind with the pistol close to the back of the head. The hair is all scorched round the wound of entry and the bullet came out at the forehead."

"Yes," agreed Miller, "that is all clear enough. But the mystery is why on earth Shemmonds didn't let himself out. He must have known that the door was unlocked. Yet instead of turning the handle, he must have stood there like a fool, battering at the door with his fists. Just look at his hands."

"The further mystery," said Thorndyke, who, all this time, had been making a minute examination of the lock both from without and within, "is how the door came to be shut. That is quite a curious problem."

"Quite," agreed Miller. "But it will keep. And there is a still more curious problem inside there. There is nearly all the swag from that Colchester robbery. Looks as if Luttrell was in it."

Half-reluctantly he re-entered the strong-room and Thorndyke and I followed. Near the angle of the passage he stooped to pick up an automatic pistol and a small, leather-bound book, which he opened and looked into by the light of the lamp. At the first glance he uttered an exclamation and shut the book with a snap.

"Do you know what this is?" he asked, holding it out to us. "It is the nominal roll, address book and journal of the gang. We've got them in the hollow of our hand; and it is dawning upon me that old Luttrell was the managing director whom I have been looking for so long. Just run your eyes along those shelves. That's loot; every bit of it. I can identify the articles from the lists that I made out."

He stood looking gloatingly along the shelves with their burden of jewellery, plate and other valuables. Then his eye lighted on a drawer in the end wall just under the lamp; an iron drawer with a disproportionately large handle and bearing a very legible label inscribed "unmounted stones."

"We'll have a look at his stock of unmounted gems," said Miller; and with that he bore down on the drawer, and seizing the handle, gave a vigorous pull. "Funny," said he. "It isn't locked, but something seems to be holding it back."

He planted his foot on the wall and took a fresh purchase on the handle.

"Wait a moment, Miller," said Thorndyke; but even as he spoke, the superintendent gave a mighty heave; the drawer came out a full two feet; there was a loud click, and a moment later the strong-room door slammed.

"Good God!" exclaimed Miller, letting go the drawer, which immediately slid in with another click. "What was that?"

"That was the door shutting," replied Thorndyke. "Quite a clever arrangement; like the mechanism of a repeater watch. Pulling out the drawer wound up and released a spring that shut the door. Very ingenious."

"But," gasped Miller, turning an ashen face to my colleague, "we're shut in!"

"You are forgetting," said I – a little nervously, I must admit – "that the lock is as we left it."

The superintendent laughed, somewhat hysterically. "What a fool I am!" said he. "As bad as Shemmonds. Still we may as well – " Here he started along the passage and I heard him groping his way to the door, and later heard the handle turn. Suddenly the deep silence of the tomb-like chamber was rent by a yell of terror.

"The door won't move! It's locked fast!"

On this I rushed along the passage with a sickening fear at my heart. And even as I ran, there rose before my eyes the horrible vision of the corpse with the battered hands that had fallen out when we opened the door of this awful trap. He had been caught as we were caught. How soon might it not be that some stranger would be looking in on our corpses.

In the dim twilight by the door I found Miller clutching the handle and shaking it like a madman. His self-possession was completely shattered. Nor was my own condition much better. I flung my whole weight on the door in the faint hope that the lock was not really closed, but the massive iron structure was as immovable as a stone wall. I was, nevertheless, gathering myself up for a second charge when I heard Thorndyke's voice close behind me.

"That is no use, Jervis. The door is locked. But there is nothing to worry about."

As he spoke, there suddenly appeared a bright circle of light from the little electric lamp that he always carried in his pocket. Within the circle, and now clearly visible, was a second indicator of the puzzle lock on the inside of the door-post. Its appearance was vaguely reassuring, especially in conjunction with Thorndyke's calm voice; and it evidently appeared so to Miller, for he remarked, almost in his natural tones:

"But it seems to be unlocked still. There is the same AAAAAA that it showed when we came in."

It was perfectly true. The slot of the letter-lock still showed the range of fifteen A's, just as it had when the door was open. Could it be that the lock was a dummy and that there was some other means of opening the door? I was about to put this question to Thorndyke when he put the lamp into my hand, and, gently pushing me aside, stepped up to the indicator.

"Keep the light steady, Jervis," said he, and forthwith he began to manipulate the milled edges of the letter discs, beginning, as I noticed, at the right, or reverse end of the slot and working backwards. I watched him with feverish interest and curiosity, as also did Miller, looking to see some word of fifteen letters develop in the slot. Instead of which, I saw, to my amazement and bewilderment, my colleague's finger transforming the row of A's into a succession of M's, which, however, were presently followed by an L and some X's. When the row was completed it looked like some remote, antediluvian date set down in Roman numerals.

"Try the handle now, Miller," said Thorndyke.

The superintendent needed no second bidding. Snatching at the handle, he turned it and bore heavily on the door. Almost instantly a thin line of light appeared at the edge; there was a sharp click, and the door swung open. We fell out immediately – at least the superintendent and I did – thankful to find ourselves outside and alive. But, as we emerged, we both became aware of a man, white-faced and horror-stricken of aspect, stooping over the two corpses at the other end of the room. Our appearance was so sudden and unexpected – for the massive solidity of the safe-door had rendered our movements inaudible outside – that, for a moment or two, he stood immovable, staring at us, wild-eyed and open-mouthed. Then, suddenly, he sprang up erect, and, darting to the door, opened it and rushed out with Miller close on his heels.

He did not get very far. Following the superintendent, I saw the fugitive wriggling in the embrace of a tall man on the pavement, who, with Miller's assistance, soon had a pair of handcuffs snapped on the man's wrists and then departed with his captive in search of a cab.

"That's one of 'em, I expect," said Miller, as we returned to the office, then, as his glance fell on the open strong-room door, he mopped his face with his handkerchief. "That door gives me the creeps to look at it," said he. "Lord! what a shake-up that was! I've never had such a scare in my life. When I heard that door shut and I remembered how that poor devil, Shemmonds, came tumbling out – phoo!" He wiped his brow again, and, walking towards the strong-room door asked: "By the way, what was the magic word after all?" He stepped up to the indicator, and, after a quick glance, looked round at me in surprise. "Why!" he exclaimed, "blow me if it isn't AAAA still! But the doctor altered it, didn't he?"

At that moment Thorndyke appeared from the strong-room, where he had apparently been conducting explorations, and to him the superintendent turned for an explanation.

"It is an ingenious device, said he; "in fact, the whole strong-room is a monument of ingenuity, somewhat misapplied, but perfectly effective, as Mr Shemmond's corpse testifies. The key-combination is a number expressed in Roman numerals, but the lock has a fly-back mechanism which acts as soon as the door begins to open. That was how Shemmonds was caught. He, no doubt purposely, avoided watching Luttrell set the lock – or else Luttrell didn't let him – but as he went in with his intended victim, he looked at the indicator and saw the row of A's, which he naturally assumed to be the key-combination. Then, when he tried to let himself out, of course, the lock wouldn't open.

"It is rather odd that he didn't try some other combination," said I.

"He probably did," replied Thorndyke; "but when they failed he would naturally come back to the A's, which he had seen when the door was open. This is how it works."

He shut the door, and then, closely watched by the superintendent and me, turned the milled rims of the letter-discs until the indicator showed a row of numerals thus: MMMMMMMCCCLXXXV. Grasping the handle, he turned it and gave a gentle pull, when the door began to open. But the instant it started from its bed, there was a loud click and all the letters of the indicator flew back to A.

"Well, I'm jiggered!" exclaimed Miller. "It must have been an awful suck in for that poor blighter, Shemmonds. Took me in, too. I saw those A's and the door open, and I thought I knew all about it. But what beats me, Doctor, is how you managed to work it out. I can't see what you had to go on. Would it be allowable to ask how it was done?"

"Certainly," replied Thorndyke; "but we had better defer the explanation. You have got those two bodies to dispose of and some other matters, and we must get back to our chambers. I will write down the key-combination, in case you want it, and then you must come and see us and let us know what luck you have had."

He wrote the numerals on a slip of paper, and when he handed it to the superintendent, we took our leave.

"I find myself," said I, as we walked home, "in much the same position as Miller. I don't see what you had to go on. It is clear to me that you not only worked out the lock-combination – from the seal inscription, as I assume – but that you identified Luttrell as the director of the gang. I don't, in the least, understand how you did it."

"And yet, Jervis," said he, "it was an essentially simple case. If you review it and cast up the items of evidence, you will see that we really had all the facts. The problem was merely to co-ordinate them and extract their significance. Take first the character of Luttrell. We saw the man in company with another, evidently a fairly intimate acquaintance. They were being shadowed by a detective, and it is pretty clear that they detected the sleuth, for they shook him off quite neatly. Later, we learn from Miller that one of these men is suspected to be a member of a firm of swell burglars and that the other is a well-to-do, rather eccentric and very miscellaneous dealer, who has a strong-room fitted with a puzzle lock. I am astonished that the usually acute Miller did not notice how well Luttrell fitted the part of the managing director whom he was looking for. Here was a dealer who bought and sold all sorts of queer but valuable things, who must have had unlimited facilities for getting rid of stones, bullion and silver, and who used a puzzle lock. Now, who uses a puzzle lock? No one, certainly, who can conveniently use a key. But to the manager of a gang of thieves it would be a valuable safeguard, for he might at any moment be robbed of his keys, and perhaps made away with. But he could not be robbed of the secret password, and his possession of it would be a security against murder. So you see that the simple probabilities pointed to Luttrell as the head of the gang.

"And now consider the problem of the lock. First, we saw that Luttrell wore on his left hand a huge, cumbrous seal ring, that he carried a Coddington lens on his watch-guard, and a small electric lamp in his pocket. That told us very little. But when Miller told us about the lock and showed us the squeeze of the seal, and when we saw that the seal bore a long inscription in minute lettering, a connection began to appear. As Miller justly observed, no man – and especially no elderly man – would trust the key-combination exclusively to his memory. He would carry about him some record to which he could refer in case his memory failed him. But that record would hardly be one that anybody could read, or the secrecy and safety of the lock would be gone. It would probably be some kind of cryptogram; and when we saw this inscription and considered it in conjunction with the lens and the lamp, it seemed highly probable that the key-combination was contained in the inscription; and that probability was further increased when we saw the nonsensical doggerel of which the inscription was made up. The suggestion was that the verses had been made for some purpose independent of their sense. Accordingly I gave the inscription very careful consideration.

"Now we learned from Miller that the puzzle lock had fifteen letters. The key might be one long word, such as 'superlativeness,' a number of short words, or some chemical or other formula. Or it was possible that it might be of the nature of a chronogram. I have never heard of chronograms being used for secret records or messages, but it has often occurred to me that they would be extremely suitable. And this was an exceptionally suitable case."

"Chronogram," said I. "Isn't that something connected with medals?"

"They have often been used on medals," he replied. "In effect, a chronogram is an inscription some of the letters of which form a date connected with the subject of the inscription. Usually the date letters are written or cut larger than the others for convenience in reading, but, of course, this is not essential. The principle of a chronogram is this. The letters of the Roman alphabet are of two kinds; those that are simply letters and nothing else, and those that are numerals as well as letters. The numeral letters are M = a thousand, D = five hundred, C = one hundred, L = fifty, X = ten, V = five, and I = one. Now, in deciphering a chronogram, you pick out all the numeral letters and add them up without regard to their order. The total gives you the date.

"Well, as I said, it occurred to me that this might be of the nature of a chronogram; but as the lock had letters and not figures, the number, if there was one, would have to be expressed in Roman numerals, and it would have to form a number of fifteen numeral letters. As it was thus quite easy to put my hypothesis to the test, I proceeded to treat the inscription as a chronogram and decipher it; and behold! It yielded a number of fifteen letters, which, of course, was as near certainty as was possible, short of actual experiment."

"Let us see how you did the decipherment," I said, as we entered our chambers and shut the door. I procured a large note-block and pencil, and, laying them on the table, drew up two chairs.

"Now," said I, "fire away."

"Very well," he said. "We will begin by writing the inscription in proper chronogram form with the numeral letters double size and treating the U's and V's and the W's as double V's according to the rules."

Here he wrote out the inscription in Roman capitals thus:

"EHEV ALAS HOVV FAST THE DAM FVGACES
LABVNTVR ANNI ESPECIALLY IN THE CASES
OF POOR OLD BLOKES LIKE YOV AND ME POSTHVMVS
VVHO ONLY VVAIT FOR VERMES TO CONSVME VS"

"Now," said he, "let us make a column of each line and add them up, thus:

	1			2			3			4	
V	=	5	L	=	50	L	=	50	VV	=	10
L	=	50	V	=	5	D	=	500	L	=	50
VV	=	10	V	=	5	L	=	50	VV	=	10
D	=	500	I	=	1	L	=	50	I	=	1
M	=	1000	C	=	100	I	=	1	V	=	5
V	=	5	I	=	1	V	=	5	M	=	1000
C	=	100	L	=	50	D	=	500	C	=	100
			L	=	50	M	=	1000	V	=	5
			I	=	1	V	=	5	M	=	1000
			C	=	100	M	=	1000	V	=	5
						V	=	5			
	1670			363			3166			2186	

"Now," he continued, "we take the four totals and add them together, thus:

$$1670$$
$$363$$
$$3166$$
$$2186$$
$$\overline{7385}$$

and we get the grand total of seven thousand three hundred and eighty-five, and this, expressed in Roman numerals, is MMMMMMMCCCLXXXV. Here, then, is a number consisting of fifteen letters, the exact number of spaces in the indicator of the puzzle lock; and I repeat that this striking coincidence, added to, or rather multiplied into, the other probabilities, made it practically certain that this was the key-combination. It remained only to test it by actual experiment."

"By the way," said I, "I noticed that you perked up rather suddenly when Miller mentioned the electric meter."

"Naturally," he replied. "It seemed that there must be a small lamp switched on somewhere in the building, and the only place that had not been examined was the strong-room. But if there was a lamp alight there, someone had been in the strong-room. And, as the only person who was known to be able to get in was missing, it seemed probable that he was in there still. But if he was, he was pretty certainly dead; and there was quite a considerable probability that someone else was in there with him, since his companion was missing, too, and both had disappeared at the same time. But I must confess that that spring drawer was beyond my expectations, though I suspected it as soon as I saw Miller pulling at it. Luttrell was an ingenious old rascal; he almost deserved a better fate. However, I expect his death will have delivered the gang into the hands of the police."

Events fell out as Thorndyke surmised. Mr Luttrell's little journal, in conjunction with the confession of the spy who had been captured on the premises, enabled the police to swoop down on the disconcerted gang before any breath of suspicion had reached them; with the result that they are now secured in strong-rooms of another kind whereof the doors are fitted with appliances as effective as, though less ingenious than, Mr Luttrell's puzzle lock.

CHAPTER TWO

The Green Check Jacket

The visits of our old friend, Mr Brodribb, even when strictly professional, usually took the outward form of a friendly call. On the present occasion there was no such pretence. The old solicitor entered our chambers carrying a small suitcase (the stamped initials on which, "R.M.," I noticed, instantly attracted an inquisitive glance from Thorndyke, being obviously not Mr Brodribb's own) which he placed on the table and then shook hands with an evident air of business.

"I have come, Thorndyke," he said, with usual directness, "to ask your advice on a matter which is causing me some uneasiness. Do you know Reginald Merrill?"

"Slightly,' was the reply. "I meet him occasionally in court; and, of course, I know him as the author of that interesting book on Prehistoric Flint-mines."

"Well," said Brodribb, "he has disappeared. He is missing. I don't like to use the expression; but when a responsible man is absent from his usual places of resort, when he apparently had no expectation of being so absent, and when he has made no provision for such absence, I think we may regard him as having disappeared in a legal sense. His absence calls for active inquiry."

"Undoubtedly," agreed Thorndyke; "and I take it that you are the person on whom the duty devolves?"

"I think so. I am his solicitor and the executor of his will – at least I believe so; and the only near relative of his whom I know is his nephew and heir, Ethelbert Crick, his sister's son. But Crick seems to have disappeared, too; and about the same time as Merrill. It is an extraordinary affair."

"You say that you believe you are Merrill's executor. Haven't you seen the will?"

"I have seen *a* will. I have it in my safe. But Merrill said he was going to draw up another, and he may have done so. But if he has, he will almost certainly have appointed me his executor, and I shall assume that he has and act accordingly."

"Was there any special reason for making a new will?" Thorndyke asked.

"Yes," replied Brodribb. "He has just come into quite a considerable fortune, and he was pretty well off before. Under the old will, practically the whole of his property went to Crick. There was a small bequest to a man named Samuel Horder, his cousin's son; and Horder was the alternative legatee if Crick should die before Merrill. Now, I understand Merrill to say that, in view of this extra fortune, he wished to do rather more for Horder, and I gathered that he proposed to divide the estate more or less equally between the two men. The whole estate was more than he thought necessary for Crick. And now, as we have cleared up the preliminaries, I will give you the circumstances of the disappearance.

"Last Wednesday, the 5th, I had a note from him saying that he would have some reports ready for me on the following day, but that he would be away from his office from 10.30 a.m. to about 6.30, and suggesting that I should send round in the evening if I wanted the papers particularly. Now it happened that my clerk, Page, had to go to a place near London Bridge on Thursday morning, and, oddly enough, he saw Mr Merrill come out of Edginton's, the ship-fitters, with a man who was carrying a largish handbag. There was nothing in it, of course, but Page is an observant man and he noticed Merrill's companion so far as to observe that he was wearing a Norfolk jacket of a greenish shepherd's plaid and a grey tweed hat. He also noted the time by the big clock in the street near to Edginton's – 11.46 – and that Merrill looked up at it, and that the two men then walked off rather quickly in the direction of the station. Well, in the evening, I sent Page round to Merrill's chambers in Figtree Court to get the papers. He arrived there just after 6.30, but he found the oak shut, and though he rapped at the door on the chance that Merrill might have come in – he lives in the chambers adjoining the office – there was no answer. So he went for a walk round the Temple, deciding to return a little later.

"Well, he had gone as far as the cloisters and was loitering there to look in the window of the wig-maker's shop when he saw a man in a greenish shepherd's plaid jacket and a tweed hat coming up Pump Court. As the man approached Page thought he recognised him; in fact, he felt so sure that he stopped him and asked him if he knew what time Mr Merrill would be home. But the man looked at him in astonishment. 'Merrill?' said he. 'I don't know anyone of that name.' Thereupon Page apologised and explained how he had been misled by the pattern and colour of the jacket.

"After walking about for nearly half an hour, Page went back to Merrill's chambers; but the oak was shut and he could get no answer by rapping with his stick, so he scribbled a note and dropped it into the letter-box and came away. The next morning I sent him round again, but the chambers were still shut up, and they have been shut up ever since; and nothing whatever has been seen or heard of Merrill.

"On Saturday, thinking it possible that Crick might be able to give me some news of his uncle, I called at his lodgings; and then, to my astonishment, I learned that he also was missing. He had gone away early on Thursday morning, saying that he had to go on business to Rochester, and that he might not be home to dinner. But he never came home at all. I called again on Sunday evening, and, as he had still not returned, I decided to take more active measures.

"This afternoon, immediately after lunch, I called at the Porter's Lodge, and, having briefly explained the circumstances and who I was, asked the porter to bring the duplicate key – which he had for the laundress – and accompany me to Mr Merrill's chambers to see if, by chance, the tenant might be lying in them dead or insensible. He assured me that this could not be the case, since he had given the key every morning to the laundress, who had, in fact, returned it to him only a couple of hours previously. Nevertheless, he took the key and looked up the laundress, who had rooms near the lodge, who was fortunately at home and who turned out to be a most respectable and intelligent elderly woman; and we went together to Merrill's chambers. The porter admitted us, and when we had been right through the set and ascertained definitely that Merrill was not there he handed the key to the laundress, Mrs Butler, and went away.

"When he was gone, I had a talk with Mrs Butler, from which some rather startling facts transpired. It seemed that on Thursday, as Merrill was going to be out all day, she took the opportunity to have a grand clean-up of the chambers, to tidy up the lobby, and to look over the chests of drawers and the wardrobe and shake out and brush the clothes and see that no moths had got in. 'When I had finished,' she said, 'the place was like the inside of a band-box; just as he liked to see it.'

" 'And, after all, Mrs Butler,' said I, 'he never did see it.'

" 'Oh, yes, he did,' says she. 'I don't know when he came in, but when I let myself in the next morning, I could see that he had been in since I left.'

" 'How did you know that?' I asked.

" 'Well,' says she, I left the carpet-sweeper standing against the wardrobe door. I remembered it after I left and would have gone back and moved it, but I had already handed the key in at the Porter's Lodge. But when I went in next morning it wasn't there. It had been moved into the corner by the fireplace. Then the looking-glass had been moved. I could see that, because, before I went away, I had tidied my hair by it, and being short, I had to tilt it to see my face in it. Now it was tilted to suit a tall person and I couldn't see myself in it. Then I saw that the shaving-brush had been moved, and when I put it back in its place, I found it was damp. It wouldn't have kept damp for twenty-four hours at this time of year,' – which was perfectly true, you know, Thorndyke."

"Perfectly," agreed Thorndyke, "that woman is an excellent observer."

"Well," continued Brodribb, "on this she examined the shaving soap and the sponge, and found them both perceptibly damp. It appeared practically certain that Merrill had been in on the preceding evening and had shaved; but by way of confirmation, I suggested that she should look over his clothes and see whether he had changed any of his garments. She did so, beginning with those that were hanging in the wardrobe, which she took down one at a time. Suddenly she gave a cry of surprise, and I got a bit of a start myself when she handed out a greenish shepherd's plaid Norfolk jacket.

" 'That jacket,' she said, 'was not here when I brushed these clothes,' and it was obvious from its dusty condition that it could not have been; and,' she added, 'I have never seen it before to my knowledge, and I think I should have remembered it.' I asked her if there was any coat missing and she answered that she brushed a grey tweed jacket that seemed to have disappeared.

"Well, it was a queer affair. The first thing to be done was to ascertain, if possible, whether that jacket was or was not Merrill's. That, I thought, you would be able to judge better than I; so I borrowed his suitcase and popped the jacket into it, together with another jacket that was undoubtedly his, for comparison. Here is the suitcase and the two jackets are inside."

"It is really a question that could be better decided by a tailor," said Thorndyke. "The difference of measurement can't be great if they could both be worn by the same person. But we shall see." He rose, and having spread some sheets of newspaper over the table, opened the suitcase and took out the two jackets, which he laid out side by side. Then, with his spring-tape, he proceeded systematically to measure the two garments, entering each pair of measurements on a slip of paper divided into two columns. Mr Brodribb and I watched him expectantly and compared the two sets of figures as they were written down; and very soon it became evident that they were, at least, not identical. At length Thorndyke laid down the tape, and picking up the paper, studied it closely.

"I think," he said, "we may conclude that these two jackets were not made for the same person. The differences are not great, but they are consistent. The elbow creases, for instance, agree with the total length of the sleeves. The owner of the green jacket has longer arms and a bigger span than Merrill, but his chest measurement is nearly two inches greater and he has much more sloping shoulders. He could hardly have buttoned Merrill's jacket."

"Then," said Brodribb, "the next question is, did Merrill come home in some other man's coat or did some other man enter his chambers? From what Page has told us it seems pretty evident that a stranger must have got into those chambers. But if that is so, the questions arise: What the deuce was the fellow's object in changing into Merrill's clothes and shaving? How did he get into Merrill's chamber? What was he doing there? What has become of Merrill? And what is the meaning of the whole affair?"

"To some of those questions," said Thorndyke, "the answers are fairly obvious. If we assume, as I do, that the owner of the green jacket is the man whom Page saw at London Bridge and afterwards in the cloisters, the reason for the change of garments becomes plain enough. Page told the man that he had identified him by this very distinctive jacket as the person with whom Merrill was last seen alive. Evidently that man's safety demanded that he should get rid of the incriminating jacket without delay. Then, as to his having shaved: did Page give you any description of the man?"

"Yes: he was a tallish man, about thirty-five, with a large dark moustache and a torpedo beard."

"Very well," said Thorndyke; "then we may say that the man who went into Merrill's chambers was a moustached bearded man in a green jacket and that the man who came out was a clean-shaved man in a grey jacket, whom Page himself would probably have passed without a second glance. And as to how he got into the chambers, evidently he let himself in with Merrill's key; and if he did, I am afraid we can make a pretty shrewd guess as to what has become of Merrill, and only hope that we are guessing wrong. As to what this man was doing in those chambers and what is the meaning of the whole affair, that is a more difficult question. If the man had Merrill's latch-key, we may assume that he had the rest of Merrill's keys; that he had, in fact, free access to any locked receptacles in those chambers. The circumstances suggest that he entered the chambers for the purpose of getting possession of some valuable objects contained in them. Do you happen to know whether Merrill had any property of considerable value on the premises?"

"I don't," replied Brodribb. "He had a safe, but I don't know what he kept in it. Principally documents, I should think. Certainly not money, in any considerable amounts. The only thing of value that I actually know of is the new will; and that would only be valuable – under certain circumstances."

The abrupt and rather ambiguous conclusion of Mr Brodribb's statement was not lost either on Thorndyke or on me. Apparently the cautious old lawyer had suddenly realised, as I had, that if anything had happened to Merrill, those "certain circumstances" had already come into being. From what he had told us it appeared that, under the new will, Crick stood to inherit a half of Mr Merrill's fortune, whereas under the old will he stood to inherit nearly the whole. And it was a great fortune. The loss or destruction of the new will would be worth a good many thousand pounds to Mr Crick.

"Well," said Brodribb, after a pause, "what is to be done? I suppose I ought to communicate with the police."

"You will have to, sooner or later," said Thorndyke; "but meanwhile, leave these two jackets – or, at least, the green one – with me for the present and let me see if I can extract any further information from it."

"You won't find anything in the pockets but dirt. I've tried them."

"I hope you left the dirt," said Thorndyke.

"I did," replied Brodribb, "excepting what came out on my fingers. Very well; I'll leave the coats with you for today, and I will see if I can get any further news of Crick from his landlady."

With this the old solicitor shook hands and went off with such an evident air of purpose that I remarked:

"Brodribb is off to find our whether Mr Crick was the proprietor of a green plaid Norfolk jacket."

Thorndyke smiled. "It was rather quaint," said he, "to see the sudden way in which he drew in his horns when the inwardness of the affair dawned on him. But we mustn't start with a preconceived theory. Our business is to get hold of some more facts. There is little enough to go on at present. Let us begin by having a good look at this green jacket."

He picked it up and carried it to the window, where we both looked it over critically.

"It is rather dusty," I remarked, "especially on the front, and there is a white mark on the middle button."

"Yes. Chalk, apparently; and if you look closely, there are white traces on the other buttons and on the front of the coat. The back is much less dirty."

As he spoke, Thorndyke turned the garment round and then, from the side of the skirt picked a small, hair-like object which he felt between his finger and thumb, looked at closely and handed to me.

"A bit of barley beard," said I, "and there are two more on the other side. He must have walked along a narrow path through a barley field – the state of the front of his coat almost suggests that he had crawled."

33

"Yes; it is earthy dust; but Polton's extractor will give us more information about that. We had better hand it over to him; but first we will go through the pockets in spite of Brodribb's discouragement."

"By Jove!" I exclaimed, as I thrust my hand into one of the side pockets, "he was right about the dirt. Look at this." I drew out my hand with a quite considerable pinch of dry earth and one or two little fragments of chalk. "It looks as if he had been crawling in loose earth."

"It does," Thorndyke agreed, inspecting his own "catch" – a pinch of reddish earth and a fragment of chalk of the size of a large pea. "The earth is very characteristic, this red-brown loam that you find overlying the chalk. All his outside pockets seem to have caught more or less of it. However, we can leave Polton to collect it and prepare it for examination. I'll take the coat up to him now, and while he is working at it I think I will walk round to Edginton's and see if I can pick up any further particulars."

He went up to the laboratory floor, where our assistant, Polton, carried on his curious and varied activities, and when he returned we sallied forth together. In Fleet Street we picked up a disengaged taxicab, by which we were whisked across Blackfriars Bridge and a few minutes later set down at the corner of Tooley Street. We made our way to the ship-chandler's shop, where Thorndyke proceeded to put a few discreet questions to the manager, who listened politely and with sympathetic interest.

"The difficulty is," said he, "that there were a good many gentlemen in here last Thursday. You say they came about 11.45. If you could tell me what they bought, we could look at the bill-duplicate book and that might help us."

"I don't actually know what they bought," said Thorndyke. "It might have been a length of rope; thinnish rope, perhaps, say twelve or fourteen fathoms, or perhaps more. But I may be wrong."

I stared at Thorndyke in amazement. Long as I had known him, this extraordinary faculty of instantaneous induction always came on me as a fresh surprise. I had supposed that in this case we had absolutely nothing to go on; and yet here he was with at least a tentative suggestion before the inquiry appeared to have begun. And that suggestion was clear evidence that he had already arrived at a hypothetical solution of the mystery. I was still pondering on this astonishing fact when the manager approached with an open book and accompanied by an assistant.

"I see," said he, "that there is an entry, apparently about midday on Thursday, of the sale of a fifteen-fathom length of deep-sea lead-line, and my friend, here, remembers selling it."

"Yes," the assistant confirmed, "I remember it because he wanted to get it into his handbag, and it took the three of us to stuff it in. Thick lead-line is pretty stiff when it's new."

"Do you remember what these gentlemen were like and how they were dressed?"

"One was a rather elderly gentleman, clean shaved, I think. The other I remember better because he had rather queer-looking eyes – very pale grey. He had a pointed beard and he wore a greenish check coat and a cloth hat. That's all I remember about him."

"It is more than most people would have remembered," said Thorndyke. "I am very much obliged to you; and I think I will ask you to let me have a fifteen-fathom length of that same lead-line."

By this time my capacity for astonishment was exhausted. What on earth could my colleague want with a deep-sea lead-line? But, after all, why not? If he had then and there purchased a Trotman's anchor, a shark-hook and a set of International code signals, I should have been prepared to accept the proceeding without comment. Thorndyke was a law unto himself.

Nevertheless, as I walked homeward by his side, carrying the coil of rope, I continued to speculate on this singular case. Thorndyke had arrived at a hypothetical solution of Mr Brodribb's problem; and it was evidently correct, so far, as the entry in the bill-book proved. But what was the connection between a dusty jacket and a length of thin rope? And why this particular length? I could make nothing of it. But I determined, as soon as we got home, to see what new facts Polton's activities had brought to light.

The results were disappointing. Polton's dust extractor – a sort of miniature vacuum cleaner – had been busy, and the products in the form of tiny heaps of dust, were methodically set out on a sheet of white paper, each little heap covered with a watch-glass and accompanied by its written particulars as to the part of the garment from which it had come. I examined a few samples under the microscope, but though curious and interesting, as all dust is, they showed nothing very distinctive. The dust might have come from anyone's coat. There was, of course, a good deal of yellowish sandy loam, a few particles of chalk, a quality of fine ash, clinker and particles of coal – railway dust from a locomotive – ordinary town and house dust and some oddments such as pollen grains, including those of the sow-thistle, mallow, poppy and valerian, and in one sample I found two scales from the wing of the common blue butterfly. That was all; and it told me nothing but that the owner of the coat had recently been in a chalk district and that he had taken a railway journey.

While I was working with the microscope, Polton was busy with an occupation that I did not understand. He had cemented the little pieces of chalk that we had found in the pockets to a plate of glass by means of pitch, and he was now brushing them under water with a soft brush and from time to time decanting the milky water into a tall sediment glass. Now, as most people know, chalk is largely composed of microscopic shells – foraminifera – which can be detached by gently brushing the chalk under water. But what was the object? There was no doubt that the material was chalk, and we knew that the foraminifera were there. Why trouble to prove what is common knowledge? I questioned Polton, but he knew nothing of the purpose of the investigation. He merely beamed on me like a crinkly old graven image and went on brushing. I dipped up a sample of the white sediment and examined it under the microscope. Of course there were foraminifera, and very beautiful they were. But what about it? The whole proceeding looked purposeless. And yet I knew that it was not. Thorndyke was the last man in the world to expend his energies in flogging a dead horse.

Presently he came up to the laboratory, and, when he had looked at the dust specimens and confirmed my opinion of them, he fell to work on the chalk sediment. Having prepared a number of slides, he sat down at the microscope with a sharp pencil and a block of smooth paper with the apparent purpose of cataloguing and making drawings of the foraminifera. And at this task I left him while I went forth to collect some books that I had ordered from a bookseller in the Charing Cross Road.

When I returned with my purchase about an hour later I found him putting back in a press a portfolio of large-scale Ordnance maps of Kent which he had apparently been consulting, and I noticed on the table his sheet of drawings and a monograph of the fossil foraminifera.

"Well, Thorndyke," I said cheerfully, "I suppose by this time, you know exactly what has become of Merrill."

"I can guess," he replied, "and so can you. But the actual data are distressingly vague. We have certain indications, as you will have noticed. The trouble will be to bring them to a focus. It is a case for constructive imagination on the one hand and the method of exclusion on the other. I shall make a preliminary circle-round tomorrow."

"Meaning by that?"

"I have a hypothesis. It is probably wrong. If it is, we must try another, and yet another. Every time we fail we shall narrow the field of inquiry, until by eliminating one possibility after another, we may hope to arrive at the solution. My first essay will take me down into Kent."

"You are not going into those wild regions alone, Thorndyke," said I. "You will need my protection and support to say nothing of my invaluable advice. I presume you realise that?"

"Undoubtedly," he replied gravely. "I was reckoning on a two-man expedition. Besides, you are as much interested in the case as

I am. And now, let us go forth and dine and fortify ourselves for the perils of tomorrow."

In the course of dinner I led the conversation to the products of Polton's labours and remarked upon their very indefinite significance; but Thorndyke was more indefinite still, as he usually was in cases of a highly speculative character.

"You are expecting too much from Polton," he said with a smile. "This is not a matter of foraminifera or pollen-grains or butterfly-scales; they are only items of circumstantial evidence. What we have to do is to consider the whole body of facts in our possession; what Brodribb has told us, what we know for ourselves and what we have ascertained by investigation. The case is still very much in the air, but it is not so vague as you seem to imply."

This was all I could get out of him; and as the "whole body of facts" yielded no suggestion at all to me, I could only possess my soul in patience and hope for some enlightenment on the morrow.

About a quarter to eleven on the following morning, while Thorndyke was giving final instructions to Polton and I was speculating on the contents of the suitcase that was going to accompany us, footsteps became audible on our stairs. Their crescendo terminated in a flourish on our little brass knocker which I recognised as Brodribb's knock. I accordingly opened the door, and in walked our old friend. His keen blue eyes took in at once our informal raiment and the suitcase and lighted up with something like curiosity.

"Off on an expedition?" he asked.

"Yes," replied Thorndyke. "A little trip down into Kent. Gravesend, in fact."

"Gravesend," repeated Brodribb with further awakened interest. "That was rather a favourite resort of poor Merrill's. By the way, your expedition is not connected with his disappearance, I suppose?"

"As a matter of fact it is," replied Thorndyke. "Just a tentative exploration, you know."

"I know," said Brodribb, all agog now, "and I'm coming with you. I've got a clear day and I'm not going to take a refusal."

"No refusal was contemplated," rejoined Thorndyke. "You'll probably waste a day, but we shall benefit by your society. Polton will let your clerk know that you haven't absconded, or you can look in at the office yourself. We have plenty of time."

Brodribb chose the latter plan, which enabled him to exchange his tall hat and morning coat for a soft hat and jacket, and we accordingly made our way to Charing Cross via Lincoln's Inn, where Brodribb's office was situated. I noticed that Brodribb, with his customary discretion, asked no questions, though he must have observed, as I had, the striking fact that Thorndyke had in some way connected Merrill with Gravesend; and in fact with the exception of Brodribb's account of his failure to get any news of Mr Crick, no reference was made to the nature of our expedition until we alighted at our destination.

On emerging from the station, Thorndyke turned to the left and led the way out of the approach into a street, on the opposite side of which a rather grimy statue of Queen Victoria greeted us with a supercilious stare. Here we turned to the south along a prosperous, suburban-looking thoroughfare, and presently crossing a main road, followed its rather sordid continuation until the urban squalor began to be tempered by traces of rusticity, and the suburb became a village. Passing a pleasant-looking inn and a smithy, which seemed to have an out-patient department for invalid carts, we came into a quiet lane offering a leafy vista with glimpses of thatched and tiled cottages whose gardens were gay with summer flowers. Opposite these, some rough stone steps led up to a stile by the side of an open gate which gave access to a wide cart-track. Here Thorndyke halted, and producing his pocket map-case, compared the surroundings with the map. At length he pocketed the case, and turning towards the cart-track, said:

"This is our way, for better or worse. In a few minutes we shall probably know whether we have found a clue or a mare's nest."

We followed the track up a rise until, reaching the crest of the hill, we saw stretching away below us a wide, fertile valley with wooded heights beyond, over the brow of which peeped the square tower of some village church.

"Well," said Brodribb, taking off his hat to enjoy the light breeze, "clue or no clue, this is perfectly delightful and well worth the journey. Just look at those charming little blue butterflies fluttering round that mallow. What a magnificent prospect! And where, but in Kent, will you see such a barley field as that?"

It was, indeed, a beautiful landscape. But as my eye travelled over the enormous barley field, its tawny surface rippling in golden waves before the summer breeze, it was not the beauty of the scene that occupied my mind. I was thinking of those three ends of barley beard that we had picked from the skirts of the green jacket. The cart-track had now contracted to a footpath; but it was a broader path than I should have looked for, running straight across the great field to a far-away stile; and halfway along it on the left-hand side I could see, rising above the barley, the top of a rough fence around a small, square enclosure that looked like a mound – though it was in an unlikely situation.

We pursued the broad path across the field until we were nearly abreast of the pound, and I was about to draw Thorndyke's attention to it, when I perceived a narrow lane through the barley – hardly a path, but rather a track, trodden through the crop by some persons who had gone by the enclosure. Into this track Thorndyke turned as if he had been looking for it, and walked towards the enclosure, closely scrutinising the ground as he went. Brodribb and I, of course, followed in single file, brushing through the barley as we went; and as we drew nearer we could see that there was an opening in the enclosing fence and that inside was a deep hollow the edges of which were fringed with clumps of pink valerian. At the opening of the fence Thorndyke halted and looked back.

"Well," said Brodribb, "is it going to be a mare's nest?"

"No," replied Thorndyke. "It is a clue, and something more!"

As he spoke, he pointed to the foot of one of the principal posts of the fence, to which was secured a short length of rope, the frayed ends of which suggested it had broken under a heavy strain. And now I could see what the enclosure was. Inside it was a deep pit, and at the bottom of the pit, to one side, was a circular hole, black as night, and apparently leading down into the bowels of the earth.

"That must be a dene hole," said I, looking at the yawning cavity.

"It is," Thorndyke replied.

"Ha," said Brodribb, "so that is a dene hole, is it? Damned unpleasant-looking place. Dene holes were one of poor Merrill's hobbies. He used to go down to explore them. I hope you are not suggesting that he went down this one."

"I am afraid that is what has happened, Brodribb," was the reply. "That end of rope looks like this. It is deep-sea lead-line. I have a length of it here, bought at the same place as he bought his, and probably cut from the same sample." He opened the suitcase, and taking out the coil of line that we had bought, flung it down by the foot of the post. Obviously it was identical with the broken end. "However," he added, "we shall see."

"We are going down, are we?" asked Brodribb.

"We?" repeated Thorndyke. "I am going down if it is practicable. Not otherwise. If it is an ordinary seventy-foot shaft with perpendicular sides, we shall have to get proper appliances. But you had better stay above, in any case."

"Nonsense!" exclaimed Brodribb. "I am not such a back number as you think. I have been a mountain-climber in my time and I'm not a bit nervous. I can get down all right if there is any foothold, and I've got a rope to hang on to. And you can see for yourself that somebody has been down with a rope only."

"Yes," replied Thorndyke, "but I don't see that that somebody has come up again."

"No," Brodribb admitted; "that's true. The rope seems to have broken; and you say your rope is the same stuff?"

Thorndyke looked at me inquiringly as I stooped and examined the frayed end of the strange rope.

"What do you say, Jervis?" he asked.

"That rope didn't break," I replied. "It has been chafed or sawn through. It is quite different in appearance from a broken end."

"That was what I decided as soon as I saw it," said Thorndyke. "Besides, a new rope of this size and quality couldn't possibly break under the weight of a man."

Brodribb gazed at the frayed end with an expression of horror.

"What a diabolical thing!" he exclaimed.

"You mean that some wretch deliberately cut the rope and let another man drop down the shaft! But it can't be. I really think you must be mistaken. It must have been a defective rope."

"Well, that is what it looks like," replied Thorndyke. He made a "running bowline" at the end of our rope and slipped the loop over his shoulders, drawing it tight under his arms. Then he turned towards the pit. "You had better take a couple of turns round the foot of the post, Jervis," said he, "and pay out just enough to keep the rope taut."

He took an electric inspection-lamp from the suitcase, slipped the battery in his pocket and hooked the bull's-eye to a button-hole, and when all was ready, he climbed down into the pit, crossed the sloping floor, and crouching down, peered into the forbidding hole, throwing down it a beam of light from his bull's-eye. Then he stood up and grasped the rope.

"It is quite practicable," said he; "only about twenty feet deep, and good foothold all the way." With this he crouched once more, backed into the hole and disappeared from view. He evidently descended pretty quickly, to judge by the rate at which I had to pay out the rope, and in quite a short time, I felt the tension slacken and began to haul up the line. As the loop came out of the hole, Mr Brodribb took possession of it, and regardless of my protests, proceeded to secure it under his arms.

"But how the deuce am I going to get down?" I demanded.

"That's all right, Jervis," he replied persuasively. "I'll just have a look round and then come up and let you down."

It being obviously useless to argue, I adjusted the rope and made ready to pay out. He climbed down into the pit with astonishing agility, backed into the hole and disappeared; and the tension of the rope informed me that he was making quite a rapid descent. He had nearly reached the bottom when there was borne to my ears the hollow reverberation of what sounded like a cry of alarm. But all was apparently well, for the rope continued to draw out steadily, and when at last its tension relaxed, I felt an unmistakable signal shake, and at once drew it up.

As my curiosity made me unwilling to remain passively waiting for Brodribb's return, I secured the end of the rope to the post with a "fisherman's bend" and let myself down into the pit. Advancing to the sinister-looking hole, I lay down and put my head over the edge. A dim light from Thorndyke's lamp came up the shaft and showed me that we were by no means the first explorers, for there were footholes cut in the chalk all the way down, apparently of some considerable age. With the aid of these and the rope, it appeared quite easy to descend and I decided to go down forthwith. Accordingly I backed towards the shaft, found the first of the foot-holes, and grasping the rope with one hand and using the other to hang on to the upper cavities, easily let myself down the well-like shaft. As I neared the bottom the light of the lamp was thrown full on the shaft-well; a pair of hands grasped me and I heard Thorndyke's voice saying; "Look where you are treading, Jervis"; on which I looked down and saw immediately below me a man lying on his face by an irregular coil of rope.

I stepped down carefully on to the chalk floor and looked round. We were in a small chamber in one side of which was the black opening of a low tunnel. Thorndyke and Brodribb were standing at the feet of the prostate figure examining a revolver which the solicitor held.

"It has certainly been fired," said the latter. "One chamber is empty and the barrel is foul."

"That may be," replied Thorndyke; "but there is no bullet wound. This man died from a knife wound in the chest." He threw the light of his lamp on the corpse and as I turned it partly over to verify his statement, he added: "This is poor Mr Merrill. We found the revolver lying by his side."

"The cause of death is clear enough," said I, "and it certainly wasn't suicide. The question is – " At this moment Thorndyke stooped and threw a beam of light down the tunnel, and Brodribb and I simultaneously uttered an exclamation. At the extreme end, about forty feet away, the body of another man lay. Instantly Brodribb started forward, and stooping to clear the low roof – it was about four feet six inches high – hurried along the tunnel and Thorndyke and I followed close behind. As we reached the body, which was lying supine with a small electric torch by its side, and the light of Thorndyke's lamp fell on the upturned face, Brodribb gasped:

"God save us! It's Crick! And here is the knife."

He was about to pick up the weapon when Thorndyke put out his hand.

"That knife," he said, "must be touched by no hand but the one that dealt the blow. It may be crucial evidence."

"Evidence of what?" demanded Brodribb. "There is Merrill with a knife wound in his chest and a pistol by his side. Here is Crick with a bullet wound in his breast, a knife by his side and the empty sheath secured round his waist. What more evidence do you want?"

"That depends on what you seek to prove," said Thorndyke. "What is your interpretation of the facts that you have stated?"

"Why, it is as plain as daylight," answered Brodribb, "incredible as the affair seems, having regard to the characters of the two men. Crick stabbed Merrill and Merrill shot him dead. Then Merrill tried to escape, but the rope broke. He was trapped and he bled to death at the foot of the shaft."

"And who do you say died first?" Thorndyke asked.

It was a curious question and it caused me to look inquisitively at my colleague. But Brodribb answered promptly:

"Why, Crick, of course. Here he lies where he fell. There is a track of blood along the floor of the tunnel, as you can see, and there is Merrill at the entrance, dead in the act of trying to escape."

Thorndyke nodded in a rather mysterious way and there was a brief silence. Then I ventured to remark:

"You seem to be losing sight of the man with the green jacket."

Brodribb started and looked at me with a frown of surprise.

"Bless my soul!" he exclaimed, "so I am. I had clean forgotten him in these horrors. But what is your point? Is there any evidence that he has been here?"

"I don't know," said I. "I bought the rope and he was seen with Merrill apparently going towards London Bridge Station. And I gather that it was the green jacket that piloted Thorndyke to this place."

"In a sense," Thorndyke admitted, "that is so. But we will talk about that later. Meanwhile there are one or two facts that I wall draw your attention to. First as to the wounds; they are almost identical in position. Each is on the left side, just below the nipple; a vital spot, which would be fully exposed by a man who was climbing down holding on to a rope. Then, if you look along the floor where I am throwing the light, you can see a distinct trace of something having been dragged along, although there seems to have been an effort to obliterate it; and the blood marks are more in the nature of smears than drops." He gently turned the body over and pointed to the back, which was thickly covered with chalk. "This corpse has obviously been dragged along the floor," he continued. "It wouldn't have been marked in that way by merely falling. Further, the rope, when last seen, was being stuffed into a handbag. The rope is here, but where is the handbag? Finally, the rope was cut by someone outside, and evidently after the murders had been committed."

As he concluded, he spread his handkerchief over the knife, and wrapping it up carefully without touching it with his fingers, placed it in his outside breast-pocket. Then we went back towards the shaft, where Thorndyke knelt down by the body of Merrill and systematically emptied the pockets.

"What are you searching for?" asked Brodribb.

"Keys," was the reply; "and there aren't any. It is a vital point, seeing that the man with the green jacket evidently let himself into Merrill's chambers that same day."

"Yes," Brodribb agreed with a reflective frown; "it is. But tell us, Thorndyke, how you reconstruct this horrible crime."

"My theory," said Thorndyke, "is that the three men came here together. They made the rope fast to the post. The stranger in the green jacket came down first and waited at the foot of the shaft. Merrill came down next, and the stranger stabbed him just as he reached the bottom, while his arms were still up hanging on to the rope. Crick followed and was shot in the same place and the same manner. Then the stranger dragged Crick's body along the tunnel, swept away the marks as well as he could, put the knife and the lamp by the body, dropped the revolver by Merrill's corpse, took the keys and went up, sawed through the rope — probably with a pocket saw — and threw the end down the shaft. Then he took the next train to London and went straight to Merrill's chambers, where he opened the safe or other receptacles and took possession of what he wanted."

Brodribb nodded. "It was a diabolically clever scheme," said he.

"The scheme was ingenious enough," Thorndyke agreed, "but the execution was contemptible. He has traces at every turn. Otherwise we shouldn't be here. He has acted on the assumption that the world contains no one but fools. But that is a fool's assumption."

When we had ascended, in the reverse order of our descent, Thorndyke detached our rope and also the frayed end, which we took with us, and we then took our way back towards the town; and I noted that as we stood by the dene hole, there was not a human creature in sight; nor did we meet a single person until we were close to the village. It was an ideal spot for a murder.

"I suppose you will notify the police?" said Brodribb.

"Yes," replied Thorndyke. "I shall call on the Chief Constable and give him the facts and advise him to keep some of them to himself for the present, and also to arrange for an adjournment of the inquest. Our friend with the green jacket must be made to think that he has played a trump card."

Apparently the Chief Constable was a man who knew all the moves of criminal investigation, for at the inquest the discovery was attributed to the local police "acting on information received" from somebody who had "noticed the broken rope."

None of us was summoned to give evidence nor were our names mentioned, but the inquest was adjourned for three weeks, for further inquiries.

But in those three weeks there were some singular developments, one of which the scene was the clerk's office at Mr Brodribb's premises in Lincoln's Inn. There, late on a certain forenoon, Thorndyke and I arrived, each provided with a bag and a sheaf of documents, and were duly admitted by Mr Page.

"Now," said Thorndyke, "are you quite confident, Mr Page, that you would recognise this man, even if he had shaved off his beard and moustache?"

"Quite confident," replied Page. "I should know him by his eyes. Very queer eyes they were; light, greenish grey. And I should know his voice too."

"Good," said Thorndyke; and as Page disappeared into the private office, we sat down and examined our documents, eyed furtively by the junior clerk. Some ten minutes later the door opened and a man entered; and the first glance at him brought my nerves to concert pitch. He was a thick-set, muscular man, clean-shaved and rather dark. But my attention was instantly arrested by his eyes – singularly pale eyes which gave an almost unhuman character to his face. He reminded me of a certain species of lemur that I once saw.

"I have got an appointment with Mr Brodribb," he said, addressing the clerk. "My name is Horder."

The clerk slipped off his stool and moved towards the door of the private office, but at that moment Page came out. As his eyes met Horder's, he stopped dead; and instantly the two men seemed to stiffen like a couple of dogs that have suddenly met at a street corner. I watched Horder narrowly. He had been rather pale when he came in. Now he was ghastly, and his whole aspect indicated extreme nervous tension.

"Did you wish to see Mr Brodribb?" asked Page, still gazing intently at the other.

"Yes," was the irritable reply; "I have given my name once – Horder."

Mr Page turned and re-entered the private office, leaving the door ajar.

"Mr Horder to see you, sir," I heard him say. Then he came out and shut the door. "If you will sit down, Mr Brodribb will see you in a minute or two," he said, offering a chair; he then took his hat from a peg, glanced at his watch and went out.

A couple of minutes passed. Once, I thought I heard stealthy footsteps out in the entry; but no one came in and knocked. Presently the door of the private office opened and a tall gentleman came out. And then, once more, my nerves sprang to attention. The tall gentleman was Detective Superintendent Miller.

The superintendent walked across the office, opened the door, looked out, and then, leaving it ajar, came back to where Horder was sitting.

"You are Mr Samuel Horder, I think," said he.

"Yes I am," was the reply. "What about it?"

"I am a police officer, and I arrest you on a charge of having unlawfully entered the premises of the late Reginald Merrill; and it is my duty to caution you – "

Here Horder, who had risen to his feet, and slipped his right hand under the skirt of his coat, made a sudden spring at the officer. But in that instant Thorndyke had gripped his right arm at the elbow and wrist and swung him round; the superintendent seized his left arm while I pounced upon the revolver in his right hand and kept its muzzle pointed to the floor. But it was an uncomfortable affair. Our prisoner was a strong man and he fought like a wild beast; and he had his finger hooked round the trigger of the revolver. The four of us, locked together, gyrated round the office, knocking over chairs and bumping against the walls, the junior clerk skipped round the room with his eyes glued on the pistol and old Brodribb charged out of his sanctum, flourishing a long ruler. However, it did not last long. In the midst of the uproar, two massive constables stole in and joined the fray. There was a yell from the prisoner, the revolver rattled to the floor and then I heard two successive metallic clicks.

"He'll be all right now," murmured the constable who had fixed on the handcuffs, with the manner of one who has administered a soothing remedy.

"I notice," said Thorndyke, when the prisoner had been removed, "that you charged him only with unlawful entry."

"Yes," replied Miller, "until we have taken his finger-prints. Mr Singleton has developed up three fingers and a thumb, beautifully clear, on that knife that you gave us. If they prove to be Horder's finger-prints, of course, it is a true bill for the murder."

The fingerprints on the knife proved undoubtedly to be Horder's. But the case did not rest on them alone. When his rooms were searched, there were found not only Mr Merrill's keys but also Mr Merrill's second will, which had been missed from the safe when it was opened by the maker's locksmith; thus illustrating afresh the perverse stupidity of the criminal mind.

"A satisfactory case," remarked Thorndyke, "in respect of the result; but there was too much luck for us to take much credit from it. On Brodribb's opening statement, it was pretty clear that a crime had been committed. Merrill was missing and someone had possession of his keys and had entered his premises. It also appeared nearly certain that the thing stolen must be the second will, since there was nothing else of value to steal; and the will was of very great value to two persons, Crick and Horder, to each of whom its destruction was worth many thousands of pounds. To both of them its value was conditional on the immediate death of Merrill, before another will could be made; and to Horder it was further conditional on the death of Crick and that he should die before Merrill – for otherwise the estate would go to Crick's heirs or next of kin. The prima facie suspicion therefore fell on these two men. But Crick was missing; and the question was, had he absconded or was he dead?

"And now as to the investigation. The green jacket showed earthy dust and chalk on the front and chalk-marks on the buttons. The indication was that the wearer had either crawled on chalky ground or climbed up a chalky face. But the marks on the buttons suggested climbing; for a horizontal surface is usually covered by soil, whereas on a vertical surface the chalk is exposed. But the time factor showed us that this man could not have travelled far from London. He was seen going towards London Bridge Station about the time when a train was due – 11.52 – to go down to Kent. That train went to Maidstone and Gillingham, calling at Gravesend, Strood, Snodland, Rochester, Chatham and other places abounding in chalk and connected with the cement industry. In that district there were no true cliffs, but there were numerous chalk-pits, railway embankments and other excavations. The evidence pointed to one of these excavations. Then Crick was know to have gone to Rochester – earlier in the day – which further suggested the district, though Rochester is the least chalky part of it.

"The question was, what kind of excavation had been climbed into? And for what purpose had the climbing been performed? But there the personality of the missing man gave us a hint. Merrill had written a book to prove that dene holes were simply prehistoric flint-mines. He had explored a number of dene holes and described them in his book. Now the district through which this train passed was peculiarly rich in dene holes; and then there was the suggestive fact that Merrill had been last seen coming out of a rope-seller's shop. This latter fact was so important that I followed it up once by calling at Edginton's. There I ascertained that Merrill or his companion had bought a fifteen-fathom length of deep-sea lead-line. Now this was profoundly significant. The maximum depth of a dene hole is about seventy feet. Fifteen fathoms – ninety feet – is therefore the exact length required, allowing for loops and fastenings. This new fact converted the dene hole hypothesis into what was virtually a certainly, especially when one considered how readily these dangerous pits lent themselves either to fatal accidents or to murder. I accordingly adopted the dene hole suggestion as a working hypothesis.

"The next question was, 'Where was this dene hole?' And an uncommonly difficult question it was. I began to fear that the inquiry would fail from the impossibility of solving it. But at this point I got some help from a new quarter. I had given the coat to Polton to extract the dust and I had told him to wash the little lumps of chalk for foraminifera."

"What are foraminifera?" asked Brodribb.

"They are minute sea shells. Chalk is largely composed of them; and although chalk is in no sense a local rock, there is nevertheless a good deal of variation in the species of foraminifera found in different localities. So I had the chalk washed out as a matter of routine. Well, the dust was confirmatory but not illuminating. There was railway dust, of the South Eastern type – I expect you know it – chalk, loam dust, pollen-grains of the mallow and valerian (which grows in chalk-pits and railway cuttings) and some wing scales of the common blue butterfly, which haunts the chalk – I expect he had touched a dead butterfly. But all this would have answered for a good part of Kent. Then I examined the information and identified the species by the plates in Warnford's *Monograph*. The result was most encouraging. There were nine species in all, and of these five were marked as 'found in the Gravesend chalk,' two more, 'from the Kentish chalk' and the other two 'from the English chalk.' This was a very striking result. More than half the contained foraminifera were from the Gravesend chalk.

"The problem now was to determine the geological meaning of the term Gravesend. I ruled out Rochester, as I had heard of no dene holes in that neighbourhood, and I consulted Merrill's book and the large-scale Ordnance map. Merrill had worked in the Gravesend district and the adjacent part of Essex and he gave a list of the dene holes that he explored, including the Clapper Napper Hole in Swanscombe Wood. But, checking his list by the Ordnance map, I found that there was one dene hole marked on the map which was not in his list. As it was evidently necessary to search all the dene holes in the district, I determined to begin with the one that he seemed to have missed. And there luck favoured us. It turned out to be the right one."

"I don't see that there was much luck in it," said Brodribb. "You calculated the probabilities and adopted the greatest."

"At any rate," said Thorndyke, "there was Merrill and there was Crick; and as soon as I saw them I knew that Horder was the murderer. For the whole tableau had obviously been arranged to demonstrate that Crick died before Merrill and establish Horder as Merrill's heir."

"A diabolical plot," commented Brodribb. "Horribly ingenious, too. By the way – which of them did die first in your opinion?"

"Merrill, I should say, undoubtedly," replied Thorndyke.

"That will be good hearing for Crick's next of kin,' said Brodribb. "And you haven't done with this case yet, Thorndyke. I shall retain you on the question of survivorship."

CHAPTER THREE

The Seal of Nebuchadnezzar

"I suppose, Thorndyke," said I, "footprints yield quite a lot of information if you think about them enough?"

The question was called forth by the circumstance of my friend halting and stooping to examine the little pit made in the loamy soil of the path by the walking-stick of some unknown wayfarer. Ever since we had entered this path – to which we had been directed by the station-master of Pinwell Junction as a short cut to our destination – I noticed my friend scanning its surface, marked with numerous footprints, as if he were mentally reconstructing the personalities of the various travellers who had trodden it before us. This I knew to be a habit of his, almost unconsciously pursued; and the present conditions certainly favoured it, for here, as the path traversed a small wood, the slightly moist, plastic surface took impressions with the sharpness of moulding wax.

"Yes," he answered, "but you must do more than think. You need to train your eyes to observe inconspicuous characteristics."

"Such as these, for instance," said I, with a grin, pointing to a blatant print of a Cox's "Invicta" rubber sole with its prancing-horse trademark.

Thorndyke smiled. "A man," said he, "who wears a sole like that is a mere advertising agent. He who runs may read those characteristics, but as there are thousands of persons wearing Invicta soles, the observation merely identifies the wearer as a member of a large genus. It has to be carried a good deal farther to identify him as an individual; otherwise, a standardised sole is apt to be rather misleading than helpful. Its gross distinctiveness tends to divert the novice's attention from the more specific characteristics which he would seek in a plain footprint like that of this man's companion."

"Why companion?" I asked. "The two men were walking the same way, but what evidence is there that they were companions?"

"A good deal, if you follow the series of tracks, as I have been doing. In the first place, there is the stride. Both men were rather tall, as shown by the size of their feet, but both have a distinctly short stride. Now the leather-soled man's short stride is accounted for by the way in which he put down his stick. He held it stiffly, leaning upon it to some extent and helping himself with it. There is one impression of the stick to every two paces; every impression of his left boot has a stick impression opposite to it. The suggestion is that he was old, weak or infirm. But the rubber-soled man walked with his stick in the ordinary way – one stick impression to every four paces. His abnormally short stride is not to be accounted for excepting by the assumption that he stepped short to keep pace with the other man.

"Then the two sets of footprints are usually separate. Neither man has trodden nor set his stick on the other man's tracks, exception in those places where the path is too narrow for them to walk abreast, and there, in the one case I noticed the rubber soles treading on the prints of the leather soles, whereas at this spot the prints of the leather soles are imposed on those of the rubber soles. That, of course, is conclusive evidence that the two men were here at the same time."

"Yes," I agreed, "that settles the question without troubling the stride. But after all, Thorndyke, this is a matter of reasoning, as I said; of thinking about the footprints and their meaning. No special acuteness of observation or training of vision comes into it. The mere facts are obvious enough; it is their interpretation that yields the knowledge."

"That is true so far," said he, "but we haven't exhausted our material. Look carefully at the impressions of the two sticks and tell me if you see anything remarkable in either of them."

I stooped and examined the little pits that the two sticks had made in the path, and, to tell the truth, found them extremely unilluminating.

"They seem very much alike," I said. "The rubber-soled man's stick is rather larger than the other and the leather-soled man's stock has made deeper holes – probably because it was smaller and he was leaning on it more heavily."

Thorndyke shook his head. "You've missed the point, Anstey, and you've missed it because you have failed to observe the visible facts. It is quite a neat point, too, and might in certain circumstances be a very important one."

"Indeed," said I. "What is the point?"

"That," said he, "I shall leave you to infer from the visible facts, which are these: first, the impressions of the smaller stick are on the right-hand side of the man who made them, and second, that each impression is shallowest towards the front and the right-hand side."

I examined the impressions carefully and verified Thorndyke's statement.

"Well," I said, "what about it? What does it prove?"

Thorndyke smiled in his exasperating fashion.

"The proof," said he, "is arrived at by reasoning from the facts. My learned friend has the facts. If he will consider them, the conclusion will emerge."

"But," said I, "I don't see your drift. The impression is shallower on one side, I suppose, because the ferrule of the stick was worn away on that side. But I repeat, what about it? Do you expect me to infer why the fool that it belonged to wore his stick away all at one side?"

"Now, don't get irritable, Anstey," said he. "Preserve a philosophic calm. I assure you that this is quite an interesting problem."

"So it may be," I replied. "But I'm hanged if I can imagine why he wore his stick down in that way. However, it doesn't really matter. It isn't my stick – and by Jingo, here is old Brodribb – caught us in the act of wasting our time on academic chin-wags and delaying his business. The debate is adjourned."

Our discussion had brought us to the opening of the wood, which now framed the figure of the solicitor. As he caught sight of us, he hurried forward, holding out his hand.

"Good men and true!" he exclaimed, "I thought you would probably come this way, and it is very good of you to have come at all, especially as it is a mere formality."

"What is?" asked Thorndyke. "Your telegram spoke of an 'alleged suicide.' I take it that there is some ground for inquiry?"

"I don't know that there is," replied Brodribb. "But the deceased was insured for three thousand pounds, which will be lost to the estate if the suicide is confirmed. So I put it to my fellow-executor that it was worth an expert's fee to make sure whether or not things are what they seem. A verdict of death by misadventure will save us three thousand pounds. *Verbum sap.*" As he concluded, the old lawyer winked with exaggerated cunning and stuck his elbow into my ribs.

Thorndyke ignored the facetious suggestion of bribery and corruption and inquired dryly:

"What are the circumstances of the case?"

"I'd better give you a sketch of them before we get to the house," replied Brodribb. "The dead man is Martin Rowlands, the brother of my neighbour in New Square, Tom Rowlands. Poor old Tom found the telegram waiting when he got to his office this morning and immediately rushed into my office with it and begged me to come down here with him. So I came. Couldn't refuse a brother solicitor. He's waiting at the house now.

"The circumstances are these. Last evening, when he had finished dinner, Rowlands went out for a walk. That is his usual habit in the summer months – it is light until nearly half-past nine nowadays. Well, that is the last time he was seen alive by the servants. No one saw him come in. But there was nothing usual in that, for he had a private entrance to the annexe in which his library, museum and workrooms were situated, and when he returned from his walk, he usually entered the house that way and went straight to his study or workroom and spent the evening there. So the servants very seldom saw him after dinner.

"Last night he evidently followed his usual custom. But, this morning, when the housemaid went to his bedroom with his morning tea, she was astonished to find the room empty and the bed undisturbed. She at once reported to the housekeeper, and the pair made their way to the annexe. There they found the study door locked, and as there was no answer after repeated knockings, they went out into the grounds to reconnoitre. The study window was closed and fastened, but the workroom window was unbolted, so that they were able to open it from outside. Then the housemaid climbed in and went to the side door, which she opened and admitted the housekeeper. The two went to the workroom, and as the door which communicated with the study was open, they were able to enter the latter, and there they found Martin Rowlands, sitting in an armchair by the table, stone-dead, cold and stiff. On the table were a whisky decanter, a siphon of soda-water, a box of cigars, an ash-bowl with stump of a cigar in it, and a bottle of photographic tabloids of cyanide of potassium.

"The housekeeper immediately sent of for a doctor and dispatched a telegram to Tom Rowlands at his office. The doctor arrived about nine and decided that the deceased had been dead about twelve hours. The cause of death was apparently cyanide poisoning, but, of course, that will be ascertained or disproved by the post-mortem. Those are all the known facts at present. The doctor helped the servants to place the body on a sofa, but as it is as stiff as a frozen sheep, they might as well have left it where it was."

"Have the police been communicated with?" I asked.

"No," replied Brodribb. "There were no suspicious circum-stances, so far as any of us could see, and I don't know that I should have felt justified in sending for you – though I always like to have Thorndyke's opinion in a case of sudden death – if it had not been for the insurance."

Thorndyke nodded. "It looks like a straightforward case of suicide," said he. "As to the state of the deceased's affairs, his brother will be able to give us any necessary information, I suppose?"

"Yes," replied Brodribb. "As a matter of fact, I think Martin has been a bit worried just lately; but Tom will tell you about that. This is the place."

We turned in at a gateway that opened into the grounds of a substantial though unpretentious house, and as we approached the front door, it was opened by a fresh-coloured, white-haired man whom we both knew well in our professional capacities. He greeted us cordially, and though he was evidently deeply shocked by the tragedy, struggled to maintain a calm, business-like manner.

"It is good of you to come down," said he; "but I am afraid we have troubled you rather unnecessarily. Still, Brodribb though it best – *ex abundantia cautelæ,* you know – to have the circumstances reviewed by a competent authority. There is nothing abnormal in the affair excepting its having happened. My poor brother was the sanest of men, I should say, and we are not a suicidal family. I suppose you had better see the body first?"

As Thorndyke assented, he conducted us to the end of the hall and into the annexe, where we entered the study, the door of which was now open, though the key was still in the lock. The table still bore the things that Brodribb had described, but the chair was empty, and its late occupant lay on a sofa, covered with a large tablecloth. Thorndyke advanced to the sofa and gently drew away the cloth, revealing the body of a man, fully dressed, lying stiffly and awkwardly on its back with the feet raised and the stiffened limbs extended. There was something strangely and horribly artificial in the aspect of the corpse, for, though it was lying down, it had the posture of a seated figure, and thus bore the semblance of a hideously realistic effigy which had been picked up from the chair and laid down. I stood looking at it from a little distance with a layman's distaste for the presence of a dead body, but still regarding it with attention and some curiosity. Presently, my glance fell on the soles of the shoes – which were, indeed, exhibited plainly enough – and I noted as an odd coincidence, that they were "Invicta" rubber soles, those which we had just been discussing in the wood; that it was even possible that those very footprints had been made by the feet of this grisly lay figure.

"I expect, Thorndyke," Brodribb said tactfully, "you would rather make your inspection alone. If you should want us, you will find us in the dining-room," and with this he retired, taking Mr Rowlands with him.

As soon as they were gone I drew Thorndyke's attention to the rubber soles.

"It is a queer thing," said I, "but we may have actually been discussing this poor fellow's own footprints."

"As a matter of fact, we were," he replied, pointing to a drawing-pin that had been trodden on and had stuck into one of the rubber heels. "I noticed this at the time, and apparently you did not, which illustrates what I was saying about the tendency of these very distinctive types of sole to distract attention from those individual peculiarities which are the ones that really matter."

"Then," said I, "if they were his footprints, the man with the remarkable stick was with him. I wonder who he was. Some neighbour who was walking home from the station with him, I expect."

"Probably," said Thorndyke, "and as the prints were quite recent – they might even have been made last night – that person may be wanted as the witness at the inquest as the last person who saw deceased alive. That depends on the time the prints were made."

He walked back to the sofa and inspected the corpse very methodically, giving close attention to the mouth and hands. Then he made a general inspection of the room, examined the objects on the table and the floor under it, strayed into the adjoining workshop, where he peered into the deep laboratory sink, took an empty tumbler from a shelf, held it up to the light and inspected the shelf – where a damp ring showed that the tumbler had been put there to drain – and from the workshop wandered into a little lobby and from thence out at the side door, down the flagged path to the side gate and back again.

"It is all very negative," he remarked discontentedly, as we returned to the study, "except that bottle of tabloids, which is pretty positive evidence of premeditation. That looks like a fresh box of cigars. Two missing. One stump in the ash-tray and more ash than one cigar would account for. However, let us go into the dining-room and hear what Rowlands has to tell us," and with that he walked out and crossed the hall and I followed him.

As we entered the dining-room, the two men looked at us and Brodribb asked:

"Well, what is the verdict?"

"At present," Thorndyke replied, "it is an open verdict. Nothing has come to light that disagrees with the obvious appearances. But I should like to hear more of the antecedents of the tragedy. You were saying that the deceased had been somewhat worried lately. What does that amount to?"

"It amounts to nothing," said Rowlands; "at least, I should have thought so, in the case of a level-headed man like my brother. Still, as it is all there is, so far as I know, to account for what has happened, I had better give you the story. It seems trivial enough.

"Some short time ago, a Major Cohen, who had just come home from Mesopotamia, sold to a dealer named Lyon a small gold cylinder seal that he had picked up in the neighbourhood of Baghdad. The Lord knows how he came by it, but he had it and he showed it to Lyon, who bought it of him for a matter of twenty pounds. Cohen, of course, knew nothing about the thing, and Lyon didn't know much more, for although he is a dealer, he is no expert. But he is a very clever faker – or rather, I should say, restorer, for he does quite a legitimate trade. He was a jeweller and watch-jobber originally, a most ingenious workman, and his line is to buy up damaged antiques and restore them. Then he sells them to miner collectors, though quite honestly as restorations, so I oughtn't to call him a faker. But, as I said, he has no real knowledge of antiques, and all he saw in Cohen's seal was a gold cylinder seal, apparently ancient and genuine, and on that he bought it for about twice the value of the gold and thought no more about it.

"About a fortnight later, my brother Martin went to his shop in Petty France, Westminster, to get some repairs done, and Lyon, knowing that my brother was a collector of Babylonian antiquities, showed him the seal; and Martin, seeing at once that it was genuine and a thing of some interest and value, bought it straightaway for forty pounds without examining it at all minutely, as it was obviously worth that much in any case. But when he got home and took a rolled impression of it on moulding wax, he made a most astonishing discovery. The impression showed a mass of minute cuneiform characters, and on deciphering these he learned with amazement and delight that this was none other than the seal of Nebuchadnezzar.

"Hardly able to believe in his good fortune, he hurried off to the British Museum and showed his treasure to the Keeper of the Babylonian Antiquities, who fully confirmed the identity of the seal and was naturally eager to acquire it for the Museum. Of course, Martin wouldn't sell it, but he allowed the keeper to take a record of its weight and measurements and to make an impression on clay to exhibit in the case of seal-rollings.

"Meanwhile, it seems that Cohen, before disposing of the seal, had amused himself by making a number of rolled impressions on clay. Some of these he took to Lyon, who bought them for a few shillings and put one of them in his shop window as a curio. There it was seen and recognised by an American Assyriologist, who went in and bought it and then began to question Lyon closely as to whence he had obtained it. The dealer made no secret of the matter, but gave Cohen's name and address saying nothing, however, about the seal. In fact, he was unaware of the connection between the seal and the rollings, as Cohen had sold him the latter as genuine clay tablets which he said he had found in

Mesopotamia. But, of course, the expert saw that it was a recent rolling and that someone must have the seal.

"Accordingly, off he went to Cohen and questioned him closely, whereupon Cohen began to smell a rat. He admitted that he had had the seal, but refused to say what had become of it until the expert told him what it was and how much it was worth. This the expert did, very reluctantly and in strict confidence, and when Cohen learned that it was the seal of Nebuchadnezzar and that it was worth anything up to ten thousand pounds, he nearly fainted, and then he and the expert together bustled off to Lyon's shop.

"But now Lyon smelt a rat, too. He refused absolutely to disclose the whereabouts of the seal; and having, by now, guessed that the seal-rollings were those of the seal, he took one of them to the British Museum, and then, of course, the murder was out. And further to complicate the matter, the Assyriologist, Professor Bateman, seems to have talked freely to his American friends at his hotel, with the result that Lyon's shop was besieged by wealthy American collectors, all roaring for the seal and all perfectly regardless of cost. Finally, as they could get no change out of Lyon, they went to the British Museum, where they learned that my brother had the seal and got his address – or rather mine, for he had, fortunately for himself, given my office as his address. Then they proceeded to bombard him with letters, as also did Cohen and Lyon.

"It was an uncomfortable situation. Cohen was like a madman. He swore that Lyon had swindled him and demanded to have the seal returned or the proper price paid. Lyon, for his part, went about like a roaring lion of Judah, making a similar demand; and the millionaire collectors offered wild sums for the seal. Poor Martin was very much worried about it. He was particularly unhappy about Cohen, who had actually found the seal and who was a disabled soldier – he had been wounded in both legs and was permanently lame. As to Lyon, he had no grievance, for he was a dealer and it was his business to know the value of his own stock: but still it was hard luck even on him. And then there were the collectors, pestering him daily with entreaties and extravagant offers. It was very worrying for him. They would probably have come down here to see him, but he kept his private address a close secret.

"I don't know what he meant to do about it. What he did was to arrange with me for the loan of my private office and have a field day, interviewing the whole lot of them – Cohen, Lyon, the Professor and the assorted millionaires. That was three days ago, and the whole boiling of them turned up; and by the same token, one of them was the kind of pestilent fool that walks off with the wrong hat or umbrella."

"Did he walk off with your hat?" asked Brodribb.

"No, but he took my stick; a nice old stick that belongs to my father."

"What kind of stick did he leave in it place?" Thorndyke asked.

"Well," replied Rowlands, "I must admit that there was some excuse, for the stick that he left was almost a facsimile of my own. I don't think I should have noticed it but for the feel. When I began to walk with it, I was aware of something unusual in the feel of it."

"Perhaps it was not quite the same length as yours," Thorndyke suggested.

"No, it wasn't that," said Rowlands. "The length was all right, but there was some more subtle difference. Possibly, as I am left-handed and carry my stick on the left side, it may in the course of years have acquired a left-handed bias, if such a thing is possible. I'll go and get the stick for you to see."

He went out of the room and returned in a few moments with an old-fashioned Malacca cane the ivory handle of which was secured by a broad silver band. Thorndyke took it from him and looked it over with a degree of interest and attention that rather surprised me. For the loss of Rowlands' stick was a trivial incident and no concern of ours. Nevertheless, my colleague inspected it most methodically, handle, silver band and ferrule: especially the ferrule, which he examined as if it were quite a rare and curious object.

"You needn't worry about your stick, Tom," said Brodribb with a mischievous smile. "Thorndyke will get it back if you ask him nicely."

"It oughtn't to be very difficult," said Thorndyke, handing back the stick, "if you have a list of the visitors who called that day."

"Their names will be in the appointments book," said Rowlands. "I must look them up. Some of them I remember – Cohen, Lyon, Bateman and two or three of the collectors. But to return to our history. I don't know what passed at the interviews or what Martin intended to do, but I have no doubt he made some notes on the subject. I must search for them, for, of course, we shall have to dispose of the seal."

"By the way," said Thorndyke, "where is the seal?"

"Why, it is here in the safe," replied Rowlands; "and it oughtn't to be. It should have been taken to the bank."

"I suppose there is no doubt that it is in the safe?" said Thorndyke.

"No," replied Rowlands; "at least – " He stood up suddenly. "I haven't seen it," he said. "Perhaps we had better make sure."

He led the way looking at the shrouded corpse.

"The key will be in his pocket," he said, almost in a whisper. Then, slowly and reluctantly, he approached the sofa, and gently drawing away the cover from the body, began to search the dead man's pockets.

"Here it is," he said at length, producing a bunch of keys and separating one, which he apparently knew. He crossed to the safe, and inserting the key, threw open the door.

"Ha!" he exclaimed with evident relief, "it is all right. Your question gave me quite a start. Is it necessary to open the packet?"

He held out a little sealed parcel on which was written "The Seal of Nebuchadnezzar," and looked inquiringly at Thorndyke.

"You spoke of making sure," the latter replied with a faint smile.

"Yes, I suppose it would be best," said Rowlands; and with that, he cut the thread with which it was fastened, broke the seal and opened the package, disclosing a small cardboard box in which lay a cylindrical object rolled up in a slip of paper.

Rowlands picked it out, and removing the paper, displayed a little cylinder of gold pitted all over with minute cuneiform characters. It was about an inch and a quarter by half an inch thick and had a hole bored through its axis from end to end.

"This paper, I see," said Rowlands "contains a copy of the keeper's description of the seal – its weight, dimensions and so on. We may as well take care of that."

He handed the little cylinder to Thorndyke, who held it delicately in his fingers and looked at it with a gravely reflective air. Indeed, small as it was, there was something very impressive in its appearance and in the thought that it had been handled by and probably worn on the person of the great king in those remote, almost mythical times, so familiar and yet so immeasurably far away. So I reflected as I watched Thorndyke inspecting the venerable little object in his queer, exact, scientific way, examining the minute characters through his lens, scrutinising the ends and even peering through the central hole.

"I notice," he said, glancing at the paper which Rowlands held, "that the keeper has given only one transverse diameter, apparently assuming that it is a true cylinder. But it isn't. The diameter varies. It is not quite circular in section and the sides are not perfectly parallel."

He produced his pocket calliper-gauge, and, closing the jaws on the cylinder, took the reading of the vernier. Then he turned the cylinder, on which the gauge became visibly out of contact.

"There is a difference of nearly two millimetres," he said when he had again closed the gauge and taken the reading.

"Ah, Thorndyke," said Brodribb, "that keeper hadn't got your mathematically exact eye; and, in fact, the precise measurements don't seem to matter much."

"On the other hand," retorted Thorndyke, "inexact measurements are of no use at all."

When we had all handled and inspected the seal, Rowlands repacked it and returned it to the safe, and we went back to the dining-room.

"Well, Thorndyke," said Brodribb, "how does the insurance question stand? What is our position?"

"I think," Thorndyke replied, "that we will leave the question open until the inquest has been held. You must insist on an expert analysis, and perhaps that may throw fresh light on the matter. And now we must be off to the station. I expect you have plenty to do."

"We have," said Brodribb, "so I won't offer to walk with you. You know the way."

Politely but firmly declining Rowlands' offer of material hospitality, Thorndyke took up his research case, and having shaken hands with our hosts, we followed them to the door and took our departure.

"Not a very satisfactory case," I remarked as we set forth along the road, "but you can't make a bull's-eye every time."

"No," he agreed; "you can only observe and note the facts. Which reminds me that we have some data to collect in the wood. I shall take casts of those footprints in case they should turn out to be of importance. It is always a useful precaution, seeing that footprints are fugitive."

It seemed to me an excessive precaution, but I made no comment: and when we arrived at the footpath through the wood and he had selected the sharpest footprints, I watched him take out from his case the plaster-tin, water-bottle, spoon and little rubber bowl, and wondered what was in his mind. The "Invicta" footprints were obviously those of the dead man. But what if they were? And of what use were the casts of the other man's feet? The man was unknown, and as far as I could see, there was nothing suspicious in his presence here. But when Thorndyke had poured the liquid plaster into the two pairs of footprints, he went on to a still more incomprehensible proceeding. Mixing some fresh plaster, he filled up with it two adjoining impressions of the strange man's stick. Then, taking a reel of thread from the case, he cut off about two yards, and stretching it taut, held it exactly across the middle of the two holes, until the plaster set and fixed it in position. After waiting for the plaster to set hard, and having, meanwhile, taken up and packed up the casts of the footprints, he gently raised, first the one and then the other cast; each of which was a snowy-white facsimile of the tip of the stick which had made the impression, the two casts being joined by a length of thread which gave the exact distance apart of the two impressions.

"I suppose," said I, as he made a pencil mark on one of the casts, "the tread is to show the length of the stride?"

"No," he answered. "It is to show the exact direction in which the man was walking and to mark the front and back of the stick."

I could make nothing of this. It was highly ingenious, but what on earth was the use of it? What could it possibly prove?

I put a few tentative questions, but could get no explanation beyond the obvious truth that it was of no use to postpone the collection of evidence until after the event. What event he was referring to, I did not gather: nor was I any further enlightened when, on arriving at Victoria, he hailed a taxicab and directed the driver to set him down at Scotland Yard.

"You had better not wait," he said, as he got out. "I have some business to talk over with Miller or the Assistant Commissioner and may be detained some time. But I shall be at home all the evening."

Taking this as an invitation to drop in at his chambers, I did so after dinner and made another ineffectual attempt to pump him.

"I am sorry to be so evasive," said he, "but this case is so extremely speculative that I cannot some to any definite conclusion until I have more data. I may have been theorising in the air. But I am going forth tomorrow morning at half-past eight in the hope of putting some of my inferences to the test. If my learned friend would care to lend his distinguished support to the expedition, his society would be appreciated. But it will be a case of passive observation and quite possibly nothing will happen."

"Well, I will come and look on," said I. "Passive observation is my speciality"; and with this I took my departure, rather more mystified than ever.

Punctually, next morning at half-past eight, I arrived at the entry of Thorndyke's chambers. A taxicab was already waiting at the kerb, and, as I stepped on the threshold, my colleague appeared on the stairs. Together we entered the cab which at once moved off, and proceeding down Middle Temple Lane to the Embankment, headed westward. Our first stopping place was New Scotland Yard, but there Thorndyke remained only a minute or two. Our further progress was in the direction of Westminster, and in a few minutes we drew up at the corner of Petty France, where we alighted and paid off the taxi. Sauntering slowly westward and passing a large, covered car that was drawn up by the pavement, we presently encountered no less a person than Mr Superintendent Miller, dressed in the height of fashion and smoking a cigar. The meeting was not, apparently, unexpected, for Miller began, without preamble:

"It's all right, so far, Doctor, unless we are too late. It will be an awful suck in if we are. Two plain-clothes men have been here ever since you called yesterday evening, and nothing has happened yet."

"You mustn't treat it as a certainty, Miller," said Thorndyke. "We are only acting on reasonable probabilities. But it may be a false shot, after all."

Miller smiled indulgently. "I know, sir. I've heard you say that sort of thing before. At any rate, he's there at present; I saw him just now through the shop window – and, by gum! Here he is!"

I followed the superintendent's glance and saw a tallish, elderly man advancing on the opposite side of the street, He walked stiffly, with the aid of a stick and with a pronounced stoop as if suffering from some weakness of the back, and he carried in his free hand a small wooden case suspended by a rug-strap. But what instantly attracted my attention was his walking-stick, which appeared, so far as I could remember, to be an exact replica of the one Tom Rowlands had shown us.

We continued to walk westward, allowing Mr Lyon − as I assumed him to be − to pass us. Then we turned back and followed at a little distance; and I noticed that two tall, military-looking men whom we had met kept close behind us. At the corner of Petty France Mr Lyon hailed a taxicab; and Miller quickened his pace and bore down on the big covered car.

"Jump in," he said, opening the door as Lyon entered the cab. "We mustn't lose sight of him," and with this he fairly shoved Thorndyke and me into the car, and having spoken a word to the driver, stepped in himself and was followed by the two plain-clothes men. The car started forward, and having made a spurt which brought it within a few yards of the taxi, slowed down to the pace of the latter and followed it through the increasing traffic until we turned into Whitehall, where our driver allowed the taxi to draw ahead somewhat. At Charing Cross, however, we closed up and kept immediately behind our quarry in the dense traffic of the Strand; and when it turned to cross opposite the Acropolis Hotel, we still followed and swept past it in the hotel courtyard so that we reached the main entrance first. By the time that Mr Lyon had paid his fare we had already entered and were waiting in the hall of the hotel.

As he followed us in, he paused and looked about him until his glance fell on the stoutish, clean-shaved man who was sitting in a wicker chair, who, on catching his eye, rose and advanced towards him. At this moment Superintendent Miller touched him on the shoulder, causing him to spin round with an expression of very distinct alarm.

"Mr Maurice Lyon, I think," said Miller. "I am a detective officer." He paused and looked hard at the dealer, who had turned deathly pale. Then he continued: "You are carrying a walking-stick which I believe is not your property."

Lyon gave a gasp of relief. "You are quite right," said he. "But I don't know whose property it is. If you do, I shall be pleased to return it in exchange for my own, which I left by mistake."

He held it our in an irresolute fashion, and Miller took it from him and handed it to Thorndyke.

"Is that the stick?" he asked.

Thorndyke looked the stick over quickly, and then, inverting it, made a minute examination of the ferrule, finishing up by taking its dimensions in two diameters and comparing the results with some written notes.

Mr Lyon fidgeted impatiently. "There's no need for all this fuss," said he. "I have told you that the stick is not mine."

"Quite so," said Miller, "but we must have a few words privately about that stick."

Here he turned to an hotel official, who had just arrived under the guidance of one of the plain-clothes men, and who suggested rather anxiously that our business would be better transacted in a private room at the back of the building than in the public hall. He was just moving off to show us the way when the clean-shaved stranger edged up to Lyon and extended his hand towards the wooden case.

"Shall I take this?" he asked suavely.

"Not just now, sir," said Miller, firmly fending him off. "Mr Lyon will talk to you presently."

"But that case is my property," the other objected truculently; "and who are you, anyway?"

"I am a police officer," replied Miller. "But if that is your property, you had better come with us and keep an eye on it."

I have never seen a man look more uncomfortable than did the owner of that case – with the exception of Mr Lyon; whose complexion had once more taken on a tallowy whiteness. But as the manager led the way to the back of the hall the two men followed silently, shepherded by the superintendent and the rest of our party, until we reached a small, marble-floored lobby or ante-room, when our conductor shut us in and retired.

"Now," said Miller, "I want to know what is in that case."

"I can tell you," said the stranger. "It is a piece of sculpture, and it belongs to me."

Miller nodded. "Let us have a look at it," said he.

There being no table, Lyon sat down on a chair, and resting the case on his knees, unfastened the straps with trembling fingers, on which a drop of sweat fell now and again from his forehead. When the case was free, he opened the lid and displayed the head of a small plaster bust, a miniature copy of Donatello's "St Cecilia," the shoulders of which were wedged in with balls of paper. These Lyon picked out clumsily, and when he had removed the last of them, he lifted out the bust with infinite care and held it out for Miller's inspection. The officer took it from him tenderly – after an eager glance into the empty case – and holding it with both hands, looked at it rather blankly.

"Feels rather damp," he remarked with a somewhat nonplussed air; and then he cast an obviously inquiring glance at Thorndyke, who took the bust from him, and holding it poised in the palm of his hand, appeared to be estimating its weight. Glancing past him at Lyon, I noticed with astonishment that the dealer was watching him with a ghastly stare of manifest terror, while the stranger was hardly less disturbed.

"For God's sake, man, be careful!" the latter exclaimed, starting forward. "You'll drop it!"

The prediction was hardly uttered before it was verified. Drop it he did; and in a perfectly deliberate, purposeful manner, so that the bust fell on its back on the marble floor and was instantly shattered into a hundred fragments. It was an amazing affair. But what followed was still more amazing. For, as the snowy fragments scattered to right and left, from one of them a little yellow metal cylinder detached itself and rolled slowly along the floor. The stranger darted forward and stooped to seize it; but Miller stopped, too, and I judged that the superintendent's cranium was the harder, for he rose, rubbing his head with one hand and with the other holding out the cylinder to Thorndyke.

"Can you tell us what this is, Doctor?" he asked.

"Yes," was the reply. "It is the seal of Nebuchadnezzar, and it is the property of the executors of the late Martin Rowlands, who was murdered the night before last."

As he finished speaking, Lyon slithered from his chair and lay upon the floor insensible, while the stranger made a sudden burst for the door, where he was instantly folded in the embrace of a massive plain-clothes man, who held him immovable while his colleague clicked on the handcuffs.

"So," I remarked, as we walked home, "your casts of the stick and the footprints were not wanted after all."

"On the contrary," he replied, "they are wanted very much. If the seal should fail to hang Mr Lyon, the casts will assuredly fit the rope round his neck." (This, by the way, actually happened. The defence that Lyon received the seal from some unknown person was countered by the unexpected production in court of the casts of Lyon's feet and the stick, which proved that the prisoner had been at Pinwell, and in the company of the deceased at or about the date of the murder, and secured his conviction.)

"By the way," said I, "how did you fix this crime on Lyon? It began, I think, with those stick impressions in the wood. What was there peculiar about those impressions?"

"Their peculiarity was that they were the impressions of a stick which apparently did not belong to the person who was carrying it."

"Good Lord, Thorndyke!" I exclaimed, "is that possible? How could an impression on the ground suggest ownership?"

"It is a curious point," he replied, "though essentially simple, which turns on the way in which the ferrule of a stick becomes worn. In a plain, symmetrical stick without a handle, the ferrule wears evenly all round; but in a stick with a crook or other definite handle, which is grasped in a particular way and always put down in the same position, the ferrule becomes worn on one side – the side opposite the handle, or the front of the stick. But the important point is that the bevel of wear is not *exactly* opposite the handle. It is to one side, for this reason. A man puts his stick down with the handle fore and aft; but as he steps forward, his hand swings away from his body, rotating the stick slightly outward. Consequently, the wear on the ferrule is slightly inward. That is to say, that in a right-handed man's stick the wear is slightly to the left and in a left-handed man's stick the wear is slightly to the right. But if a right-handed man walks with a left-handed stick, the impression on the ground will show the bevel of wear on the right side – which is the wrong side; and the right-handed rotation will throw it still farther to the right. Now in this case, the impression showed a shallow part, corresponding to the bevel of wear on the right side. Therefore it was a left-handed stick. But it was being carried in the right hand. Therefore it – apparently – did not belong to the person who was carrying it.

"Of course, as the person was unknown, the point was merely curious and did not concern us. But see how quickly circumstantial evidence mounts up. When we saw the feet of deceased, we knew that the footprints in the wood were his. Consequently the man with the stick was in his company: and that man at once came into the picture. Then Tom Rowlands told us that he had lost his stick and that he was left-handed; and he showed us the stick that he had got in exchange, and behold! That is a right-handed stick, as I ascertained by examining the ferrule. Here, then, is a left-handed man who has lost a stick and got a right-handed one in exchange; and there, in the wood, was a right-handed man who was carrying a left-handed stick and who was in company with the deceased. It was a striking coincidence. But further, the suggestion was that this unknown man was one of those who had called at Tom's office, and therefore one who wanted to get possession of the seal. This instantly suggested the question. Did he succeed in getting possession of the seal? We went to the safe; and at once it became obvious that he did."

"The seal in the safe was a forgery, of course?"

"Yes; and a bad forgery, though skilfully done. It was an electrotype; it was unsymmetrical; it did not agree with the keeper's measurements; and the perforation, though soiled at the ends, was bright in the middle from the boring tool."

"But how did you know that Lyon had made it?"

"I didn't. But he was by far the most probable person. He had a seal-rolling, from which an electro could be made, and he had the great skill that was necessary to turn a flat electro into a cylinder. He was an experienced faker of antiques, and he was a dealer who would have facilities for getting rid of the stolen seal. But it was only a probability, though, as time pressed, we had to act on it. Of course, when we saw him with the stick in his hand, it became virtually a certainty."

"And how did you guess that the seal was in the bust?"

"I had expected to find it enclosed in some plaster object, that being the safest way to hide it and smuggle it out of this country and into the United States. When I saw the bust, it was obvious. It was a hastily-made copy of one of Brucciani's busts. The plaster was damp – Brucciani's bake theirs dry – and had evidently been made only a few hours. So I broke it. If I had been mistaken I could have replaced it for five shillings, but the whole circumstances made it practically a certainty."

"Have you any idea as to how Lyon administered the poison?"

"We can only surmise," he replied. "Probably he took with him some solution of cyanide – if that was what was used – and poured it into Rowlands' whisky when his attention was otherwise occupied. It would be quite easy; and a single gulp of a quick-acting poison like that would finish the business in a minute or two. But we are not likely ever to know the details."

The evidence at the inquest showed that Thorndyke was probably right, and his evidence at the trial clinched the case against Lyon. As to the other man – who proved to be an American dealer well known to the New York Customs officials – the case against him broke down from lack of evidence that he was privy either to the murder or the theft. And so ended the case of Nebuchadnezzar's seal: a case that left Mr Brodribb more than ever convinced that Thorndyke was either gifted with a sixth sense which enabled him to smell out evidence or was in league with some familiar demon who did it for him.

CHAPTER FOUR

Phyllis Annesley's Peril

"One is sometimes disposed to regret," said Thorndyke, as we sat waiting for the arrival of Mr Mayfield, the solicitor, "that our practice is so largely concerned with the sordid and the unpleasant."

"Yes," I agreed. "Medical Jurisprudence is not always a particularly delicate subject. But it is our line of practice and we have got to take it as we find it."

"A philosophic conclusion, Jervis," he rejoined, "and worthy of my learned friend. It happens that the most intimate contact of Law and Medicine is in crimes against the person and consequently the proper study of the Medical Jurist is crime of that type. It is a regrettable fact, but we must accept it."

"At the same time," said I, "there don't seem to be any Medico-legal issues in this Bland case. The woman was obviously murdered. The only question is, who murdered her? And the answer to that question seems pretty obvious."

"It does," said Thorndyke. "But we shall be better able to judge when we have heard what Mayfield has to tell us. And I think I hear him coming up the stairs now."

I rose to open the door for our visitor, and, as he entered, I looked at him curiously. Mr Mayfield was quite a young man, and the mixture of deference and nervousness in his manner as he entered the room suggested no great professional experience.

"I am afraid, sir," said he, taking the easy chair that Thorndyke offered him, "that I ought to have come to you sooner, for the inquest, or, at least, the police court proceedings."

"You reserved your defence, I think?" said Thorndyke.

"Yes," replied the solicitor, with a wry smile. "I had to. There seemed to be nothing to say. So I put in a plea of Not Guilty and reserved the defence in the hope that something might turn up. But I am gravelled completely. It looks a perfectly hopeless case. I don't know how it strikes you, sir."

"I have seen only the newspaper reports," said Thorndyke. "They are certainly not encouraging. But let us disregard them. I suggest that you recite the facts of the case and I can ask any questions that are necessary to elucidate it further."

"Very well, sir," said Mayfield. "Then I will begin with the disappearance of Mrs Lucy Bland. That occurred about the eighteenth of last May. At that time she was living, apart from her husband, at Wimbledon, in furnished lodgings. After lunch on the eighteenth she went out, saying that she should not be home until night. She was seen by some one who knew her, at Wimbledon Station on the down side about three o'clock. At shortly after six probably on the same day, she went to the Post Office at Lower Ditton to buy some stamps. The postmistress, who knew her by sight, is certain that she called there, but cannot swear to the exact date. At any rate, she did not go home that night and was never seen alive again. Her landlady communicated with her husband and he at once applied to the police. But all the inquiries that were made led to nothing. She had disappeared without leaving a trace.

"The discovery was made four months later, on the sixteenth of September. On that day some workmen went to 'The Larches,' a smallish, old-fashioned, riverside house just outside Lower Ditton, to examine the electric wiring. The house was let to a new tenant, and as the meter had shown an unaccountable leakage of current during the previous quarter, they went to see what was wrong.

"To get at the main, they had to take up part of the floor of the dining-room; and when they got the boards up, they were horrified to discover a pair of feet – evidently a woman's feet – projecting from under the next board. They immediately went to the police station and reported what they had seen, whereupon the inspector and a sergeant accompanied them back to the house and directed them to take up several more boards, which they did; and there, jammed in between the joists, was the body of a woman who was subsequently identified as Mrs Lucy Bland. The corpse appeared to be perfectly fresh and only quite recently dead; but at the post-mortem it was discovered that it had been embalmed or preserved by injecting a solution of formaldehyde and might have been dead three or four months. The cause of death was given at the inquest as suffocation, probably preceded by the forcible administration of chloroform."

"The house, I understand," said Thorndyke, "belongs to one of the accused?"

"Yes. Miss Phyllis Annesley. It is her freehold, and she lived in it until recently. Last autumn, however, she took to travelling about and then partly dismantled the house and stored most of the furniture; but she kept two bedrooms furnished and the kitchen and dining-room in just usable condition, and she used to put up there for a day or two in the intervals, of her journeys, either alone or with her maid."

"And as to Miss Annesley's relations with the Blands?"

"She had known them both for some years. With Leonard Bland she was admittedly on affectionate terms, though there is no suggestion of improper relations between them. But Bland used to visit her when she lived there and they used to go for picnics on the river in the boat belonging to the house. Mrs Bland also occasionally visited Miss Annesley, and they seem to have been on quite civil terms. Of course, she knew about her husband's affection for the lady, but she doesn't seem to have had any strong feeling about it."

"And what were the relations of the husband and wife?" asked Thorndyke.

"Rather queer. They didn't suit one another, so they simply agreed to go their own ways. But they don't seem to have been unfriendly, and Mr Bland was most scrupulous in regard to his financial obligations to his wife. He not only allowed her liberal maintenance but went out of his way to make provision for her. I will give you an instance, which impressed me very much.

"An old acquaintance of his, a Mr Julius Wicks, who had been working for some years in the film studio at Los Angeles, came to England about a year ago and proposed to Bland that they should start one or two picture theatres in the province, Bland to find the money – which he was able to do – and Wicks to provide the technical knowledge and do the actual management. Bland agreed, and a partnership was arranged on the basis of two-thirds of the profits to Bland and one-third to Wicks; with the proviso that if Bland should die, all his rights as partner should be vested in his wife."

"And supposing Wicks should die?"

"Well, Wicks was not married, though he was engaged to a film actress. On his death, his share would go to Bland, and similarly, on Bland's death, if he should die after his wife, his share would go to his partner."

"Bland seems to have been a fairly good business man," said I.

"Yes," Mayfield agreed. "The arrangement was all in his favour. But he was the capitalist, you see. However, the point is that Bland was quite mindful of his wife's interests. There was nothing like enmity."

"Then," said Thorndyke, "one motive is excluded. Was the question of divorce ever raised?"

"It couldn't be," said Mayfield. "There were no grounds on either side. But it seems to have been recognised and admitted that if Bland had been free he would have married Miss Annesley. They were greatly attached to one another."

"That seems a fairly solid motive," said I.

"It appears to be," Mayfield admitted. "But to me, who have known these people for years and have always had the highest opinion of them, it seems – well, I can't associate this atrocious crime with them at all. However, that is not to the point. I must get on with the facts."

"Very soon after the discovery at 'The Larches,' the police learned that there had been rumours in Lower Ditton for some time past of strange happenings at the house and that two labourers named Brodie and Stanton knew something definite. They accordingly looked up these two men and examined them separately, when both men made substantially identical statements, which were to this effect:

"About the middle of May – neither of them was able to give an exact date – between nine and ten in the evening, they were walking together along the lane in which 'The Larches' is situated when they saw a man lurking in the front garden of the house. As they were passing, he came to the gate and beckoned to them, and when they approached he whispered; 'I say, mates, there's something rummy going on in this house.'

" 'How do you know?' asked Brodie.

" 'I've been looking in through a hole in the shutter,' the man replied. 'They seem to be hiding something under the floor. Come and have a look.'

"The two men followed him up the garden to the back of the house, where he took them to one of the windows of a ground-floor room and pointed to two holes in the outside shutters.

" 'Just take a peep in through them,' said he.

"Each of the men put an eye to one of the holes and looked in; and this is what they both saw: there were two rooms, communicating, with a wide arch between. Through the arch and at the far end of the second room were two persons, a man and a woman. They were on their hands and knees, apparently doing something to the floor. Presently the man, who had on a painter's white blouse, rose and picked up a board which he stood on end against the wall. Then he stooped again and seemed to lay hold of something that lay on the floor – something that looked like a large bundle or a roll of carpet. At this moment something passed across in front of the holes and shut out the view – so that there must have been a third person in the room. When the obstructing body moved away again, the man was kneeling on the floor looking down at the bundle and the woman had come forward and was standing just in the arch with a pair of pincers in her hand. She was dressed in a spotted pinafore with a white sailor collar, and both the men recognised her at once as Miss Annesley."

"They knew her by sight, then?" said Thorndyke.

"Yes. They were Ditton men. It is a small place and everybody in it must have known Miss Annesley – and Bland, too, for that matter. Well, they saw her standing in the archway quite distinctly. Neither of the men has the least doubt as to her identity. They watched her for, perhaps, half a minute. Then the invisible person inside moved in front of the peepholes and shut out the scene.

"When the obstruction moved away, the woman was back in the farther room, kneeling on the floor. The bundle had disappeared and the man was in the act of taking the board, which he had rested against the wall, and laying it in its place in the floor. After this, the obstruction kept coming and going, so that the watchers only got occasional glimpses of what was going on. They saw the man apparently hammering nails into the floor and they heard faint sounds of knocking. On one occasion, towards the end of the proceedings, they saw the man standing in the archway with his face towards them, apparently looking at something in his hand. They couldn't see what the thing was, but they clearly recognised the man as Mr Bland, whom they both knew well by sight. Then the view was shut out again, and when they next saw Mr Bland, he was standing by Miss Annesley in the farther room, looking down at the floor and taking off his blouse. As it seemed that the business was over and that Bland and Miss Annesley would probably be coming out, the men thought it best to clear off, lest they should be seen.

"As they walked up the lane, they discussed the mysterious proceedings that they had witnessed, but could make nothing of them. The stranger suggested that perhaps Miss Annesley was hiding her plate or valuables to keep them safe while she was travelling, and hinted that it might be worth someone's while to take the floor up later on and see what was there. But this suggestion Brodie and Stanton, who are most respectable men, condemned strongly, and they agreed that, as the affair was no concern of theirs, they had better say nothing about it. But they evidently must have talked to some extent, for the affair got to be spoken about in the village, and, of course, when the body was discovered under the floor, the gossip soon reached the ears of the police."

"Has the third man come forward to give evidence?" Thorndyke asked.

"No, he has not been found yet. He was a stranger to both men; apparently a labourer or farm-hand or tramp. But nothing is known about him. So that is the case; and it is about as hopeless as it is possible to be. Of course, there is the known character of the accused; but against that is a perfectly intelligible motive and the evidence of two eye-witnesses. Do you think you would be disposed to undertake the defence, sir? I realise that it is asking a great deal of you."

"I should like to think the matter over," said Thorndyke, "and make a few preliminary inquiries. And I should want to read over the depositions in full details. Can you let me have them?"

"I have a verbatim report of the police court proceedings and of the inquest. I will leave them with you now. And when may I hope to have your decision?"

"By the day after tomorrow at the latest," was the reply, on which the young solicitor produced a bundle of papers from his bag, and having laid them on the table, thanked us both and took his leave.

"Well, Thorndyke," said I when Mayfield had gone, "I am fairly mystified. I know you would not undertake a merely formal defence, but what else you could do is, I must confess, beyond my imagination. It seems to me that the prosecution have only to call the witnesses and the verdict of 'Guilty' follows automatically."

"That is how it appears to me," said Thorndyke. "And if it still appears so when I have read the reports and made my preliminary investigations, I shall decline the brief. But appearances are sometimes misleading."

With this he took the reports and the note-book, in which he had made a few brief memoranda of Mayfield's summary of the case, and drawing a chair to the table, proceeded, with quiet concentration, to read through and make notes on the evidence. When he had finished, he passed the reports to me and rose, pocketing his note-book and glancing at his watch.

"Read the evidence through carefully, Jervis," said he, "and tell me if you see any possible way out. I have one or two calls to make, but I shall not be more than an hour. When I come back, I should like to hear your views on the case."

During his absence I read the reports through with the closest attention. Something in Thorndyke's tone had seemed to hint at a possible flaw in the case for the prosecution. But I could find no escape from the conviction that these two persons were guilty. The reports merely amplified what Mayfield had told us; and the added detail, especially in the case of the eye-witnesses, only made the evidence more conclusive. I could not see the material for even a formal defence.

In less than an hour my colleague re-entered the room, and I was about to give him my impressions of the evidence when he said:

"It is rather early, Jervis, but I think we had better go and get some lunch. I have arranged to go down to Ditton this afternoon and have a look at the house. Mayfield has given me a note to the police sergeant, who has the key and is virtually in possession."

"I don't see what you will gain by looking at the house," said I.

"Neither do I," he replied. "But it is a good rule always to inspect the scene of a crime and check the evidence as far as possible."

"Well," I said, "it is a forlorn hope. I have read through the evidence and it seems to me that the accused are as good as convicted. I can see no line of defence at all. Can you?"

"At present I cannot," he replied. "But there are one or two points that I should like to clear up before I decide whether or not to undertake the defence. And I have a great belief in first-hand observation."

We consumed a simplified lunch at one of our regular haunts in Fleet Street and from thence were conveyed by a taxi to Waterloo, where we caught the selected train to Lower Ditton. I had put the reports in my pocket, and during our journey I read them over again, to see if I could discover any point that would be cleared up by an inspection of the premises.

For, in spite of the rather vague purpose implied by Thorndyke's explanation, something in my colleague's manner, coupled with long experience of his methods, made me suspect that he had some definite object in view. But nothing was said by either of us during the journey, nor did we discuss the case; indeed, so far as I could see, there was nothing to discuss.

Our reception at the Lower Ditton Police Station was something more than cordial. The sergeant recognised Thorndyke instantly – it appeared that he was an enthusiastic admirer of my colleague – and after a brief glance at Mayfield's note, took a key from his desk and put on his helmet.

"Lord bless you, sir," said he, "I don't need to be told who you are. I've seen you in court, and heard you. I'll come along with you to the house myself."

I suspected that Thorndyke would have gladly dispensed with this attention, but he accepted it with genial courtesy, and we went forth through the village and along the quiet lane in which the ill-omened house was situated. And as we went, the sergeant commented on the case with curiously unofficial freedom.

"You've got your work cut out, sir, if you are going to conduct the defence. But I wish you luck. I've know Miss Annesley for some years – she was well known in the village here – and a nicer, gentler, more pleasant lady you wouldn't wish to meet. To think of her in connection with a murder – and such a murder, too – such a brutal, callous affair! Well, it's beyond me. And yet there it is, unless those two men are lying."

"Is there any reason to suppose that they are?" I asked.

"Well, no; there isn't. They are good, sober, decent men. And it would be such an atrociously wicked lie. And they both knew the prisoners, and liked them. Everybody like Mr Bland and Miss Annesley, though their friendship for one another may not have been quite in order. But I can tell you, sir, these two men are frightfully cut up at having to give evidence. This is the house."

He opened a gate and we entered the garden, beyond which was a smallish, old-fashioned house, of which the ground-floor windows were protected by outside shutters. We walked round to the back of the house, where was another garden with a lawn and a path leading down to the river.

"Is that a boat-house?" Thorndyke asked, pointing to a small gable that appeared above a clump of lilac bushes.

"Yes," replied the sergeant. "And there is a boat in it; a good, beamy, comfortable tub that Miss Annesley and her friend used to go out picnicking in. This is the window that the men peeped in at, but you can't see much now because the room is all dark."

I looked at the two French windows, which opened on to the lawn, and reflected on this new instance of the folly of wrong-doers. Each window was fitted with a pair of strong shutters, which bolted on the inside, and each shutter was pierced, about five feet from the sill, by a circular hole a little over an inch in diameter. It seemed incredible that two sane persons, engaged in the concealment of a murdered body, should have left those four holes uncovered for any chance eavesdropper to spy on their doings.

But my astonishment at this lack of precaution was still greater when the sergeant admitted us and we stood inside the room, for both the windows, as well as the pair in the farther room, were furnished with heavy curtains.

"Yes," said the sergeant, in answer to my comment, "it's a queer thing how people overlook matters of vital importance. You see, they drew the drawing-room curtains all right, but they forgot these. Is there anything in particular that you want to see, sir?"

"I should like to see where the body was hidden," said Thorndale, "But I will just look round the rooms first."

He walked slowly to and fro, looking about him and evidently fixing the appearance of the rooms on his memory. Not that there was much to see or remember. The two nearly square rooms communicated through a wide arch, once closed by curtains, as shown by the brass curtain-rod. The back room had been completely dismantled with the exception of the window curtains, but the front room, although the floor and the walls were bare, was not entirely unfurnished. The sideboard was still in position and bore at each end a tall electric light standard, as did also the mantelpiece. There were three dining chairs and a good-sized gate-leg table stood closed against the wall.

"I see you have not had the floorboards nailed down," said Thorndyke.

"No, sir; not yet. So we can see where the body was hidden and where the electric main is. The electricians took up the wrong board at first – that is how they came to discover the body. And one of them said that the boards over the main had been raised recently, and he thought that the – er – the accused had meant to hide the body there, but when they got the floor up they struck the main and had to choose a fresh place."

He stooped, and lifting the loose boards, which he stood on end against the mantelpiece, exposed the joist and the earth floor about a foot below them. In one of the spaces the electric main ran and in the adjoining one the apparently disused gas main.

"This is where we found poor Mrs Bland," said the sergeant, pointing to an empty space. "It was an awful sight. Gave me quite a turn. The poor lady was lying on her side, jammed down between the joists and her nose flattened up against one of the timbers. They must have been brutes that did it, and I can't – I really can't believe that Miss Annesley was one of them."

"It looks a narrow place for a body to lie in," said I.

"The joist are sixteen inches apart," said Thorndyke, laying his pocket rule across the space, "and two and a half inches thick. Heavy timber and wide spaces."

He stood up, and turning round, looked towards the windows of the back room. I followed his glance and noted, almost with a start, the two holes in the shutter of the left-hand window (the right-hand window, of course, from outside) glaring into the darkened room like a pair of inquisitive, accusing eyes. The holes in the other window were hardly visible, and the reason for the difference was obvious. The one window had small panes and thick muntins, or sash-bars, whereas the other was glazed with large sheets of plate glass and had no muntins.

"Of course it would be dark at the time," I said in response to his unspoken comment, "and this room would be lighted up, more or less."

"Not so very dark in May," he replied. "There is a furnished bedroom, isn't there, Sergeant?"

"Two, sir," was the reply; and the sergeant forthwith opened the door and led the way across the hall and up the stairs.

"This is Miss Annesley's room," he said, opening a door gingerly and peering in.

We entered the room and looked about us with vague curiosity. It was a simple-furnished room, but dainty and tasteful, with its small four-post bedstead, light easy chair and little, ladylike writing-table.

"That's Mr Bland," said the sergeant, pointing to a double photograph-frame on the table, "and the lady is Miss Annesley herself."

I took up the frame and looked curiously at the two portraits. For a pair of murderers they were certainly uncommonly prepossessing. The man, who looked about thirty-five, was a typical good-looking, middle-class Englishman, while the woman was distinctly handsome, with a thoughtful, refined and gentle cast of face.

"She has something of a Japanese air," said I, "with that coil on the top of the head and the big ivory hairpin stuck through it."

I passed the frame to Thorndyke, who regarded each portrait attentively, and then, taking both photographs out of the frame, closely examined each in turn, back and front, before replacing them.

"The other bedroom," said the sergeant as Thorndyke laid down the frame, "is the spare room. There's nothing to see in it."

Nevertheless he conducted us into it, and when we had verified his statement we returned downstairs.

"Before we go," said Thorndyke, "I will just see what is opposite those holes."

He walked to the window and was just looking out though one of the holes when the sergeant, who had followed him closely, suddenly slid along the floor and nearly fell.

"Well, I never!" he exclaimed, recovering himself and stooping to pick up some small object. "There's a dangerous thing to leave lying about the floor. Bit of slate pencil – at least, that is what it looks like."

He handed it to Thorndyke, who glanced at it and remarked:

"Yes, things that roll under the foot are apt to produce broken bones; but I think you had better take care of it. I may have to ask you something about it at the trial."

We bade the sergeant farewell at the bottom of the lane and as we turned into the footpath to the station, I said:

"We don't seem to have picked up very much more than Mayfield told us – excepting that bit of slate pencil. By the way, why did you tell the sergeant to keep it?"

"On the broad principle of keeping everything, relevant or irrelevant. But it wasn't slate pencil; it was a fragment of a small carbon rod."

"Presumably dropped by the electricians who had been working in the room," said I, and then asked; "Have you come to any decision about this case?"

"Yes; I shall undertake the defence."

"Well," I said, "I can't imagine what line you will take. Strong suspicion would have fallen on these two persons even if there had been no witnesses; but the evidence of those two eye-witnesses seems to clinch the matter."

"Precisely," said Thorndyke. "That is my position. I rest my case on the evidence of those two men – as I hope it will appear under cross-examination."

This statement of Thorndyke's gave me much food for reflection during the days that followed. But it was not very nourishing food, for the case still remained perfectly incomprehensible. To be sure, if the evidence of the two eye-witnesses could be shown to be false, the case against the prisoners would break down, since it would bring another suspected person into view. But their evidence was clearly not false. They were men of known respectability and no one doubted the truth of their statements.

Nor was the obscurity of the case lightened in any way by Thorndyke's proceedings. We called together on the two prisoners, but from neither did we elicit any fresh facts.

Neither could establish a clear alibi or suggest any explanation of the eye-witnesses' statements. They gave a simple denial of having been in the house at that time or of having ever taken up the floor.

Both prisoners, however, impressed me favourably. Bland, whom we interviewed at Brixton, seemed a pleasant, manly fellow, frank and straightforward though quite shrewd and business-like; while Miss Annesley, whom we saw at Holloway, was a really charming young lady – sweet-faced, dignified and very gracious and gentle in manner. In one respect, indeed, I found her disappointing. The picturesque coil had disappeared from the top of her head and her hair had been shortened ("bobbed" is, I believe, the correct term) into a mere fringe. Thorndyke also noticed the change, and in fact commented on it.

"Yes," she admitted, "it is a disimprovement in my case. It doesn't suit me. But I really had no choice. When I was in Paris in the spring I had an accident. I was having my hair cleaned with petrol when it caught fire. It was most alarming. The hairdresser had the presence of mind to throw a damp towel over my head, and that saved my life. But my hair was nearly all burnt. There was nothing for it but to have it trimmed as evenly as possible. But it looked horrid at first. I had my photograph taken by Barton soon after I came home, just as a record, you know, and it looks awfully odd. I look like a Bluecoat boy."

"By the way," said Thorndyke, "when did you return?"

"I landed in England about the middle of April and went straight to my little flat at Paddington, where I have been living ever since."

"You don't remember where you were on the eighteenth of May?"

"I was living at my flat, but I can't remember what I did on that day. You don't, as a rule, unless you keep a diary, which I do not."

This was not very promising. As we came away from the prison, I felt, on the one hand, a conviction that this sweet, gracious lady could have had no hand in this horrible crime, and on the other an utter despair of extricating her from the web of circumstances in which she had become enmeshed.

From Thorndyke I could gather nothing, except that he was going on with his investigation – a significant fact, in his case. To my artfully disguised questions he had one invariable reply: "My dear Jervis, you have read the evidence, you have seen the house, you have all the facts. Think the case over and consider the possibilities of the cross-examination." And that was all I could get out of him.

He was certainly very busy, but his activities only increased my bewilderment. He sent a well-known architect down to make a scale-plan of the house and grounds; and he dispatched Polton to take photographs of the place from every possible point of view. The latter, indeed, was up to his eyes in work, and enjoying himself amazingly, but as secret as an oyster. As he went about, beaming with happiness and crinkling with self-complacency, he exasperated me to the extent that I could have banged his little head against the wall. In short, though I had watched the development of the case from the beginning, I was still without a glimmer of understanding of it even when I took my seat in court on the morning of the trial.

It was a memorable occasion, and every incident in it is still in my memory. Particularly do I remember looking with a sort of horrified fascination at the female prisoner, standing by her friend in the dock, pale but composed and looking the very type and picture of womanly beauty and dignity; and reflecting with a shudder that the graceful neck – looking longer and more slender from the shortness of the hair – might very probably be, within a matter of days, encircled by the hangman's rope. These lugubrious reflections were interrupted by the entrance of two persons, a man and a woman, who were apparently connected with the case, since as they took their seats they both looked towards the dock and exchanged silent greetings with the prisoners.

"Do you know who those people are, Mayfield?" I asked.

"That is Mr Julius Wicks, Mr Bland's partner, and his fiancée, Miss Eugenia Kropp, the film actress," he replied.

I was about to ask him if they were here to give evidence when, the preliminaries having come to an end, the counsel for the Crown, Sir John Turville, rose and began his opening speech.

It was a good speech and eminently correct; but its very moderation made it the more damaging. It began with an outline of the facts, almost identical with Mayfield's summary, and a statement of the evidence which would presently be given by the principal witnesses.

"And now," said Sir John, when he had finished his recital, "let us bring these facts to a focus. Considered as a related group, this is what they show us. On the sixteenth of September there is found, concealed under the floor of a certain room in a certain house, the body of a woman who has evidently been murdered. That woman is the separated wife of a man who is on affectionate terms with another woman whom he would admittedly wish to marry and who would be willing to marry him. This murdered woman is, in short, the obstacle to the marriage desired by these two persons. Now the house in which the corpse is concealed is the property of one of those two persons, and both of them have access to it; and no other person has access to it. Here, then, to begin with, is a set of profoundly suspicious circumstances.

"But there are others far more significant. That unfortunate lady, the unwanted wife of the prisoner, Bland, disappeared mysteriously on the eighteenth of last May; and witnesses will prove that the body was deposited under the floor on or about that date. Now, on or about that same date, in that same house, in that same room, in the same part of that room, those two persons, the prisoners at the bar, were seen by the two eminently respectable witnesses in the act of concealing some large object under the floor. What could that object have been? The floor of the room has been taken up and nothing whatever but the corpse of this poor murdered lady has been found under it. The irresistible conclusion is that those two persons were then and there engaged in concealing that corpse.

"To sum up, then, the reasons for believing that the prisoners are guilty of the crime with which they are charged are threefold. They had an intelligible and strong motive to commit that crime; they had the opportunity to commit it; and we have evidence from two eye-witnesses which makes it practically an observed fact that the prisoners did actually commit that crime."

As the Crown counsel sat down, pending the swearing of the first witness, I turned to Thorndyke and said anxiously:

"I can't imagine what you are going to reply to that."

"My reply," he answered quietly, "will be largely governed by what I am able to elicit in cross-examination."

Here the first witness was called – the electrician who discovered the body – and gave his evidence, but Thorndyke made no cross-examination. He was followed by the sergeant, who described the discovery in more detail. As the Crown counsel sat down, Thorndyke rose, and I picked up my ears.

"Have you mentioned everything that you saw or found in this room?" he asked.

"Yes, at that time. Later – on the second of October – I found a small piece of carbon pencil on the floor of the front room near the window."

He produced from his pocket an envelope from which he extracted the fragment of the alleged "slate pencil" and passed it to Thorndyke, who, having passed it to the judge with the intimation that he wished it to be put in evidence, sat down. The judge inspected the fragment curiously and then cast an inquisitive glance at Thorndyke – as he had done once or twice before. For my colleague's appearance in the role of counsel was a rare event, and one usually productive of surprises.

To the long succession of witnesses who followed Thorndyke listened attentively but did not cross-examine. I saw the judge look at him curiously from time to time and my own curiosity grew more and more intense. Evidently he was saving himself up for the crucial witnesses. At length the name of James Brodie was called, and a serious-looking elderly workman entered the box. He gave his evidence clearly and confidently, though with manifest reluctance, and I could see that this vivid description of that sinister scene made a great impression on the jury. When the examination in chief was finished, Thorndyke rose, and the judge settled himself to listen with an air of close attention.

"Have you ever been inside 'The Larches'?" Thorndyke asked.

"No sir. I've passed the house twice every day for years, but I've never been inside it."

"When you looked in through the shutter, was the room well lighted?"

"No 'twas very dim. I could only just see what the people were doing."

"Yet you recognised Miss Annesley quite clearly?"

"Not at first, I didn't. Not until she came and stood in the archway. The light seemed quite good there."

"Did you see her come out of the front room and walk to the arch?"

"No. I saw her in the front room and then something must have stopped up the hole, for 'twas all dark. Then the hole got clear again and I saw her standing in the arch. But I only saw her for a moment or two. Then the hole got stopped again and when it opened she was back in the front room."

"How did you know that the woman in the front room was Miss Annesley? Could you see her face in that dim light?"

"No, but I could tell her by her dress. She wore a striped pinafore with a big, white sailor-collar. Besides, there wasn't nobody else there."

"And with regard to Mr Bland. Did you see him walk out of the front room and up to the arch?"

"No. 'Twas the same as with Miss Annesley. Something kept passing across the hole. I see him in the front room; then I see him in the arch and then I see him in the front room again."

"When they were in the archway, were they moving or standing still?"

"They both seemed to be standing quite still."

"Was Miss Annesley looking straight towards you?"

"No. Her face was turned away a little."

"I want you to look at these photographs and tell us if any of them shows the head in the position in which you saw it."

He handed a bundle of photographs to the witness, who looked at them, one after another, and at last picked out one.

"That is exactly how she looked," said he. "She might have been standing for this very picture."

He passed the photograph to Thorndyke, who noted the number written on it and passed it to the judge, who also noted the number and laid it on his desk. Thorndyke then resumed:

"You say the light was very dim in the front room. Were the electric lamps alight?"

"None that I could see were alight."

"How many electric lamps could you see?"

"Well, there was three hanging from the ceiling and there was two standards on the mantelpiece and one on the sideboard. None of them was alight."

"Was there only one standard on the sideboard?"

"There may have been more, but I couldn't see 'em because I could only see just one corner of the sideboard."

"Could you see the whole of the mantelpiece?"

"Yes. There was a standard lamp at each end."

"Could you see anything on the near side of the mantelpiece?"

"There was a table there; a folding table with twisted legs. But I could only see part of that. The side of the arch cut it off."

"You have said that you could see Miss Annesley quite clearly and could see how she was dressed. Could you see how her hair was arranged?"

"Yes. 'Twas done up on the top of her head in what they calls a bun and there was a sort of a skewer stuck through it."

As the witness gave this answer, a light broke on me. Not a very clear light, for the mystery was still unsolved. But I could see that Thorndyke had a very definite strategic plan. And, glancing at the dock, I was immediately aware that the prisoners had seen the light, too.

"You have described what looked like a hole in the floor," Thorndyke resumed, "where some boards had been raised, near the middle of the room. Was that hole nearer the sideboard or nearer the mantelpiece?"

"It was nearer the mantelpiece," the witness replied; on which Thorndyke sat down, the witness left the box, and both the judge and the counsel for the prosecution rapidly turned over their notes with evident surprise.

The next witness was Albert Stanton and his evidence was virtually a repetition of Brodie's: and when, in cross-examination, Thorndyke put over again the same series of questions, he elicited precisely the same answers even to the recognition of the same photograph. And again I began to see a light. But only a glimmer.

Stanton being the last of the witnesses for the Crown, his brief re-examination by Sir John Turville completed the case for the prosecution. Thereupon Thorndyke rose and announced that he called witnesses, and forthwith the first of them appeared in the box. This was Frederick Stokes, a RIBA architect, and he deposed that he had made a careful survey of the house called 'The Larches' at Lower Ditton and prepared a plan on the scale of half an inch to a foot. He swore that the plan − of which he produced the original and a number of lithographed duplicates − was true and exact in every respect. Thorndyke took the plans from him and passing them to the judge asked that the original should be put in evidence and the duplicates handed to the jury.

The next witness was Joseph Barton of Kensington, photographer. He deposed to having taken photographs of Miss Annesley on various occasions, the last being on the twenty-third of last April. He produced copies of them all with the date written on each. He swore that the dates written were correct dates. The photographs were handed up to the judge, who looked them over, one by one. Suddenly he seemed, as it were, to stiffen, and turned quickly from the photograph to his notes; and I knew that he had struck the last portrait − the one with the short hair.

As the photographs left the box, his place was taken by no less a person than our ingenious laboratory assistant; who, having taken his place, beamed on the judge, the jury and the court in general, with a face wreathed in crinkly smiles. Nathaniel Polton, being sworn, deposed that, on the fifteenth of October, he proceeded to 'The Larches' at Lower Ditton and took three photographs of the ground-floor rooms. The first was taken through the right-hand hole of the shutter marked A in the plan; the second through the left-handed hole, and the third from a point inside the back room between the windows and nearer to the window marked B. He produced those photographs with the particulars written on each. He had also made some composite photographs showing the two prisoners dressed as the witnesses, Brodie and Stanton, had described them. The bodies in those photographs were the bodies of Miss Winifred Blake and Mr Robert Anstey, KC, respectively. On these bodies the heads of the prisoners had been printed; and here Polton described the method of substitution in detail. The purpose of the photographs was to show that a photograph could be produced with the head of one person and the body of another. He also deposed to having seen and taken possession of two photographs, one of each of the two prisoners, which he found in the bedroom and which he now produced and passed to the judge. And this completed his evidence.

Thorndyke now called the prisoner, Bland, and having elicited from him a sworn denial of the charge, proceeded to examine him respecting the profits from his three picture theatres; which, it appeared, amounted to over six thousand pounds per annum.

"In the event of your death, what becomes of this valuable property?"

"If my wife had been alive it would have gone to her, but as she is dead, it goes to my partner and manager, Mr Julius Wicks."

"In whose custody was the house at Ditton while Miss Annesley was in France?"

"In mine. The keys were in my possession."

"Were the keys ever out of your possession?"

"Only for one day. My partner, Mr Wicks, asked to be allowed to use the boat for a trip on the river and to take a meal in the house. So I lent him the keys, which he returned the next day."

After a short cross-examination, Bland returned to the dock and was succeeded by Miss Annesley, who, having given a sworn denial of the charge, described her movements in France and in London about the period of the crime. She also described, in answer to a question, the circumstances under which she had lost her hair.

"Can you remember the date on which this accident happened?" Thorndyke asked.

"Yes. It was on the thirtieth of March. I made a note of the date, so that I could see how long my hair took to grow."

As Thorndyke sat down, the counsel for the prosecution rose and made a somewhat searching cross-examination, but without in any way shaking the prisoner's evidence. When this was concluded and Miss Annesley had returned to the docks, Thorndyke rose to address the court for the defence.

"I shall not occupy your time, gentlemen," he began, "by examining the whole mass of evidence nor by arguing the question of motive. The guilt of innocence of the prisoners turns on the accuracy or inaccuracy of the evidence of the two witnesses, Brodie and Stanton; and to the examination of that evidence I shall confine myself.

"Now that evidence, as you may have noticed, presents some remarkable discrepancies. In the first place, both witnesses describe what they saw in identical terms. They saw exactly the same things in exactly the same relative positions. But this is a physical impossibility, if they were really looking into a room; for they were looking in from different points of view; through different holes, which were two feet six inches apart. But there is another much more striking discrepancy. Both these men have described, most intelligently, fully and clearly, a number of objects in that room which were totally invisible to both of them; and they have described as only partly visible other objects which were in full view. Both witnesses, for instance, have described the mantelpiece with its two standard lamps and a table with twisted legs on the near side of it; and both saw one corner only of the sideboard. But if you look at the architect's plan and test it with a straight-edge, you will see that neither the mantelpiece nor the table could possibly be seen by either. The whole of that side of the room was hidden from them by the jamb of the arch. While as to the sideboard, the whole of it, with its two standards, was visible to Brodie and Stanton, the whole of it excepting a small portion of the near side. But further, if you lay the straight-edge on the point marked C and test it against the sides of the arch, you will see that a person standing at that spot would get the exact view described by both the witnesses. I pass round duplicate plans with pencil lines ruled on them; but in case you find any difficulty in following the plans, I have put in the photographs of the room taken by Polton. The first photograph was taken through the hole used by Brodie, and shows exactly what he would have seen on looking through that hole; and you see that it agrees completely with the plan but disagrees totally with his description. The second photograph shows what was visible to Stanton; and the third photograph, taken from the point marked C, shows exactly the view description by both the witnesses, but which neither of them could possibly have seen under the circumstances stated.

"Now what is the explanation of these extraordinary discrepancies? No one, I suppose, doubts the honesty of these witnesses. I certainly do not. I have no doubt whatever that they were telling the truth to the best of their belief. Yet they have stated that they saw things which it is physically impossible that they could have seen. How can these amazing contradictions be reconciled?"

He paused, and in the breathless silence, I noticed that the judge was gazing at him with an expression of intense expectancy; an expression that was reflected on the jury and indeed on every person present.

"Well, gentlemen," he resumed, "there is one explanation which completely reconciles these contradictions; and that explanation also reconciles all the other strange contradictions and discrepancies which you may have noticed. If we assume that these two men, instead of looking through an arch into a room, as they believed, were really looking at a moving picture thrown on a screen stretched across the arch, then all the contradictions

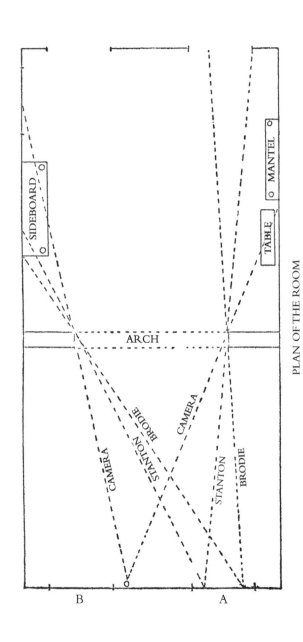

SIDEBOARD

MANTEL

TABLE

ARCH

CAMERA

BRODIE

STANTON

CAMERA

STANTON

BRODIE

B

A

PLAN OF THE ROOM

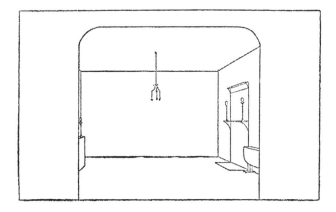

THE ROOM AS DESCRIBED BY BRODIE

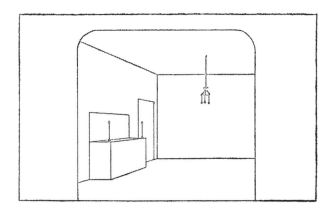

THE ROOM AS SEEN FROM BRODIE'S SPYHOLE

vanish. Everything becomes perfectly plain, consistent and understandable.

"Thus both men, from two different points of view, saw exactly the same scene; naturally, if they were both looking at the same picture, but otherwise quite impossible. Again, both men, from the point A, saw a view which was visible only from the point C. Perfectly natural if they were both looking at a picture taken from the point C; for a picture is the same picture from whatever point of view it is seen. But otherwise a physical impossibility.

"You may object that these men would have seen the difference between a picture and a real room. Perhaps they would, even in that dim light – if they had looked at the scene with both eyes. But each man was looking with only one eye – through a small hole. Now it requires the use of both eyes to distinguish between a solid object and a flat picture. To a one-eyed man there is no difference – which is probably the reason that one-eyed artists are such accurate draughtsmen; they see the world around them as a flat picture, just as they draw it, whereas a two-eyed artist has to turn the solid into a flat. For the same reason, if you look at a picture with one eye shut it tends to look solid, really because the frame and the solid objects around it have gone flat. So that, if this picture was coloured, as it must have been, it would have been indistinguishable, to these one-eyed observers, from the solid reality.

"Then, let us see how the other contradictions disappear. There is the appearance of the prisoner Annesley. She was seen – on or after the eighteenth of May – with her long hair coiled on the top of her head. But at that date her hair was quite short. You have heard the evidence and you have the photograph taken on the twenty-third of April showing her with short hair, like a man's. Here is a contradiction which vanishes at once if you realise that these men were not looking at Miss Annesley at all, but at a photograph of her taken more than a year previously."

"And everything agrees with this assumption. The appearance of Miss Annesley has been declared by the witnesses to be identical with that photograph – a copy of which was in the house and could have been copied by anyone who had access to the house. Her figure was perfectly stationary. She appeared suddenly in the arch and then disappeared; she was not seen to come or to go. And the light kept coming and going, with intervals of darkness which are inexplicable, but that exactly fitted these appearances and disappearances. Then the figure was well lighted, though the room was nearly dark. Of course it was well lighted. It had to be recognised. And of course the rest of the room was dimly lighted, because the film-actors in the background had to be unrecognised.

"Then there is the extraordinary dress; the striped pinafore with the great white collar and the painter's blouse worn by Bland. Why this ridiculous masquerade? Its purpose is obvious. It was to make these observers believe that the portraits in the arch – which they mistook for real people – were the same persons as the film-actors in the background, whose features they could not distinguish. And Mr Polton has shown us how the clothing of the portraits was managed.

"Then there is the lighting of the room. How was it lighted? None of the electric lamps was alight. *But* – a piece of a carbon pencil from an arch lamp, such as cinematographers use, has been found near the point C, from which spot the picture would have been taken and exhibited; and the electric light meter showed, about this date, an unaccountable leakage of current such as would be explained by the use of an arch lamp.

"Then the evidence of the witnesses shows the hole in the floor in the wrong place. Of course it could not have been a real hole, for the gas and electric mains were just underneath. It was probably an oblong of black paper. But why was it in the wrong place? The explanation, I suggest, is that the picture was taken before the murder (and probably shown before the murder, too); that the spot shown was the one in which it was intended to bury the body, but that when the floor was taken up after the murder, the mains were found underneath and a new spot had to be chosen.

"Finally – as to the discrepancies – what has become of the third spectator? The mysterious man who came to the gate and called in these two men from the lane – along which they were known to pass every day at about the same time? Who is this mysterious individual? And where is he? Can we give him a name? Can we say that he is at this moment in this court, sitting amongst the spectators, listening to the pleadings in defence of his innocent victims, the prisoners who stand at the bar on their deliverance? I affirm, gentlemen, that we can. And more than that it is not permitted to me to say."

He paused, and a strange, impressive hush fell on the court. Men and women furtively looked about them: the jury stared openly into the body of the court, and the judge, looking up from his notes, cast a searching glance among the spectators. Suddenly my eye lighted on Mr Wicks and his fiancée. The man was wiping away the sweat that streamed down his ashen, ghastly face; the woman had rested her head in her hands, and was trembling as if in an ague-fit.

I was not the only observer. One after another – spectators, ushers, jurymen, counsel, judge – noticed the terror-stricken pair, until every eye in the court was turned on them. And the silence that fell on the place was like the silence of the grave.

It was a dramatic moment. The air was electric; the crowded court tense with emotion. And Thorndyke, looking, with his commanding figure and severe, impassive face, like a personification of Fate and Justice, stood awhile motionless and silent, letting emotion set the coping-stone on reason.

At length he resumed his address. "Before concluding," he began, "I have to say a few words on another aspect of the case. The learned counsel for the prosecution, referring to the motive for this crime, has suggested a desire on the part of the prisoners to remove the obstacle to their marriage. But it has been given in evidence that there are other persons who had a yet stronger and more definite motive for getting rid of the deceased Lucy Bland. You have heard that in the event of Bland's death, his partner, Julius

Wicks, stood to inherit property of the value of six thousand pounds per annum, provided that Bland's wife was already dead. Now, the murder of Lucy Bland has fulfilled one of the conditions for the devolution of this property; and if you should convict and his lordship should sentence the prisoner, Bland, then his death on the gallows would fulfil the other condition and this great property would pass to his partner, Julius Wicks. This is a material point; as is also the fact that Julius Wicks is, as you have heard, an expert film-producer and cinema operator; that he has been proved to have had access to the house at Ditton, and that he is engaged to a film-actress.

"In conclusion, I submit that the evidence of Brodie and Stanton makes it certain that they were looking at a moving picture, and that all the other evidence confirms that certainty. But the evidence of this moving picture is the evidence of a conspiracy to throw suspicion on the prisoners. But a conspiracy implies conspirators. And there can be no doubt that those conspirators were the actual murderers of Lucy Bland. But if this be so, and I affirm that there can be no possible doubt that it is so, then it follows that the prisoners are innocent of the crime with which they are charged, and I accordingly ask you for a verdict of 'Not Guilty.' "

As Thorndyke sat down a faint hum arose in the court; but still all eyes were turned towards Wicks and Eugenia Kropp. A moment later the pair rose and walked unsteadily towards the door. But here, I noticed, Superintendent Miller had suddenly appeared and stood at the portal with a uniformed constable. As Wicks and Miss Kropp reached the door, I saw the constable shake his head. With, or without authority, he was refusing to let them leave the court. There was a brief pause. Suddenly there broke out a confused uproar; a scuffle, a loud shriek, the report of a pistol and the shattering of glass; and then I saw Miller grasping the man's wrists and pinning him to the wall, while the shrieking woman struggled with the constable to get to the door.

After the removal of the disturbers – in custody – events moved swiftly. The Crown counsel's reply was brief and colourless, practically abandoning the charge, while the judge's summing-up was a mere précis of Thorndyke's argument with a plain direction for an acquittal. But nothing more was needed; for the jury had so clearly made up their minds that the clerk had hardly uttered his challenges when the foreman replied with the verdict of "Not Guilty." A minute later, when the applause had subsided and after brief congratulations by the judge, the prisoners came down from the dock, into the court, moist-eyed but smiling, to wring Thorndyke's hands and thank him for this wonderful deliverance.

"Yes," agreed Mayfield – himself disposed furtively to wipe his eyes – "that is the word. It was wonderful. And yet it was all so obvious – when you knew."

CHAPTER FIVE

A Sower of Pestilence

The affectionate relations that existed between Thorndyke and his devoted follower, Polton, were probably due, at least in part, to certain similarities in their characters. Polton was an accomplished and versatile craftsman, a man who could do anything, and do it well; and Thorndyke has often said that if he had not been a man of science, he would, by choice, have been a skilled craftsman. Even as things were, he was a masterly manipulator of all instruments of research, and a good enough workman to devise new appliances and processes and to collaborate with his assistant in carrying them out.

Such a collaboration was taking place when the present case opened. It had occurred to Thorndyke that lithography might be usefully applied to medico-legal research, and on this particular morning he and Polton were experimenting in the art of printing from the stone. In the midst of their labours the bell from our chambers below was heard to ring, and Polton, reluctantly laying down the inking roller and wiping his hands on the southern aspect of his trousers, departed to open the door.

"It's a Mr Rabbage," he reported on his return. "Says he has an appointment with you, sir."

"So he has," said Thorndyke. "And, as I understand that he is going to offer us a profound mystery for solution, you had better come down with me, Jervis, and hear what he has to say." Mr

Rabbage turned out to be a benevolent-looking elderly gentleman, who, as we entered, peered at us through a pair of deep, concave spectacles and greeted us "with a smile that was childlike and bland." Thorndyke looked him over and adroitly brought him to the point.

"Yes," said Mr Rabbage, "it is really a most mysterious affair that has brought me here. I have already laid it before a very talented detective officer whom I know slightly – a Mr Badger; but he frankly admitted that it was beyond him and strongly advised me to consult you."

"Inspector Badger was kind enough to pay me a very handsome compliment," said Thorndyke.

"Yes. He said that you would certainly be able to solve this mystery without any difficulty. So here I am. And perhaps I had better explain who I am, in case you don't happen to know my name. I am the director of the St Francis Home of Rest for aged, invalid and destitute cats: an institution where these deserving animals are enabled to convert the autumn of their troubled lives into a sort of Indian summer of comfort and repose. The home is, I may say, my own venture, I support it out of my own means. But I am open to receive contributions; and to that end there is secured to the garden railings a large box with a wide slit and an inscription inviting donations of money, of articles of value, or of food or delicacies for the inmates."

"And do you get much?" I asked.

"Of money," he replied, "very little. Of articles of value, none at all. As to gifts of food, they are numerous, but they often display a strange ignorance of the habits of the domestic cat. Such things, for instance, as pickles and banana-skins, though doubtless kindly meant, are quite unsuitable as diet. But the most singular donation that I have ever received was that which I found in the box the day before yesterday. There were a number of articles, but all apparently from the same donor; and their character was so mysterious that I showed them to Mr Badger, as I have told you, who was as puzzled as I was and referred me to you. The collection comprised three ladies' purses, a morocco leather wallet and a small aluminium case. I have brought them with me to show you."

"What did the purses contain?" Thorndyke asked.

"Nothing," replied Mr Rabbage, gazing at us with wide-open eyes. "They were perfectly empty. That is the astonishing circumstance."

"And the leather wallet?"

"Empty, too, excepting for a few papers."

"And the aluminium case?"

"Ah!" exclaimed Mr Rabbage, "that was the most amazing of all. It contained a number of glass tubes; and those tubes contained – now, what do you suppose?" He paused impressively, and then, as neither of us offered a suggestion, he answered his own question. "Fleas and lice! Yes, actually! Fleas and lice! Isn't that an extraordinary donation?"

"It is certainly," Thorndale agreed. "Anyone might have known that, with a houseful of cats, you could produce your own fleas."

"Exactly," said Mr Rabbage. "That is what instantly occurred to me, and also, I may say, to Mr Badger. But let me show you the things."

He produced from a handbag and spread out on the table a collection of articles which were, evidently, the "husks" of the gleanings of some facetious pickpocket, to whom Mr Rabbage's donation-box must have appeared as a perfect godsend. Thorndyke picked up the purses, one after the other, and having glanced at their empty interiors, put them aside. The leather wallet he looked through more attentively, but without disturbing its contents, and then he took up and opened the aluminium case. This certainly was a rather mysterious affair. It opened like a cigarette case. One side was fitted with six glass specimen-tubes, each provided with a well-fitted parchment cap, perforated with a number of needle-holes; and of the six tubes, four contained fleas – about a dozen in each tube – some of which were dead, but others still alive, and the remaining two lice, all of which were dead. In the opposite side of the case, secured with a catch, was a thin celluloid note-tablet on which some numbers had been written in pencil.

"Well," said Mr Rabbage, when the examination was finished, "can you offer any solution of the mystery?"

Thorndyke shook his head gravely. "Not offhand," he replied. "This is a matter which will require careful consideration. Leave these things with me for further examination and I will let you know, in the course of a few days, what conclusion we arrive at."

"Thank you," said Mr Rabbage, rising and holding out his hand. "You have my address, I think."

He glanced at his watch, snatched up his handbag and darted to the door; and a moment later we heard him bustling down the stairs in the hurried, strenuous manner that is characteristic of persons who spend most of their lives doing nothing.

"I'm surprised at you, Thorndyke," I said when he had gone, "encouraging that ass, Badger, in his silly practical jokes. Why didn't you tell this old nincompoop that he had just got a pick-pocket's leavings and have done with it?"

"For the reason, my learned brother, that I haven't done with it. I am a little curious as to whose pocket has been picked, and what that person was doing with a collection of fleas and lice."

"I don't see that it is any business of yours," said I. "And as to the vermin, I should suggest that the owner of the case is an entomologist who specialises in epizoa. Probably he is collecting varieties and races."

"And how," asked Thorndyke, opening the case and handing it to me, "does my learned friend account for the faint scent of aniseed that exhales from this collection?"

"I don't account for it at all," said I. "It is a nasty smell. I noticed it when you first opened the case. I can only suppose that the flea-merchant likes it, or thinks that the fleas do."

"The latter seems the more probable," said Thorndyke, "for you notice that the odour seems to come principally from the parchment caps of the four tubes that contain fleas. The caps of the louse tubes don't seem to be scented. And now let us have a little closer look at the leather wallet."

He opened the wallet and took out its contents which were unilluminating enough. Apparently it had been gutted by the pickpocket and only the manifestly valueless articles left. One or two bills, recording purchasing at shops, a timetable, a brief letter in French, without its envelope and bearing neither address, date, nor signature, and a set of small maps mounted on thin card: this was the whole collection, and not one of the articles appeared to furnish the slightest clue to the identity of the owner.

Thorndyke looked at the letter curiously and read it aloud.

"It is just a little singular," he remarked, "that this note should be addressed to nobody by name, should bear neither address, date, nor signature, and should have had its envelope removed. There is almost an appearance of avoiding the means of identification. Yet the matter is simple and innocent enough: just an appointment to meet at the Mile End Picture Palace. But these maps are more interesting; in fact, they are quite curious."

He took them out of the wallet – lifting them carefully by the edges, I noticed – and laid them out on the table. There were seven cards, and each had a map, or rather a section, pasted on both sides. The sections had been cut out of a three-inch map of London, and as each card was three inches by four and a half, each section represented an area of one mile by a mile and a half. They had been very carefully prepared: neatly stuck on the cards and varnished, and every section bore a distinguishing letter. But the most curious feature was a number of small circles drawn in pencil on various parts of the maps, each circle enclosing a number.

"What do you make of those circles, Thorndyke?" I asked.

"One can only make a speculative hypothesis," he replied. "I am disposed to associate them with fleas and lice. You notice that the maps all represent the most squalid parts of East London – Spitalfields, Bethnal Green, Whitechapel, and so forth, where the material would be plentiful; and you also notice that the celluloid tablet in the insect case bears a number of pencilled jottings that might refer to these maps. Here, for instance is a note, 'B 21 $a+b-$' and you observe that each entry has an a and a b with either a plus or a minus sign. Now, if we assume that a means fleas and b means lice, or vice versa, the maps and the notes together might form a record of collections or experiments with a geographical basis."

"They might," I agreed, "but there isn't a particle of evidence that they do. It is a most fantastic hypothesis. We don't know, and we have no reason to suppose, that the insect-case and the wallet were the property of the same person. And we have no means of finding out whether they were or were not."

"There I think you do us an injustice, Jervis," said he. "Are we not lithographers?"

"I don't see where the lithography come in," said I.

"Then you ought to. This is a test case. These maps are varnished, and are thus virtually lithographic transfer paper; and the celluloid tablet also has a non-absorbent surface. Now, if you handle transfer paper carelessly when drawing on it, you are apt to find, when you have transferred to the stone, that your fingerprints ink up, as well as the drawing. So it is possible that if we put these maps and the note-tablet on the stone, we may be able to ink up the prints of the fingers that have handled them and so prove whether they were or were not the same fingers."

"That would be interesting as an experiment," said I, "though I don't see that it matters two straws whether they were the same or not."

"Probably it doesn't, " he replied, "though it may. But we have a new method and we may as well try it."

We took the things up to the laboratory and explained the problem to Polton, who entered into the inquiry with enthusiasm. Producing from the cupboard a fresh stone, he picked the maps out of the wallet one by one (with a pair of watchmaker's tweezers) and fell to work forthwith on the task of transferring the invisible – and possibly non-existent – fingerprints from the maps and the note-tablet to the stone. I watched him go through the various processes in his neat, careful, dextrous fashion and hoped that all his trouble would not be in vain. Nor was it; for when he began cautiously to ink up the stone, it was evident that something was there, though it was not so evident what that something was. Presently, however, the vague markings took more definite shape, and now could be recognised as eight rather confused masses of fingerprints, some badly smeared, some incomplete, and all mixed up and superimposed so as to make the identification of any one print almost an impossibility.

Thorndyke looked them over dubiously. "It is a dreadful muddle," said he, "but I think we can pick out the prints well enough for identification if that should be necessary. Which of these is the note-tablet, Polton?"

"The one in the right-hand top corner, sir," was the reply.

"Ah!" said Thorndyke, "then that answers our question. Confused as the impressions are, you can see quite plainly that the left thumb is the same thumb as that on the maps."

"Yes," I agreed after making the comparison, "there is not much doubt that they are the same. And now the question is, what about it?"

"Yes," said Thorndyke; "that is the question." And with this we retired from the laboratory, leaving Polton joyfully pulling off proofs.

During the next few days I had a vague impression that my colleague was working at this case, though with what object I could not imagine. Mr Rabbage's problem was too absurd to take seriously, and Thorndyke was beyond working out cases, as he used to at one time, for the sake of mere experience. However, a day or two later, a genuine case turned up and occupied our attention to some purpose.

It was about six in the evening when Mr Nicholas Balcombe called on us by appointment, and proceeded, in a business-like fashion, to state his case.

"I was advised by my friend Stalker, of the Griffin Life Assurance Office, to consult you," said he. "Stalker tells me that you have got him out of endless difficulties, and I am hoping that you will be able to help me out of mine, though they are not so clearly within your province as Stalker's. But you will know about that better than I do.

"I am the manager of Rutherford's Bank – the Cornhill Branch – and I have just had a very alarming experience. The day before yesterday, about three in the afternoon, a deed-box was handed in with a note from one of our customers – Mr Pilcher, the solicitor, of Pilcher, Markham and Sudburys – asking us to deposit it in our strong-room and give the bearer a receipt for it. Of course this was done, in the ordinary way of business; but there was one exceptional circumstance that turns out to have been, as it would appear, providential. Owing to the increase of business our strong-room had become insufficient for our needs, and we have lately had a second one built on the most modern lines and perfectly fire-proof. This had not been taken into use when Pilcher's deed-box arrived, but as the old room was very full, I opened the new room and saw the deed-box deposited in it.

"Well, nothing happened up to the time that I left the bank, but about two o'clock in the morning the night watchman noticed a smell of burning, and on investigation, located the smell as apparently proceeding from the door of the new strong-room. He at once reported to the senior clerk, whose turn it was to sleep on the premises, and the latter at once telephoned to the police station. In a few minutes a police officer arrived with a couple of firemen and a hand-extinguisher. The clerk took them down to the strong-room and unlocked the door. As soon as it was opened, a volume of smoke and fumes burst out, and then they saw the deed-box – or rather the distorted remains of it – lying on the floor. The police took possession of what was left, but a very cursory examination on the spot showed that the box was, in effect, an incendiary bomb, with a slow time fuse or some similar arrangement."

"Was any damage done?" Thorndyke asked.

"Mercifully, no," replied Mr Balcombe. "But just think of what might have happened! If I had put the box in the old strong-room it is certain that thousands of pounds' worth of valuable property would have been destroyed. Or again, if instead of an incendiary bomb the box had contained a high explosive, the whole building would probably have been blown to pieces."

"What explanation does Pilcher give?"

"A very simple one. He knows nothing about it. The note was a forgery; and on the firm's headed paper or a perfect imitation of it. And mind you," Mr Balcombe continued, "my experience is not a solitary one. I have made private inquiries of other bank managers, and I find that several of them have been subjected to similar outrages, some with serious results. And probably there are more. They don't talk about these things, you know. Then there are those fires: the great timber fire at Stepney, and those big warehouse fires near the London Docks; there is something queer about them. It looks as if some gang was at work for purposes of pure mischief and destruction."

"You have consulted the police, of course?"

"Yes. And they know something, I feel sure. But they are extremely reticent; so I suppose they don't know enough. At any rate, I should like you to investigate the case independently, and so would my directors. The position is most alarming."

"Could you let me see Pilcher's letter?" Thorndyke asked.

"I have brought it with me," said Balcombe. "Thought you would probably want to examine it. I will leave it with you; and if we can give you any other information or assistance, we shall be only too glad."

"Was the box brought by hand?" inquired Thorndyke.

"Yes," replied Balcombe, "but I didn't see the bearer. I can get you a description from the man who received the package, if that would be any use."

"We may as well have it," said Thorndyke, "and the name and address of the person giving it, in case he is wanted as a witness."

"You shall have it," said Balcombe, rising and picking up his hat. "I will see to it myself. And you will let me know, in due course, if any information comes to hand?"

Thorndyke gave the required promise and our client took his leave.

"Well," I said with a laugh, as the brisk footsteps died away on the stairs, "you have had a very handsome compliment paid you. Our friend seems to think that you are one of those master craftsmen who can make bricks, not only without straw, but without clay. There's absolutely nothing to go on."

"It is certainly rather in the air," Thorndyke agreed. "There is this letter and the description of the man who left the packet, when we get it, and neither of them is likely to help us much."

He looked over the letter and its envelope, held the former up to the light and then handed them to me.

"We ought to find out whether this is Pilcher's own paper or an imitation," said I, when I had examined the letter and envelope without finding anything in the least degree distinctive or characteristic; "because it is their paper, the unknown man must have had some sort of connection with their establishment or staff."

"There must have been some sort of connection in any case," said Thorndyke. "Even an imitation implies possession of an original. But you are quite right. It is a line of inquiry, and practically the only one that offers."

The inquiry was made on the following day, and the fact clearly established that the paper was Pilcher's paper, but the ink was not their ink. The handwriting appeared to be disguised, and no one connected with the firm was able to recognise it. The staff, even to the caretaker, were all eminently respectable and beyond suspicion of being implicated in an affair of the kind.

"But after all," said Pilcher, "there are a hundred ways in which a sheet of paper may go astray if anyone wants it; at the printer's, the stationer's, or even in this office – for the paper is always in the letter-rack on the table."

Thus our only clue – if so it could be called – came to an end, and I waited with some curiosity to see what Thorndyke would do next. But so far as I could see, he did nothing, nor did he make any reference to this obscure case during the next few days. We had a good deal of other work on hand, and I assumed that this fully occupied his attention.

One evening, about a week later, he made the first reference to the case, and a very mysterious communication it seemed to me.

"I have projected a little expedition for tomorrow," said he. "I am proposing to spend the day, or part of it, in the pastoral region of Bethnal Green."

"In connection with any of our cases?" I asked.

"Yes," he replied. "Balcombe's. I have been making some cautious inquiries with Polton's assistance, principally among hawkers and coffee-shop keepers, and I think I have struck a promising track."

"What kind of inquiries have you been making?" said I.

"I have been looking for a man, or men, engaged in giving street entertainments. That is what our data seemed to suggest, among other possibilities."

"Our data!" I exclaimed. "I didn't know we had any."

"We had Balcombe's account of the attempt to burn the bank. That gave us some hint as to the kind of man to look for. And there were certain other data, which my learned friend may recall."

"I don't recall anything suggesting a street entertainer," said I.

"Not directly," he replied. "It was one of several hypotheses, but it is probably the correct one, as I have heard of such a person as I had assumed, and have ascertained where he is likely to be found on certain days. Tomorrow I propose to go over his beat in the hope of getting a glimpse of him. If you think of coming with me, I may remind you that it is not a dressy neighbourhood."

On the following morning we set forth about ten o'clock, and as raiment which is inconspicuous at Bethnal Green may be rather noticeable in the Temple, we slipped out by the Tudor Street gate and made our way to Blackfriars Station. In place of the usual "research case," I noticed that Thorndyke was carrying a somewhat shabby wood-fibre attaché case, and that he had no walking-stick. We got out at Aldgate and presently struck up Vallance Street in the direction of Bethnal Green; and by the brisk pace and the direct route adopted, I judged that Thorndyke had a definite objective. However, when we entered the maze of small streets adjoining the Bethnal Green Road, our pace was reduced to a saunter, and at corners and cross-roads Thorndyke halted from time to time to look along the streets; and occasionally he referred to a card which he produced from his pocket, on which was written the names of streets and days of the week.

A couple of hours passed in this apparently aimless perambulation of the back streets.

"It doesn't look as if you are going to have much luck," I remarked, suppressing a yawn. "And I am not sure that we are not, in our turn, being 'spotted.' I have noted a man – a small, shabby-looking fellow – apparently keeping us in view from a distance, though I don't see him at the moment."

"It is quite likely," said Thorndyke. "This is a shady neighbourhood, and any native could see that we don't belong to it. Good morning! Taking a little fresh air?"

The latter question was addressed to a man who was standing at the door of a small coffee-shop, having apparently come to the surface for a 'breather.'

"Dunno about fresh," was the reply, "but it's the best there is. By the by, I saw one of them blokes what I was a-tellin' you about go by just now. Foreigner with the rats. If you want to see him give a show, I expect you'll find him in that bit of waste ground off Bolter's Rents."

"Bolter's Rents?" Thorndyke repeated. "Is that a turning out of Salcombe Street?"

"Quite right," was the reply. "Half-way up on the right-hand side."

Thanking our informant, Thorndyke strode off up the street, the next corner I glanced back. At that moment, whom I had noticed before stepped out of a after us at a pace suggesting anxiety not to lose

Bolter's Rents turned out to be a wide paved alley, one side of which opened into a patch of waste ground where a number of old houses had been demolished. This space had an unspeakably squalid appearance; for not only had the debris of the demolished houses been left in unsavoury heaps, but the place had evidently been adopted by the neighbourhood as a general dumping-ground for household refuse. The earth was strewn with vegetable, and even animal, leavings; flies and bluebottles hummed around and settled in hundreds on the garbage, and the air was pervaded by an odour like that of an old-fashioned brick dust-bin.

But in spite of these trifling disadvantages, a considerable crowd had collected, mainly composed of women and children; and at the centre of the crowd a man was giving an entertainment with a troupe of performing rats. We had sauntered slowly up the "rents" and now halted to look on. At the moment, a white rat was climbing a pole at the top of which a little flag was stuck in a socket. We watched him rapidly climb the pole, seize the flagstaff in his teeth, lift it out of the socket, climb down the pole and deliver the flag to his master. Then a little carriage was produced and the rat harnessed into it, another white rat being dressed in a cloak and placed in the seat, and the latter – introduced to the audience as Lady Murphy – was taken for a drive round the stage.

While the entertainment was proceeding I inspected the establishment and its owner. The stage was composed of light hinged boards opened out on a small four-wheeled hand cart, apparently home-made. At one end was a largish cage, divided by a wire partition into two parts, one of which contained a number of white and piebald rats, while the inmates of the other compartment were all wild rats; but not, I noted, the common brown or Norway rat, but the old-fashioned British black rat. I remarked upon the circumstance to Thorndyke.

"Yes," he said, "they were probably caught locally. The sewers will be inhabited by brown rats, but the houses, in an old neighbourhood like this, will be infested principally by the black rat. What do you make of the exhibitor?"

119

I had already noticed him, and now unobtrusively examined him again. He was a medium-sized man with a sallow complexion, dark, restless eyes – which frequently wandered in our direction – a crop of stiff, bushy, upstanding hair – he wore no hat – and a ragged beard.

"A Slav of some kind, I should think," was my reply; "a Russian, or perhaps a Lett. But the beard is not perfectly convincing."

"No," Thorndyke agreed, "but it is a good make-up. Perhaps we had better move on now; we have a deputy, you observe."

As he spoke, the small man whom I had observed following us strolled up the Rents; and as he drew nearer, revealed to my astonished gaze no less a person than our ingenious laboratory assistant, Polton. Strangely altered, indeed, was our usually neat and spruce artificer, with his seedy clothing and grubby hands; but as he sauntered up, profoundly unaware of our existence, a faint reminiscence of the familiar crinkly smile stole across his face.

We were just moving off when a chorus of shrieks mingled with laughter arose from the spectators, who hastily scattered right and left, and I had a momentary glimpse of a big black rat bounding across the space, to disappear into one of the many heaps of debris. It seemed that the exhibitor had just opened the cage to take out a black rat when one of the waiting performers – presumably a new recruit – had seized the opportunity to spring our and escape.

"Well," a grinning woman remarked to me, genially, "there's plenty more where that one came from. You should see this place on a moonlit night! Fair alive with 'em it is."

We sauntered up the Rents and along the cross street at the top; and as we went, I reflected on the very singular inquiry in which Thorndyke seemed to be engaged. The rat-tamer's appearance was suspicious. He didn't quite look the part, and his beard was almost -up – and a skilful one, too, for it was no mere ; and the restless, furtive eyes, and a certain ment in his bearing hinted at something more But if this was Mr Balcombe's incendiary, how had Thorndyke arrived at his identity, and, above all, by what process of reasoning had he contrived to associate the bank outrage with performing rats? That he had done so, his systematic procedure made quite clear. But how? It had seemed to me that we had not a single fact on which to start an investigation.

We had walked the length of the cross street, and had halted before turning, when a troop of children emerged from the Rents. Then came the exhibitor, towing his cart, with the cage shrouded in a cloth, then more children, and finally, at a little distance, Polton, slouching along idly but keeping the cart in view.

"I think," said Thorndyke, "it would be instructive, as a study in urban sanitation, to have a look round the scene of the late exhibition."

We retraced our steps down Bolter's Rents, now practically deserted, and wandered around the patch of waste land and in among the piles of bricks and rotting timber where the houses had been pulled down.

"Your lady friend was right," said Thorndyke. "This is a perfect Paradise for rats. Convenient residences among the ruins and unlimited provisions to be had for the mere picking up."

"Apparently you were right, too," said I, "as to the species inhabiting these eligible premises. That seems to be a black rat," and I pointed to a deceased specimen that lay near the entrance to a burrow.

Thorndyke stooped over the little corpse, and after a brief inspection, drew a glove on his right hand.

"Yes," he said, "this is a typical specimen of *mus rattus*, though it is unusually light in colour. I think it will be worth taking away to examine at our leisure."

Glancing round to see that we were unobserved, he opened his attaché case and took from it a largish tin canister and removed the lid – which, I noted, was anointed at the joint with vaseline. Stooping, he picked up the dead rat by the tail with his gloved fingers, dropped it into the canister, clapped on the lid, and replaced it in the attaché case. Then he pulled off the glove and threw it on the rubbish heap.

"You are mighty particular," said I.

"A dead rat is a dirty thing," said he, "and it was only an old glove."

On our way home I made various cautious attempts to extract from Thorndyke some hint as to the purpose of his investigation and his mode of procedure. But I could extract nothing from him beyond certain generalities.

"When a man," said he, "introduces an incendiary bomb into the strong-room of a bank, we may reasonably inquire as to his motives. And when we have reached the fairly obvious conclusion as to what those motives must be, we may ask ourselves what kind of conduct such motives will probably generate; that is, what sort of activities will be likely to be associated with such motives and with the appropriate state of mind. And when we have decided on that, too, we may look for a person engaged in those activities; and if we find such a person we may consider that we have a *prima facie* case. The rest is a matter of verification."

"That is all very well, Thorndyke," I objected, "but if I find a man trying to set fire to a bank, I don't immediately infer that his customary occupation is exhibiting performing rats in a back street of Bethnal Green."

Thorndyke laughed quietly. "My learned friend's observation is perfectly just. It is not a universal rule. But we are dealing with a specific case in which certain other facts are known to us. Still, the connection, if there is one, has yet to be established. This exhibitor may turn out not to be Balcombe's man after all."

"And if he is not?"

"I think we shall want him all the same; but I shall know better in a couple of hours' time."

What transpired during those two hours I did not discover at the time, for I had an engagement to dine with some legal friend and must needs hurry away as soon as I had purified myself from the effects of our travel in the unclean East. When I returned to our chambers, about half-past ten, I found Thorndyke seated in his easy chair immersed in a treatise on old musical instruments. Apparently he had finished with the case.

"How did Polton get on?" I asked.

"Admirably," replied Thorndyke. "He shadowed our entertaining friend from Bethnal Green to a by-street in Ratcliff, where he apparently resides. But he did more than that. We had made up a little book of a dozen leaves of transfer paper in which I wrote in French some infallible rules for taming rats. Just as the man was going into his house, Polton accosted him and asked him for an expert opinion on these directions. The foreign gentleman was at first impatient and huffy, but when he had glanced at the book, he became interested, and a good deal amused, and finally read the whole set of rules through attentively. Then he handed the book back to Polton and recommended him to follow the rules carefully, offering to supply him with a few rats to experiment on, an offer which Polton asked him to hold over for a day or two.

"As soon as he got home, Polton dismembered the book and put the leaves down on the stone, with this result."

He took from his pocket-book a number of small pieces of paper, each of which was marked more or less distinctly with lithographed reproductions of fingerprints, and laid them on the table. I looked through them attentively, and with a faint sense of familiarity.

"Isn't that left thumb," said I, "rather similar to the print on the maps from Mr Rabbage's wallet?"

"It is identical," he replied. "Here are the proofs of the map-prints and the note-tablet. If you compare them you can see that not only the left but the other prints are the same in all."

Careful comparison showed that this was so.

"But," I exclaimed, "I don't understand this at all. These are the finger-prints of Mr Rabbage's mysterious entomologist. I though you were looking for Balcombe's man."

"My impression," he replied, "is that they are the same person though the evidence is far from conclusive. But we shall soon know. I have sworn an information against the foreign gent, and Miller has arranged to raid the house at Ratcliff early tomorrow morning; and as it promises to be a highly interesting event, I propose to be present. Shall I have the pleasure of my learned friend's company?"

"Most undoubtedly," I replied, "though I am absolutely in the dark as to the meaning of the whole affair."

"Then," said Thorndyke, "I recommend you to go over the history of both cases systematically in the interval."

Six o'clock on the following morning found us in an empty house in Old Gravel Lane, Ratcliff, in company with Superintendent Miller and three stalwart plain-clothes men, awaiting the report of a patrol. We were dressed in engineers' overalls, reeking with naphthalin. Our trousers were tucked into our socks, and socks and boots were thickly smeared with vaseline, as were our wrists, around which our sleeves were bound closely with tape. These preparations, together with an automatic pistol served out to each of us, gave me some faint inkling of the nature of the case, though it was still very confused in my mind.

About a quarter-past six a messenger arrived and reported that the house which was to be raided was open. Thereupon Miller and one of his men set forth, and the rest of us followed at short intervals. On arriving at the house, which was but a short distance from our rendezvous, we found a solid plain-clothes man guarding the open door and a frowsy-looking woman, who carried a jug of milk, angrily demanding in very imperfect English to be allowed to pass into her house. Pushing past the protesting housekeeper, we entered the grimy passage, where Miller was just emerging from a ground-floor room.

"That is the woman's quarters," said he, "and the kitchen seems to be a sort of rat-menagerie. We'd better try the first floor."

He led the way up the stairs, and when he reached the landing he tried the handle of the front room. Finding the door locked or bolted, he passed on to the back room and tried the door of that, with the same result. Then, holding up a warning finger, he proceeded to whistle a popular air in a fine, penetrating tone, and to perform a double shuffle on the bare floor. Almost immediately an angry voice was heard in the front room, and slippered feet padded quickly across the floor. Then a bolt was drawn noisily, the door flew open, and for an instant I had a view of the rat-showman, clothed in a suit of very soiled pyjamas. But it was only for an instant. Even as our eyes met, he tried to slam the door to, and failing – in consequence of an intruding constabulary foot – he sprang back, leaped over a bed and darted through a communicating doorway into the back and shut and bolted the door.

"That's unfortunate," said Miller. "Now we're going to have trouble."

The superintendent was right. On the first attempts to force the door, a pistol-shot from within blew a hole in the top panel and made a notch in the ear of the would-be invader. The latter replied through the hole, and there followed a sort of snarl and the sound of a shattered bottle. Then, as the constable stood aside and shot after shot came from within, the door became studded with ragged holes. Meanwhile Miller, Thorndyke and I tiptoed out on the landing, and taking as long a run as was possible, flung ourselves, simultaneously on the back-room door. The weight of three large men was too much for the crazy woodwork. As we fell on it together, there was a bursting crash, the hinges tore away, the door flew inwards, and we staggered into the room.

It was a narrow shave for some of us. Before we could recover our footing, the showman had turned with his pistol pointing straight at Miller's head. But a bare instant before it exploded, Thorndyke, whose momentum had carried him half-way across the room, caught it with an upward snatch, and its report was followed by a harmless shower of plaster from the ceiling. Immediately our quarry changed his tactics. Leaving the pistol in Thorndyke's grasp, he darted across the room towards a workbench on which stood a row of upright, cylinder tins. He was in the act of reaching out for one of these when Thorndyke grasped his pyjamas between the shoulders and dragged him back, while Miller rushed forward and seized him. For a few moments there was a frantic and furious struggle, for the fellow fought with hands and feet and teeth with the ferocity of a wild cat, and overpowered as he was, still strove to drag his captors towards the bench. Suddenly, once more, a pistol-shot rang out, and then all was still. By accident or design the struggling man had got hold of the pistol that Thorndyke still grasped and pressed the trigger, and the bullet had entered his own head just above the ear.

"Pooh!" exclaimed Miller, rising and wiping his forehead, "that was a near one. If you hadn't stopped him, doctor, we'd all have gone up like rockets."

"You think those things are bombs, then?" said I.

"Think!" he repeated. "I removed two exactly like them from the General Post Office, and they turned out to be charged with TNT. And those square ones on the shelf are twin brothers of the one that went off in Rutherford's Bank."

As we were speaking, I happened to glance round at the doorway, and there, to my surprise, was the woman whom we had seen below, still holding the jug of milk and staring in with an expression of horror at the dead revolutionary. Thorndyke also observed her, and stepping across to where she stood, asked:

"Can you tell me if there has been, or is now, anyone sick in this house?"

"Yes," the woman replied, without removing her eyes from the dead man. "Dere is a chentleman sick upstairs. I haf not seen him. *He* used to look after him," and she nodded to the dead body of the showman.

"I think we will go up and have a look at this sick gentleman," said Thorndyke. "You had better not come, Miller."

We started together up the stairs, and as we went I asked:

"Do you suppose this is a case of plague?"

126

"No," he replied. "I fancy the plague department is in the kitchen; but we shall see."

He looked round the landing which we had now reached and then opened the door of the front room. Immediately I was aware of a strange, intensely foetid odour, and glancing into the room, I perceived a man lying, apparently in a state of stupor, in a bed covered with indescribably filthy bed-clothes. Thorndyke entered and approached the bed, and I followed. The light was rather dim, and it was not until we were quite close that I suddenly recognised the disease.

"Good God!" I exclaimed, "it is typhus!"

"Yes," said Thorndyke; "and look at the bed-clothes, and look at the poor devil's neck. We can see now how that villain collected his specimens."

I stooped over the poor, muttering, unconscious wretch and was filled with horror. Bed-clothes, pillow and patient were all alike crawling with vermin.

"Of course," I said as we walked homewards, "I see the general drift of this case, but what I can't understand is how you connected up the facts."

"Well," replied Thorndyke, "let us set out the argument and trace the connections. The starting point was the aluminium case that Mr Rabbage brought us. Those tubes of fleas and lice were clearly an abnormal phenomenon. They might, as you suggested, have belonged to a scientific collector; but that was not probable. The fleas were alive, and were meant to remain alive, as the perforated caps of the tubes proved. And the lice had merely died, as lice quickly do if they are not fed. They did not appear to have been killed. But against your view there were two very striking facts, one of which I fancy you did not observe. The fleas were not the common human flea; they were Asiatic rat-fleas."

"You are quite right," I admitted. "I did not notice that."

"Then," he continued, "there was the aniseed with which the parchment caps of the tubes were scented. Now aniseed is irresistible to rats. It is an infallible bait. But it is not specially attractive to fleas. What then was the purpose of the scent? The answer, fantastic as it was, had to be provisionally accepted because it was the only one that suggested itself. If one of these tubes had been exposed to rats – dropped down a rat-hole, for instance – it is certain that the rats would have gnawed off the parchment cap. Then the fleas have been liberated, and as they were rat-fleas, they would have immediately fastened upon the rats. The tubes, therefore, appeared to be an apparatus for disseminating rat-fleas."

"But why should anyone want to disseminate rat-fleas? That question at once brought into view another striking fact. Here, in these tubes, were rat-fleas and body-lice: both carries of deadly disease. The rat-flea is a carrier of plague; the body-louse is a carrier of typhus. It was an impressive coincidence. It suggested that the dissemination of rat-fleas might be really the dissemination of plague; and if the lice were distributed, too, that might mean the distribution of typhus.

"And new consider the maps. The circles on them all marked old slum-areas tenanted by low-class aliens. But old slums abound in rats; and low-class aliens abound in body-lice. Here was another coincidence. Then there was the note-tablet bearing numbers associated with the letters a and b and plus and minus signs. The letters a and b might mean rat and louse or plague and typhus, and the plus and minus might mean a success or a failure to produce an outbreak of disease. That was merely speculative, but it was quite consistent.

"So far we were dealing with a hypothesis based on simple observation. But that hypothesis could be proved or disproved. The question was: Were these insects infected insects, or were they not? To settle this I took one flea from each of the four tubes and 'sowed' it on agar, with the result that from each flea I got a typical culture of plague bacillus, which I verified with Haffkine's 'Stalactite test.' I also examined one louse from each of the two tubes, and in each case got a definite typhus reaction. So the insects were infected and the hypothesis was confirmed.

"The next thing was to find the owner of the tubes. Now the circles on the maps indicated some sort of activity, presumably connected with rats and carried on in these areas.

"I visited those areas and got into conversation with the inhabitants on the subject of rats, rat-catchers, rat-pits, sewermen, and everything bearing on rats; and at length I heard of an exhibitor of performing rats. You know the rest. We found the man, we observed that all his rats, excepting the tame white ones, were black rats – the special plague-carrying species – and we found on this spot a dead rat, which I ascertained, on examining the body, had died of plague. Finally there was Polton's little book giving us the fingerprints of the owner of the aluminium case. That completed the identification; and inquiries at the Local Government Board showed that cases of plague and typhus had occurred in the marked areas."

"Had not the authorities taken any steps in the matter?" I asked.

"Oh, yes," he replied. "They had carried out an energetic rat campaign in the London Docks, the likeliest source of infection. Naturally they would not think of a criminal lunatic industriously sowing plague broadcast."

"Then how did you connect this man with the bank outrage?"

"I never did, very conclusively," he replied. "It was mostly a matter of inference. You see, the two crimes were essentially similar. They were varieties of the same type. Both were cases of idiotic destructiveness, and the agent in each was evidently a moral imbecile who was a professed enemy of society. Such persons are rare in this country, and when they occur are usually foreigners, most commonly Russian, or East European of some kind. The only clue was the date on Pilcher's letter, the rather peculiar figures of which were extraordinarily like those on the maps and the note-tablet. Still, it was little more than a guess, though it happens to have turned out correct."

"And how do you suppose this fellow avoided getting plague and typhus himself?"

"It was quite likely that he had had both. But he could easily avoid the typhus by keeping himself clean and his clothing disinfected; and as to the plague, he could have used Haffkine's plague-prophylactic and given it to the woman. Clearly it would not have suited him to have a case of plague in the house and have the health officer inspecting the premises."

That was the end of the case, unless I should include in the history a very handsome fee sent to my colleague by the President of the Local Government Board.

"I think we have earned it," said Thorndyke; "and yet I am not sure that Mr Rabbage is not entitled to a share."

And in fact, when that benevolent person called a few days later to receive a slightly ambiguous report and tender his fee, he departed beaming, bearing a donation wherewith to endow an additional bed, cot, or basket, in the St Francis Home of Rest.

CHAPTER SIX

Rex v. Burnaby

It is a normal incident in general medical practice that the family doctor soon drifts into the position of a family friend. The Burnabys had been among my earliest patients, and mutual sympathies had quickly brought about the more intimate relationship. It was a pleasant household, pervaded by a quiet geniality and a particularly attractive homely, unaffected culture. It was an interesting household, too, for the disparity in age between the husband and wife made the domestic conditions a little unusual and invited speculative observation. And there were other matters, to be referred to presently.

Frank Burnaby was a somewhat delicate man of about fifty: quiet, rather shy, gentle, kindly, and singularly innocent and trustful. He held a post at the Record Office, and was full of quaint and curious lore derived from the ancient documents on which he worked: selections from which he would retail in the family circle with a picturesque imagination and a fund of quiet, dry humour that made them delightful to listen to. I have never met a more attractive man, or one whom I liked better or respected more.

Equally attractive, in an entirely different way, was his wife: an extremely charming and really beautiful woman of under thirty – little more than a girl, in fact, amiable, high-spirited and full of fun and frolic, but nevertheless an accomplished, cultivated woman with a strong interest in her husband's pursuits. They appeared to me an exceedingly happy and united couple, deeply attached to one another and in perfect sympathy. There were four children – three boys and a girl – of Burnaby's by his first wife; and their devotion to their young stepmother spoke volumes for her care of them.

But there was a fly in the domestic ointment: at least, that was what I felt. There was another family friend, a youngish man named Cyril Parker. Not that I had anything against him, personally, but I was not quite happy about the relationship. He was a markedly good-looking man, pleasant, witty, and extremely well informed; for he was a partner in a publishing house and acted as reader for the firm; whence it happened that he, like Mr Burnaby, gathered stores of interesting matter from his professional reading, But I could not disguise from myself that his admiration and affection for Mrs Burnaby were definitely inside the danger zone, and that the intimacy – on his side, at any rate – was growing rather ominously. On her side there seemed nothing more than frank, though very pronounced, friendship. But I looked at the relationship askance. She was a woman whom any man might have fallen in love with, and I did not like the expression that I sometimes detected in Parker's eyes when he was looking at her. Still, there was nothing in the conduct of either to which the slightest exception could have been taken or which in any way foreshadowed the terrible disaster which was so shortly to befall.

The starting point of the tragedy was a comparatively trivial event. By much poring over crabbed manuscripts, Mr Burnaby developed symptoms of eye-strain, which caused me to send him to an oculist for an opinion and a prescription for suitable spectacles. On the evening of the day on which he had consulted the oculist, I received an urgent summons from Mrs Burnaby, and, on arriving at the house, found her husband somewhat seriously ill. His symptoms were rather puzzling, for they corresponded to no known disease. His face was flushed, his temperature slightly raised, his pulse rapid, though the breathing was slow, his throat was excessively dry, and his pupils widely dilated. It was an extraordinary condition, resembling nothing within my knowledge excepting atropine poisoning.

"Has he been taking medicine of any kind?" I asked.

Mrs Burnaby shook her head. "He never takes any drugs or medicines but what you prescribe; and it couldn't be anything that he has taken, because the attack came on quite soon after he came home, before he had either food or drink."

It was very mysterious, and the patient himself could throw no light on the origin of the attack. While I was reflecting on the matter, I happened to glance at the mantelpiece, on which I noticed a drop-bottle labelled "The Eye Drops" and a prescription envelope. Opening the latter I found the oculist's prescription for the drops – a very weak solution of atropine sulphate.

"Has he had any of these drops?" I asked.

"Yes," replied Mrs Burnaby. "I dropped some into his eyes as soon as he came in; two drops in each eye, according to the directions."

It was very odd. The amount of atropine in those four drops was less than a hundredth of a grain; an impossibly small dose to produce the symptoms. Yet he had all the appearance of having taken a poisonous dose, which he obviously had not, since the drop-bottle was nearly full. I could make nothing of it. However, I treated it as a case of atropine poisoning; and as the treatment produced marked improvement, I went home, more mystified than ever.

When I called on the following morning, I learned that he was practically well, and had gone to his office. But that evening I had another urgent message, and on hurrying round to Burnaby's house, found him suffering from an attack similar to, but even more severe than, the one the previous day. I immediately administered an injection of pilocarpine and other appropriate remedies, and had the satisfaction of seeing a rapid improvement in his condition. But whereas the efficacy of the treatment proved that the symptoms were really due to atropine, no atropine appeared to have been taken excepting the minute quantity contained in the eye-drops.

It was very mysterious. The most exhaustive inquiries failed to suggest any possible source of poison excepting the drops; and as each attack had occurred a short time after the use of them, it was impossible to ignore the apparent connection, in spite of the absurdly minute dose.

"I can only suppose," said I, addressing Mrs Burnaby and Mr Parker, who had called to make inquiries, "that Burnaby is the subject of an idiosyncrasy – that he is abnormally sensitive to this drug."

"Is that a known condition?" asked Parker.

"Oh, yes," I replied. "People vary enormously in the way which they react to drugs. Some are so intolerant of particular drugs – iodine, for instance – that ordinary medicinal doses produce poisonous effects, while others have the most extraordinary tolerance. Christison, in his *Treatise on Poisons,* gives a case of a man, unaccustomed to opium, who took nearly an ounce of laudanum without any effect – a dose that would have killed an ordinary man. These drug-idiosyncrasies are terrible pitfalls for the doctor who doesn't know his patient. Just think what might have happened to Burnaby if someone had given him a full medical dose of belladonna."

"Does belladonna have the same effect as atropine?" asked Mrs Burnaby.

"It is the same," I replied. "Atropine is the active principle of belladonna."

"What a mercy," she exclaimed, "that we discovered this idiosyncrasy in time. I suppose he had better discontinue the drops?"

"Yes," I answered, "most emphatically; and I will write to Mr Haines and let him know that the atropine is impracticable."

I accordingly wrote to the oculist, who was politely sceptical as to the connection between the drops and the attacks. However, Burnaby settled the matter by refusing point-blank to have any further dealings with atropine; and his decision was so far justified that, for the time being, the attacks did not recur.

A couple of months passed. The incident had, to great extent, faded from my mind. But then it was revived in a way that not only filled me with astonishment but caused me very grave anxiety. I was just about to set out on my morning round when Burnaby's housemaid met me at my door, breathing quickly and carrying a note. It was from Mrs Burnaby, begging me to call at once and telling me that her husband had been seized by an attack similar to the previous ones. I ran back for my emergency bag and then hurried round to the house, where I found Burnaby lying on a sofa, very flushed, rather alarmed, and exhibiting well-marked symptoms of atropine poisoning. The attack, however, was not a very severe one, and the application of the appropriate remedies soon produced a change for the better.

"Now, Burnaby," I said, as he sat up with a sigh of relief, "what have you been up to? Haven't been tinkering with those drops again?"

"No," he replied. "Why should I? Haines has finished with my eyes."

"Well, you've been taking something with atropine in it."

"I suppose I have, but I can't imagine what. I have had no medicine of any kind."

"No pills, lozenges, liniment, plaster, or ointment?"

"Nothing medicinal of any sort," he replied. "In fact, I have swallowed nothing today but my breakfast; and the attack came on directly after, though it was a simple enough meal, goodness knows – just a couple of pigeon's eggs and some toast and tea."

"Pigeon's eggs," said I, with a grin, "why not sparrow's?"

"Cyril sent them – as a joke, I think," Mrs Burnaby explained (Cyril, of course, was Mr Parker), "but I must say Frank enjoyed them. You see, Cyril has taken lately to keeping pigeons and rabbits and other edible beasts, and I think he has done it principally for Frank's sake, as you have ordered him a special diet. We are constantly getting things from Cyril now – pigeons and rabbits especially; and much younger than we can buy them at the shops."

"Yes," said Burnaby, "he is most generous. I should think he supplies more than half my diet. I hardly like to accept so much from him."

"It gives him pleasure to send these gifts," said Mrs Burnaby; "but I wish it gave him pleasure to slaughter the creatures first. He always brings or sends them alive, and the cook hates killing them. As to me, I couldn't do it, though I deal with the corpses afterwards. I prepare nearly all Frank's food myself."

"Yes," said Burnaby, with a glance of deep affection at his wife, "Margaret is an artist in kickshaws; and I consume the works of art. I can tell you, Doctor, I live like a fighting cock."

This was all very interesting but it was beside the question; which was, where did the atropine come from? If Burnaby had swallowed nothing but his breakfast, it would seem that the atropine must have been in that. I pointed this out.

"But you know, Doctor," said Burnaby, "that isn't possible. We can write the eggs off. You can't get poison into an egg without making a hole in the shell, and these eggs were intact. And as to the bread, the butter, and the tea, we all had the same, and none of the others seem any the worse."

"That isn't very conclusive," said I. "A dose of atropine that would be poisonous to you would probably have no appreciable effect on the others. But, of course, the real mystery is how on earth atropine could have got into any of the food."

"It couldn't," said Burnaby; and that really was my own conviction. But it was an unsatisfactory conclusion, for it left the mystery unexplained; and when at length I took my leave, to continue my round of visits, it was with the uncomfortable feeling that I had failed to trace the origin of the danger or to secure my patient against its recurrence.

Nor was my uneasiness unjustified. Little more than a week had passed when a fresh summons brought me to Burnaby's house, full of bewilderment and apprehensions. And indeed there was good cause for apprehension; for when I arrived, to find Burnaby lying speechless and sightless, his blue eyes turned to blank discs of black, glittering with the unnatural "belladonna sparkle," – when I felt his racing pulse and watched his vain effort to swallow a sip of water – I began to ask myself whether he was not beyond recall. The same question was asked mutely by the terrified eyes of his wife, who rose like a ghost from his bedside as I entered the room. But once more he responded to the remedies, though more slowly this time, and at the end of an hour I was relieved to see that the urgent danger was past, although he still remained very ill.

Meanwhile, inquiries failed utterly to elicit any explanation of the attack. The symptoms had set in shortly after dinner; a simple meal, consisting of a pigeon cooked *en casserole* by Mrs Burnaby herself, vegetables, and a light pudding which had been shared by the rest of the family, and a little Chablis from a bottle that had been unsealed and opened in the dining-room. Nothing else had been taken and no medicaments of any kind used. On the other hand, any doubts as to the nature of the attack were set at rest by a chemical test made by me and confirmed by the Clinical Research Association. Atropine was demonstrably present, though the amount was comparatively small. But its source remained an impenetrable mystery.

It was a profoundly disturbing state of affairs. This last attack had narrowly missed a fatal termination, and the poison was still untraced. From the same unknown source a fresh charge might be delivered at any moment, and who could say what the result might be? Poor Burnaby was in a state of chronic terror and his wife began to look haggard and worn with constant anxiety and apprehension. Nor was I in much better case myself, for, whatever should befall, the responsibility was mine. I racked my brains for some possible explanation, but could think of none, though there were times when a horrible thought would creep into my mind, only to be indignantly cast out.

One evening, a few days after the last attack, I received a visit from Burnaby's brother, a pathologist attached to one of the

London Hospitals, but not in practice. Very different was Dr Burnaby from his gentle, amiable brother; a strong, resolute, energetic man and none too suave in manner. We were already acquainted, so no introductions were necessary, and he came to the point with characteristic directness.

"You can guess what I have come about, Jardine – this atropine business. What is being done in the matter?"

"I don't know that anything is being done," I answered lamely. "I can make nothing of it."

"Waiting for the next attack and the inquest, h'm! Well, that won't do, you know. This affair has got to be stopped before it is too late. If you don't know where the poison comes from, somebody does. H'm! And it is time to find out who that somebody is. There aren't many to choose from. I am going there now to have a look round and make a few inquiries. You'd better come with me."

"Are they expecting you?" I asked.

"No," he answered gruffly; "but I'm not a stranger and neither are you."

I decided to go round with him, though I didn't much like his manner. This was evidently meant to be a surprise visit, and I had no great difficulty in guessing at what was in his mind. On the other hand, I was not sorry to share the responsibility with a man of his position and a relative of the patient. Accordingly, I set forth with him willingly enough; and it is significant of my state of mind at this time, that I took my emergency bag with me.

When we arrived Burnaby and his wife were just sitting down to dinner – the children took their evening meal by themselves – and they welcomed us with the ready hospitality that made this such a pleasant household. Dr Burnaby's place was laid opposite mine, and I was faintly amused to note his eye furtively travelling over the table, evidently assessing each article of food as a possible vehicle of atropine.

"If you had only let us know you were coming, Jim," said Mrs Burnaby when the joint made its appearance, "we would have had something better than saddle of mutton. As it is, you must take pot-luck."

"Saddle of mutton is good enough for me," replied Dr Burnaby. "But what on earth is that stuff that Frank has got?" he added, as Burnaby lifted the lid from a little casserole.

"That," she answered, "is a fricassee of rabbit. Such a tiny creature it was; a mere infant. Cook nearly wept at having to kill it."

"Kill it!" exclaimed the doctor; "do you buy your rabbits alive?"

"We didn't buy this one," she replied. "It was brought by Cyril – Mr Parker, you know," she added hastily and with a slight flush, as she caught a grim glance of interrogation. "He sends quite a lot of poultry and rabbits and things for Frank from his little farm."

"Ha!" said the doctor with a reflective eye on the casserole. "H'm! Breeds them himself, hey? Whereabouts is his farm?"

"At Eltham. But it isn't a farm. He just keeps rabbits and fowls and pigeons in a place at the back of his garden."

"Is your cook English?" Dr Burnaby asked, glancing again at the casserole. "That affair of Frank's has rather a French look."

"Bless you, Jim," said Burnaby. "I am not dependent on mere cooks. I am a pampered gourmet. Margaret prepares most of my food with her own sacred hands. Cooks can't do this sort of thing;" and he helped himself afresh from the casserole.

Dr Burnaby seemed to reflect profoundly upon this explanation. Then he abruptly changed the subject from cookery to the Lindisfarne Gospels and thereby set his brother's chin wagging to a new tune. For Burnaby's affections as a scholar were set on seventh and eight century manuscripts and his knowledge of them was as great as his enthusiasm.

"Oh, get on with your dinner, Frank, you old windbag," exclaimed Mrs Burnaby. "You are letting everything get cold."

"So I am, dear," he admitted, "but – I won't be a minute. I just want Jim to see those collotypes of the Durham Book. Excuse me."

He sprang up from the table and darted into the adjoining library, whence he returned almost immediately carrying a small portfolio.

"These are the plates," he said, handing the portfolio to his brother. "Have a look at them while I dispose of the arrears."

He took up his knife and fork and made as if to resume his meal. Then he laid them down and leaned back in his chair.

"I don't think I want any more, after all," he said.

The tone in which spoke caused me to look at him critically; for my talk with his brother had made me a little nervous and apprehensive of further trouble. What I now saw was by no means reassuring. A slight flush and a trace of anxiety in his expression made me ask, with outward composure but inward alarm:

"You are feeling quite fit, I hope, Burnaby?"

"Well, not so very," he replied. "My eyes are going a bit misty and my throat – " Here he worked his lips and swallowed as if with some effort.

I rose hastily, and, catching a terrified glance from his wife, went to him and looked into his eyes. And thereupon my heart sank. For already his pupils were twice their natural size and the darkened eyes exhibited the too-familiar sparkle. I was sensible of a thrill of terror, and, as I looked into Burnaby's now distinctly alarmed face, his brother's ominous words echoed in my ears. Had I waited "for the next attack and the inquest?"

The symptoms, once started, developed apace. From moment to moment he grew worse, and the rapid enlargement of the pupils gave an alarming hint as to the intensity of the poisoning. I darted out into the hall for my bag, and as I re-entered, I saw him rise, groping blindly with his hands, until his wife, ashen-faced and trembling, took his arm and led him to the door.

"I had better give him a dose of pilocarpine at once," I said, getting out my hypodermic syringe and glancing at Dr Burnaby, who watched me with stony composure.

"Yes," he agreed, "and a little morphine, too; and he will probably need some stimulant presently. I won't come up; only be in the way."

I followed the patient up to the bedroom and administered the antidotes forthwith. Then, while he was getting partially undressed with his wife's help, I went downstairs in search of brandy and hot water. I was about to enter the dining-room when, though the partly-open door, I saw Dr Burnaby standing by the fireplace with his open handbag – which he had fetched in from the hall – on the table before him, and in his hand a little Bohemian glass jar from the mantelpiece. Involuntarily, I halted for a moment; and as I did so, he carefully deposited the little ornament in the bag and closed the latter, locking it with a small key which he then put in his pocket.

It was an excessively odd proceeding, but, of course, it was no concern of mine. Nevertheless, instead of entering the dining-room, I stole softly towards the kitchen and fetched the hot water myself. When I returned, the bag was back on the hall table and I found Dr Burnaby grimly pacing up and down the dining-room. He asked me a few questions while I was looking for the brandy, and then, somewhat to my surprise, proposed to come up and lend a hand with the patient.

On entering the bedroom, we found poor Burnaby lying half-undressed on the bed and in a very pitiable state; terrified, physically distressed and inclined to ramble mentally. His wife knelt by the bed, white-faced, red-eyed and evidently panic-stricken, though she was quite quiet and self-restrained. As we entered, she rose to make way for us, and while we were examining the patient's pulse and listening to his racing heart, she silently busied herself with the preparations for administering the stimulants.

"You don't think he is going to die, do you?" she whispered, as Dr Burnaby handed me back my stethoscope.

"It is no use thinking," he replied dryly – and I thought rather callously – "we shall see;" and with this he turned his back to her and looked at his brother with a gloomy frown.

For more than an hour that question was an open one. From moment to moment I expected to feel the wildly-racing pulse flicker out; to hear the troubled breathing die away in an expiring rattle. From time to time we cautiously increased the antidotes and administered restoratives, but I must confess that I had little hope. Dr Burnaby was undisguisedly pessimistic. And as the weary minutes dragged on, and I looked momentarily for the arrival of the dread messenger, there would keep standing into my mind a question that I hardly dared to entertain. What was the meaning of it all? Whence had the poison come? And why, in this household, had it found its way to Burnaby alone – the one inmate to whom it was specially deadly?

At last – at long last – there came a change; hardly perceptible at first, and viewed with little confidence. But after a time it became more pronounced; and then, quite rapidly, the symptoms began to clear up. The patient swallowed with ease, and great relish, a cup of coffee; the heart slowed down, the breathing became natural, and presently, as the morphine began to take effect, he sank into a doze which passed by degrees into a quiet sleep.

"I think he will do now," said Dr Burnaby, "so I won't stay any longer. But it was a near thing, Jardine; most uncomfortably near."

He walked to the door, where, as he went out, he turned and bowed stiffly to his sister-in-law. I followed him down the stairs, rather expecting him to revert to the subject of his visit to me. But he made no reference to it, nor, indeed, did he say anything until he stood on the doorstep with his bag in his hand. Then he made a somewhat cryptic remark:

"Well, Jardine," he said, "the Durham Book saved him. But for those collotypes, he would be a dead man;" and with that he walked away, leaving me to interpret as best I could this decidedly obscure remark.

A quarter of an hour later, as Burnaby was now peacefully asleep and apparently out of all danger, I took my own departure, and as soon as I was outside the house, I proceeded to put into execution a plan that had been forming in my mind during the last hour. There was some mystery in this case that was evidently beyond my powers to solve. But solved it had to be, if Burnaby's life was to be saved, to say nothing of my own reputation; so I decided to put the facts before my friend and former teacher, Dr Thorndyke, and seek his advice, and if necessary, his assistance.

It was now past ten o'clock, but I determined to take my chance on finding him at his chambers, and accordingly, having found a taxi, I directed the driver to set me down at the gate of Inner Temple Lane. My former experience of Thorndyke's habits led me to be hopeful, and my hopes were not unjustified on this occasion, for when I had mounted to the first pair landing of No. 5A, King's Bench Walk, and assaulted the knocker of the inner door, I was relieved to find him not only at home, but alone and disengaged.

"It's a deuce of a time to come knocking you up," I said, as he shook my hand, "but I am in rather a hole, and the matter is urgent, so – "

"So you paid me the compliment of treating me as a friend," said he. "Very proper of you. What is the nature of your difficulty?"

"Why, I've got a case of recurrent atropine poisoning and I can make absolutely nothing of it."

Here I began to give a brief outline sketch of the facts, but after a minute or two he stopped me.

"It is of no use being sketchy, Jardine," said he. "The night is young. Let us have a complete history of the case, with particulars of all the persons concerned and their mutual relations. And don't spare details."

He seated himself with a note-book on his knee, and when he had lighted his pipe, I plunged into the narrative of the case, beginning with the eye-drop incident and finishing with the alarming events of the present evening. He listened with close

143

attention, refraining from interrupting me excepting occasionally to ask for a date, which he jotted down with a few other notes. When I had finished, he laid aside his note-book, and, as he knocked out his pipe, observed;

"A very remarkable case, Jardine, and interesting by reason of the unusual nature of the poison."

"Oh, hang the interest!" I exclaimed. "I am not a toxicologist. I am a general practitioner; and I want to know what the deuce I ought to do."

"I think," said he, "that your duty is perfectly obvious. You ought to communicate with the police, either alone or in conjunction with some member of the family."

I looked at him in dismay. "But," I faltered, "what have I got to tell the police?"

"What you have told me," he replied; "which, put in a nutshell, amounts to this: Frank Burnaby has had three attacks of antropine poisoning, disregarding the eye-drops. Each attack has appeared to be associated with some article of food prepared by Mrs Burnaby and supplied by Mr Cyril Parker."

"But, good God!" I exclaimed, "you don't suspect Mrs Burnaby?"

"I suspect nobody," he replied. "It may not be criminal poisoning at all. But Mr Burnaby has to be protected, and the case certainly needs investigation."

"You don't think I could make a few inquiries myself first?" I suggested.

He shook his head. "The risk is too great," he replied. "The man might die before you reached a conclusion; whereas a few inquiries made by the police would probably put a stop to the affair, unless the poisoning is in some inconceivable way inadvertent."

That was what his advice amounted to, and I felt that he was right. But it put on me a horribly unpleasant duty; and as I wended homewards I tried to devise some means of mitigating its

144

unpleasantness. Finally I decided to try to persuade Mrs Burnaby to make a joint communication with me.

But the necessity never arose. When I made my morning visit, I found a taxicab drawn up opposite the door and the housemaid who admitted me looked as if she had seen a ghost.

"Why, what is the matter, Mabel?" I asked, as she ushered me funereally into the drawing-room.

She shook her head. "I don't know, sir. Something awful, I'm afraid. I'll tell them you are here." With this she shut the door and departed.

The housemaid's manner and the unusually formal reception filled me with vague forebodings. But even as I was wondering what could have happened, the question was answered by the entry of a tall man who looked like a guardsman in mufti.

"Dr Jardine?" he asked; and as I nodded, he explained, presenting his card:

"I am Detective-sergeant Lane. I have been instructed to make some inquiries in respect of certain information which we have received. It is stated that Mr Frank Burnaby is suffering from the effects of poison. So far as you know, is that true?"

"I hope he is recovered now," I replied, "but he was suffering last night from what appeared to be atropine poisoning."

"Have there been any previous attacks of the same kind?" the sergeant asked.

"Yes," I answered. "This was the fifth attack; but the first two were evidently due to some eye-drops that he had used."

"And in the case of the other three; have you any idea as to how the poison came to be taken? Whether it was in the food, for instance?"

"I have no idea, Sergeant. I know nothing more than what I have told you; and of course, I am not going to make any guesses. Is it admissible to ask who gave the information?"

"I am afraid not, sir," he replied. "But you will soon know. There is a definite charge against Mrs Burnaby – I have just made the arrest – and we shall want your evidence for the prosecution."

I stared at him in utter consternation. "Do you mean," I gasped, "that you have arrested Mrs Burnaby?"

"Yes," he replied; "on charges of having administered poison to her husband."

I was absolutely thunderstruck. And yet, when I remembered Thorndyke's words and recalled my own dim and hastily-dismissed surmises, there was nothing so very surprising in this shocking turn of events.

"Could I have a few words with Mrs Burnaby?" I asked.

"Not alone," he replied, "and better not at all. Still, if you have any business – "

"I have," said; whereupon he led the way to the dining-room, where I found Mrs Burnaby seated rigidly in a chair, pale as death, but quite calm though rather dazed. Opposite her a military-looking man sat stiffly by the table with an air of being unconscious of her presence, and he took no notice as I walked over to his prisoner and silently pressed her hand.

"I've come, Mrs Burnaby," said I, "to ask if there is anything that you want me to do. Does Burnaby know about this horrible affair?"

"No," she answered. "You will have to tell him, if he is fit to hear it; and if not, I want you to let my father know as soon as you can. That is all; and you had better go now, as we mustn't detain these gentlemen. Goodbye."

She shook my hand unemotionally, and when I had faltered a few words of vague encouragement and sympathy, I went out of the room, but waited in the hall to see the last of her.

The police officers were most polite and considerate. When she came out, they attended her in quite a deferential manner. As the sergeant was in the act of opening the street door, the bell rang; and when the door opened it disclosed Mr Parker standing on the threshold. He was about to address Mrs Burnaby, but she passed him with a slight bow, and descended the steps, preceded by the sergeant and followed by the detective. The former held the door of the cab open while she entered, when he entered also and shut the door. The detective took his seat beside the driver and the cab moved off.

"What is in the wind, Jardine?" Parker asked, looking at me with a distinctly alarmed expression. "Those fellows look like plain-clothes policemen."

"They are," said I. "They have just arrested Mrs Burnaby on a charge of having attempted to poison her husband."

I thought Parker would have fallen. As it was, he staggered to a hall chair and dropped on it in a state of collapse.

"Good God!" he gasped. "What a frightful thing! But there can't possibly be any evidence – any real grounds for suspecting her. It must be just a wild guess. I wonder who started it."

On this subject I had pretty strong suspicions, but I did not mention them; and when I had seen Parker into the dining-room and explained matters a little further I went upstairs, bracing myself for my very disagreeable task.

Burnaby was quite recovered, though rather torpid from the effects of the morphine. But my news roused him most effectively. In a moment he was out of bed, hurriedly preparing to dress; and though his pale, set face told how deeply the catastrophe had shocked him, he was quite collected and had all his wits about him.

"It's of no use letting our emotions loose, Doctor," said he, in reply to my expression of sympathy. "Margaret is in a very dangerous position. You have only to consider what she is – a young, beautiful woman – and what I am, to realise that. We must act promptly. I shall go and see her father; he is a very capable layer; and we must get a first-class counsel."

This seemed to be an opportunity for mentioning Thorndyke's peculiar qualifications in a case of kind, and I did so. Burnaby listened attentively, apparently not unimpressed; but he replied cautiously:

"We shall have to leave the choice of the counsel to Harratt; but if you care, meanwhile, to consult with Dr Thorndyke, you have my authority. I will tell Harratt."

R A<small>USTIN</small> F<small>REEMAN</small>

On this I took my departure, not a little relieved at the way he
had taken the evil tidings; and as soon as I had disposed of the
more urgent part of my work, I betook myself to Thorndyke's
chambers, just in time to catch him on his return from the Courts.

"Well, Jardine," he said, when I had brought the history up to
date, "what is it that you want me to do?"

"I want you to do what you can to establish Mrs Burnaby's
innocence," I replied.

He looked at me reflectively for a few moments; then he said,
quietly but rather significantly:

"It is not my practice to give *ex parte* evidence. An expert
witness cannot act as an advocate. If I investigate the evidence in
this case, it will have to be at your risk, as representing the accused,
since any fact, no matter how damaging, which is in the possession
of the witness must be disclosed in accordance with the terms of
the oath, to say nothing of the obvious duty of every person to
further the ends of justice. Speaking as a lawyer, and taking the
known facts at their face value, I do not advise you to employ me
to investigate the case at large. You might find that you had merely
strengthened the hand of the prosecution.

"But I will make a suggestion. There seems to me to be in this
case a very curious and interesting possibility. Let me investigate
that independently. If my inquiries yield a positive result, I will let
you know and you can call me as a witness. If they yield a negative
result, you had better leave me out of the case."

To this suggestion I necessarily agreed; but when I took my
leave of Thorndyke I went away with a sense of discouragement
and failure. His reference to "the face value of the known facts,"
clearly implied that those facts were adverse to the accused; while
the "curious possibility" suggested nothing but a forlorn hope
from which he had no great expectations.

I need not follow the weary business in detail. At the first
hearing before the magistrate the police merely stated the charge
and gave evidence of arrest, both they and the defence asking for
a remand and neither apparently desiring to show their hand.

Accordingly the case was adjourned for seven days, and as bail was refused, the prisoner was detained in custody.

During those seven dreary days I spent as much time as I could with Burnaby, and though I was filled with admiration of his fortitude and self-control, his drawn and pallid face wrung my heart. In those few days he seemed to have changed into an old man. At his house I also met Mr Harratt, Mrs Barnaby's father, a fine, dignified man and a typical old-fashioned lawyer; and it was unspeakably pathetic to see the father and the husband of the accused woman each trying to support the courage of the other while both were torn with anxiety and apprehension. On one occasion Mr Parker was present and looked more haggard and depressed than either. But Mr Harratt's manner towards him was so frigid and forbidding that he did not repeat his visit. At these meetings we discussed the case freely, which was a further affliction to me. For even I could not fail to see that any evidence that I could give directly supported the case for the prosecution.

So six of the seven days ran out, and all the time there was no word from Thorndyke. But on the evening of the sixth day I received a letter from him, curt and dry, but still giving out a ray of hope. This was the brief message:

"I have gone into the question of which I spoke to you and consider that the point is worth raising. I have accordingly written to Mr Harratt advising him to that effect."

It was a somewhat colourless communication. But I knew Thorndyke well enough to realise that his promises usually understated his intentions. And when, on the following morning, I met Mr Harratt and Burnaby at the court, something in their manner – a new vivacity and expectancy – suggested that Thorndyke had been more explicit in his communication to the lawyer. But, all the same, their anxiety, for all their outward courage, was enough to have touched a heart of stone.

The spectacle that that court presented when the case was called forms a tableau that is painted on my memory in indelible colours. The mingling of squalor and tragedy, of frivolity and dread solemnity – the grave magistrate on the bench, the stolid policemen, the busy, preoccupied lawyers, and the gibbering crowd of spectators, greedy for sensation, with eager eyes riveted on the figure in the dock – offered such a medley of contrasts as I hope never to look upon again.

As to the prisoner herself, her appearance brought my heart into my mouth. Rigid as a marble statue and nearly as void of colour, she stood in the dock, guarded by two constables, looking with stony bewilderment on the motley scene, outwardly calm, but with the calm of one who looks death in the face; and when the prosecuting counsel rose to open the case for the police, she looked at him as a victim on the scaffold might look upon the executioner.

As I listened to the brief opening address, my heart sank, though the counsel, Sir Harold Layton, KC, presented his case with that scrupulous fairness to the accused that makes an English court of justice a thing without parallel in the world. But the mere facts, baldly stated without comment, were appalling. No persuasive rhetoric was needed to show that they led direct to the damning conclusion.

Frank Burnaby, an elderly man, married to a young and beautiful woman, had on three separate occasions had administered to him a certain deadly poison, to wit, atropine. It would be proved that he had suffered from the effects of that poison; that the symptoms followed the taking of certain articles of food of which he alone had partaken; that the said food did actually contain the said poison; and that the food which contained the poison was specially prepared for his sole consumption by his wife, the accused, with her own hands. No evidence was at present available as to how the accused obtained the poison or that she had any such poison in her possession, nor would any suggestion be offered as to the motive of the crime. But, on the evidence of the actual administration of the poison, he would ask the prisoner be committed for trial. He then proceeded to call the witnesses, of whom I was naturally the first. When I had been sworn and given my description the counsel asked a few questions which elicited the history of the case and which I need not repeat. He then continued:

"Have you any doubt as to the cause of Mr Burnaby's symptoms?"

"No. They were certainly due to atropine poisoning."

"Has Mr Burnaby any constitutional peculiarity in respect of atropine?"

"Yes. He is abnormally susceptible to the effects of atropine."

"Was this peculiar susceptibility known to the accused?"

"Yes. It was communicated to her by me."

"Was it known, so far as you are aware, to any other persons?"

"Mr Parker was present when I told her, and Mr Burnaby and his brother, Dr Burnaby, were also informed."

"Is there any way, so far as you know, in which the accused could have obtained possession of atropine?"

"Only by having the oculist's prescription for the eye-drops made up."

"Do you know of any medium, other than the food, by which atropine might have been taken by Mr Burnaby?"

"I do not," I replied; and this concluded my evidence. But as I stepped out of the witness-box, I reflected gloomily that every word that I had spoken was a rivet in the fetters of the silent figure in the dock.

The next witness was the cook. She testified that she had killed and skinned the rabbit and had then handed it to the accused, who made it into a fricassee and prepared it for the table. Witness took no part in the preparation and she was absent from the kitchen on one occasion for several minutes, leaving the accused there alone.

When the cook had concluded her evidence, the name of James Burnaby was called, and the doctor entered the witness-box, looking distinctly uncomfortable, but grim and resolute. The first few questions elicited the circumstances of his visit to his brother's house and of the sudden attack of illness. That illness he had at once recognised as acute atropine poisoning, and had assumed that the poison was in the specially prepared food.

"Did you take any measures to verify this opinion?" counsel asked.

"Yes. As soon as I was alone, I took part of the remainder of the rabbit and put it in a glass jar which I found on the mantelpiece and which I first rinsed out with water. Later, I carried the sample of food to Professor Berry, who analysed it in my presence and found it to contain atropine. He obtained from it a thirtieth of a grain of atropine sulphate."

"Is that a poisonous dose?"

"Not to an ordinary person, though it is considerably beyond the medicinal dose. But it would have been a poisonous dose to Frank Burnaby. If he had swallowed this, in addition to what he had already taken, I feel no doubt that it would have killed him."

This concluded the case for the prosecution, and a black case it undoubtedly looked. There was no cross-examination; and as Thorndyke had arrived some time previously and conferred with Mr Harratt and his counsel, I concluded that the defence would take the form of a counter-attack by the raising of a fresh issue. And so it turned out. When Thorndyke entered the witness-box and had disposed of the preliminaries, the counsel for the defence "gave him his head."

"You have made certain investigations in regard to this case, I believe?" Thorndyke assented, and the counsel continued: "I will not ask you specific questions, but will request you to describe your investigations and their result, and tell us what caused you to make them."

"This case," Thorndyke began, "was brought to my notice by Dr Jardine, who gave me all the facts known to him. These facts were very remarkable, and, taken together, they suggested a possible explanation of the poisoning. There were four striking points in the case. First, there was the very unusual nature of the poison. Second the abnormal susceptibility of Mr Burnaby to this particular poison. Third, the fact that all the food in which the poison appeared to have been conveyed came from the same source: it was sent by Mr Cyril Parker. Fourth, that food consisted of pigeon's eggs, pigeon's flesh, and rabbit's flesh."

"What is there remarkable about that?" the counsel asked.

"The remarkable point is that the pigeon and the rabbit have an extraordinary immunity to atropine. Most vegetable-feeding birds and animals are more or less immune to vegetable poisons. Many birds and animals are largely immune to atropine; but among birds the pigeon is exceptionally immune, while the rabbit is the most extreme instance among animals. A single rabbit can take without the slightest harm more than a hundred times the quantity of atropine that would kill a man; and rabbits habitually feed freely on the leaves and berries of the belladonna or deadly nightshade."

"Does the deadly nightshade contain atropine?" the counsel asked.

"Yes. Atropine is the active principle of the belladonna plant and gives to it its poisonous properties."

"And if an animal, such as a rabbit, were to feed on the nightshade plant, would its flesh be poisonous?"

"Yes. Cases of belladonna poisoning from eating rabbit have been recorded – by Firth and Bentley, for instance."

"And you suspected that the poison in this case has been contained in the pigeon and the rabbit themselves?"

"Yes. It was a striking coincidence that the poisoning should follow the consumption of these two specially immune animals. But there was a further reason for connecting them. The symptoms were strictly proportionate to the probable amount of poison in each case. Thus the symptoms were only slight after eating the pigeon's eggs. But the eggs of a poisoned pigeon could contain only a minute quantity of the poison. After eating the pigeon the symptoms were much more severe; and the body of the pigeon which had fed on belladonna would contain much more atropine than could be contained in an egg. Finally, after eating the rabbit, the symptoms were extremely violent; but a rabbit has the greatest immunity and is the most likely to have eaten large quantities of belladonna leaves."

"Did you take any measures to put your theory to the test?"

"Yes. Last Monday I went to Eltham, where I had ascertained that Mr Cyril Parker lives, and inspected his premises from the outside. At the end of his garden is a small paddock enclosed by a wall. Approaching this across a meadow and looking over the wall, I saw that the enclosure was provided with small fowl-houses, pigeon-cotes, and rabbit hutches. All these were open and their inmates were roaming about the paddock. On one side of the enclosure, by the wall, was a dense mass of deadly nightshade plants, extending the whole length of the wall and about a couple of yards in width. At one part of this was a ring fence of wire netting, and inside it were five half-grown rabbits. There was a basket containing a small quantity of cabbage leaves and other green stuff, but as I watched, I saw the young rabbits browsing freely on the nightshade plants in preference to the food provided for them.

"On the following day I went to Eltham again, taking with me an assistant who carried a young rabbit in a small hamper. We watched the paddock until the coast was clear. Then my assistant got over the wall and abstracted a young rabbit from inside the ring fence and handed it to me. He then took the rabbit from the hamper and dropped it inside the fence. As soon as we were clear of the meadow, we killed the captured rabbit – to prevent any possible elimination of any poison that it might have swallowed. On arriving in London, I at once took the dead rabbit to St Margaret's Hospital, where, in the chemical laboratory, and in the presence of Dr Woodford, the Professor of Chemistry, I skinned it and prepared it as if for cooking by removing the viscera. I then separated the flesh from the bones and handed the former to Dr Woodford, who, in my presence, carried out an exhaustive chemical test for atropine. The result was that atropine was found to be present in all the muscles; and, on making a quantitative test, the muscles alone yielded no less than 1.93 grains."

"Is that a poisonous dose?" the counsel asked.

"Yes; it is a poisonous dose for a normal man. In the case of an abnormally susceptible person like Mr Burnaby it would certainly be a fatal dose."

This completed Thorndyke's evidence. There was no cross-examination, and the magistrate put no questions. When Dr Woodford had been called and had given confirmatory evidence, Mrs Burnaby's counsel proceeded to address the bench. But the magistrate cut him short.

"There is really no case to argue," said he. "The evidence of the expert witnesses makes it perfectly clear that the poison was already in the food when it came into the hands of the accused. Consequently the charge against her of introducing the poison falls to the ground and the case must be dismissed. I am sure everyone will sympathise with the unfortunate lady who has been the victim of these extraordinary circumstances, and will rejoice, as I do, at the clearing up of the mystery. The prisoner is discharged."

It was a dramatic moment when, amidst the applause of the spectators, Mrs Burnaby stepped down from the dock and clasped her husband's outstretched hands. But, overwhelmed as they both were by the sudden relief, I though it best not to linger, but, after brief congratulations, to take myself off with Thorndyke. But one pleasant incident I witnessed before I went. Dr Burnaby had been standing apart, evidently somewhat embarrassed, when suddenly Mrs Burnaby ran to him and held out her hand.

"I suppose, Margaret," he said gruffly, "you think I'm an old beast?"

"Indeed, I don't," she replied. "You acted quite properly, and I respect you for having the moral courage to do it. And don't forget, Jim, that your action has saved Frank's life. But for you, there would have been no Dr Thorndyke; and but for Dr Thorndyke, there would have been another poisoned rabbit."

"What do you make of this case?" I asked, as Thorndyke and I walked away from the court. "Do you suppose the poisoning was accidental?"

He shook his head. "No, Jardine," he replied. "There are too many coincidences. You notice that the poisoned animals did not appear until after Mr Parker had learned from you that Burnaby was abnormally sensitive to atropine and could consequently be poisoned by an ordinary medicinal dose. Then the sending of the animals alive looks like a precaution to divert suspicion from himself and confuse the issues. Again, that ring fence among the belladonna plants has a fishy look, and the plants themselves were not only abnormally numerous but many of them were young and looked as if they had been planted. Further, I happen to know that Parker's firm published, only last year, a book on toxicology in which the immunity of pigeons and rabbits was mentioned and which Parker probably read."

"Then do you believe that he intended to let Mrs Burnaby – the woman with whom he was in love – bear the brunt of his crime? It seems incredibly villainous and cowardly."

"I do not," he replied. "I imagine that the rabbit that I captured, or one of the others, would have been sent to Burnaby in a few day' time. The cook would probably have prepared it for him and it would almost certainly have killed him; and his death would have been proof of Mrs Burnaby's innocence. Suspicion would have been transferred to the cook. But I don't suppose any action will be taken against him, for it is practically certain that no jury would convict him on my evidence."

Thorndyke was right in his opinion. No proceedings were taken against Parker. But the house of the Burnabys knew him no more.

CHAPTER SEVEN

A Mystery of the Sand-hills

I have occasionally wondered how often Mystery and Romance present themselves to us ordinary men of affairs only to be passed by without recognition. More often, I suspect, than most of us imagine. The uncanny tendency of my talented friend John Thorndyke to become involved in strange, mysterious and abnormal circumstances has almost become a joke against him. But yet, on reflection, I am disposed to think that his experiences have not differed essentially from those of other men, but that his extraordinary powers of observation and rapid inference have enabled him to detect abnormal elements in what, to ordinary men, appeared to be quite commonplace occurrences. Certainly this was so in the singular Roscoff case, in which, if I had been alone, I should assuredly have seen nothing to merit more than a passing attention.

It happened that on a certain summer morning – it was the fourteenth of August, to be exact – we were discussing this very subject as we walked across the golf-links from Sandwich towards the sea. I was spending a holiday in the old town with my wife, in order that she might paint the ancient streets, and we had induced Thorndyke to come down and stay with us for a few days. This was his last morning, and we had come forth betimes to stroll across the sand-hills to Shellness.

It was a solitary place in those days. When we came off the sand-hills on to the smooth, sandy beach, there was not a soul in sight, and our own footprints were the first to mark the firm strip of sand between high-water mark and the edge of the quiet surf.

We had walked a hundred yards or so when Thorndyke stopped and looked down at the dry sand above the tide-marks and then along the wet beach.

"Would that be a shrimper?" he cogitated, referring to some impressions of bare feet in the sand. "If so, he couldn't have come from Pegwell, for the River Stour bars the way. But he came out of the sea and seems to have made straight for the sand-hills."

"Then he probably was a shrimper," said I, not deeply interested.

"Yet," said Thorndyke, "it was an odd time for a shrimper to be at work."

"What was an odd time?" I demanded. "When was he at work?"

"He came out of the sea at this place," Thorndyke replied, glancing at his watch, "at about half-past eleven last night, or from that to twelve."

"Good Lord, Thorndyke!" I exclaimed, "how on earth do you know that?"

"But it is obvious, Anstey," he replied. "It is now half-past nine, and it will be high-water at eleven, as we ascertained before we came out.

"Now, if you look at those footprints on the sand, you see that they stop short – rather begin – about two-thirds of the distance from high-water mark to the edge of the surf. Since they are visible and distinct, they must have been made after last high-water. But since they do not extend to the water's edge, they must have been made when the tide was going out; and the place where they begin is the place where the edge of the surf was when the footprints were made. But that place is, as we see, about an hour below the high-water mark. Therefore, when the man came out of the sea, the tide had been going down for an hour, roughly. As it is high-water at eleven this morning, it was high-water at about ten-forty last night; and as the man came out of the sea about an hour after high-water, he must have come out at, or about, eleven-forty. Isn't that obvious?"

"Perfectly," I replied, laughing. "It is as simple as sucking eggs when you think it out. But how the deuce do you manage always to spot these obvious things at a glance? Most men would have just glanced at those footprints and passed them without a second thought."

"That," he replied, "is a mere matter of habit; the habit of trying to extract the significance of simple appearances. It has become almost automatic with me."

During our discussion we had been walking forward slowly, straying on to the edge of the sand-hills. Suddenly, in a hollow between the hills, my eye lighted upon a heap of clothes, apparently, to judge by their orderly disposal, those of a bather. Thorndyke also had observed them and we approached together and looked down on them curiously.

"Here is another problem for you," said I. "Find the bather. I don't see him anywhere."

"You won't find him here," said Thorndyke. "These clothes have been out all night. Do you see the little spider's web on the boots with a few dewdrops still clinging to it? There has been no dew forming for a good many hours. Let us have a look at the beach."

We strode out through the loose sand and stiff, reedy grass to the smooth beach, and here we could plainly see a line of prints of naked feet leading straight down to the sea, but ending abruptly about two-thirds of the way to the water's edge.

"This looks like your nocturnal shrimper," said I. "He seems to have gone into the sea here and come out at the other place. But if they are the same footprints, he must have forgotten to dress before he went home. It is a quaint affair."

"It is a most remarkable affair," Thorndyke agreed; "and if the footprints are not the same it will be still more inexplicable."

He produced from his pocket a small spring tape-measure with which he carefully took the lengths of two of the most distinct footprints and the length of the stride. Then we walked back along the beach to the other set of tracks, two of which he measured in the same manner.

"Apparently they are the same," he said, putting away his tape; "indeed, they could hardly be otherwise. But the mystery is, what has become of the man? He couldn't have gone away without his clothes, unless he is a lunatic, which his proceedings rather suggest. There is just the possibility that he went into the sea again and was drowned. Shall we walk along towards Shellness and see if we can find any further traces?"

We walked nearly half a mile along the beach, but the smooth surface of the sand was everywhere unbroken. At length we turned to retrace our steps; and at this moment I observed two men advancing across the sand-hills. By the time we had reached the mysterious heap of garments they were quite near, and, attracted no doubt by the intentness with which we were regarding the clothes, they altered their course to see what we were looking at. As they approached, I recognised one of them as a barrister named Hallett, a neighbour of mine in the Temple, whom I had already met in the town, and we exchanged greetings.

"What is the excitement?" he asked, looking at the heap of clothes and then glancing along the deserted beach; "and where is the owner of the togs? I don't see him anywhere."

"That is the problem," said I. "He seems to have disappeared."

"Gad!" exclaimed Hallett, "if he has gone home without his clothes, he'll create a sensation in the town! What?"

Here the other man, who carried a set of golf clubs, stooped over the clothes with a look of keen interest.

"I believe I recognise these things, Hallett; in fact, I am sure I do. That waistcoat, for instance. You must have noticed that waistcoat. I saw you playing with the chap a couple of days ago. Tall, clean-shaved, dark fellow. Temporary member, you know. What was his name? Popoff, or something like that?"

"Roscoff," said Hallett, "Yes, by Jove, I believe you are right. And now I come to think of it, he mentioned to me that he sometimes came up here for a swim. He said he particularly liked a paddle by moonlight, and I told him he was a fool to run the risk of bathing in a lonely place like this, especially at night."

"Well, that is what he seems to have done," said Thorndyke, "for these clothes have certainly been here all night, as you can see by that spider's web."

"Then he has come to grief, poor beggar!" said Hallett; "probably got carried away by the current. There is a devil of a tide here on the flood."

He started to walk towards the beach, and the other man, dropping his clubs, followed.

"Yes," said Hallett, "that is what has happened. You can see his footprints plainly enough going down to the sea; but there are no tracks coming back."

"There are some tracks of bare feet coming out of the sea farther up the beach," said I, "which seem to be his."

Hallett shook his head. "They can't be his," he said, "for it is obvious that he never did come back. Probably they are the tracks of some shrimper. The question is, what are we to do? Better take his things to the dormy-house and then let the police know what has happened."

We went back and began to gather up the clothes, each of us taking one or two articles.

"You were right, Morris," said Hallett, as he picked up the shirt. "Here's his name, 'P. Roscoff,' and I see it is on the vest and the shorts, too. And I recognise the stick now – not that that matters, as the clothes are marked."

On our way across the links to the dormy-house mutual introductions took place. Morris was a London solicitor, and both he and Hallett knew Thorndyke by name.

"The coroner will have an expert witness," Hallett remarked as we entered the house. "Rather a waste in a simple case like this. We had better put the things in here."

He opened the door of a small room furnished with a good-sized table and a set of lockers, into one of which he inserted a key.

"Before we lock them up," said Thorndyke, "I suggest that we make and sign a list of them and of the contents of the pockets to put with them."

"Very well," agreed Hallett. "You know the ropes in these cases. I'll write down the descriptions, if you will call them out."

Thorndyke looked over the collection and first enumerated the articles: a tweed jacket and trousers, light, knitted wool waistcoat, black and yellow stripes, blue cotton shirt, net vest and shorts, marked in ink "P. Roscoff," brown merino socks, brown shoes, tweed cap, and a walking-stick – a mottled Malacca cane with a horn crooked handle. When Hallett had written down this list, Thorndyke laid the clothes on the table and began to empty the pockets, one at a time, dictating the descriptions of the articles to Hallett while Morris took them from him and laid them on a sheet of newspaper. In the jacket pockets were a handkerchief, marked "P. R."; a letter-case containing a few stamps, one or two hotel bills and local tradesmen's receipts, and some visiting-cards inscribed "Mr Peter Roscoff, Bell Hotel, Sandwich"; a leather cigarette-case, a 3B pencil fitted with a point-protector, and a fragment of what Thorndyke decided to be vine charcoal.

"That lot is not very illuminating," remarked Morris, peering into the pockets of the letter-case. "No letter or anything indicating his permanent address. However, that isn't our concern." He laid aside the letter-case, and picking up a pocket-knife that Thorndyke had just taken from the trousers pocket, examined it curiously. "Queer knife, that," he remarked. "Steel blade – mighty sharp, too – nail file and an ivory blade. Silly arrangement, it seems. A paper-knife is more convenient carried loose, and you don't want a handle to it."

"Perhaps it was meant for a fruit-knife," suggested Hallett, adding it to the list and glancing at a little heap of silver coins that Thorndyke had just laid down. "I wonder," he added, "what has made that money turn so black. Looks as if he had been taking some medicine containing sulphur. What do you think, doctor?"

"It is quite a probable explanation," replied Thorndyke, "though we haven't the means of testing it. But you notice that this vesta-box from the other pocket is quite bright, which is rather against your theory."

He held out a little silver box bearing the engraved monogram "P.R.," the burnished surface of which contrasted strongly with the dull brownish-black of the coins. Hallett looked at it with an affirmative grunt, and having entered it in his list and added a bunch of keys and a watch from the waistcoat pocket, laid down his pen.

"That's the lot, is it?" said he, rising and beginning to gather up the clothes. "My word! Look at the sand on the table! Isn't it astonishing how saturated with sand one's clothes become after a day on the links here? When I undress at night, the bathroom floor is like the bottom of a birdcage. Shall I put the things in the locker now?"

"I think," said Thorndyke, "that, as I may have to give evidence, I should like to look them over before you put them away."

Hallett grinned. "There's going to be some expert evidence after all," he said. "Well, fire away, and let me know when you have finished. I am going to smoke a cigarette outside."

With this, he and Morris sauntered out, and I thought it best to go with them, though I was a little curious as to my colleague's object in examining these derelicts. However, my curiosity was not entirely balked, for my friends went no farther than the little garden that surrounded the house, and from the place where we stood I was able to look in through the window and observe Thorndyke's proceedings.

Very methodical they were. First he laid on the table a sheet of newspaper and on this deposited the jacket, which he examined carefully all over, picking some small object off the inside near the front, and giving special attention to a thick smear of paint which I had noticed on the left cuff. Then, with his spring tape he measured the sleeves and other principal dimensions. Finally, holding the jacket upside down, he beat it gently with his stick, causing a shower of sand to fall on the paper. He then laid the jacket aside, and, taking from his pocket one or two seed-envelopes (which I believe he always carried), very carefully shot the sand from the paper into one of them and wrote a few words on it – presumably the source of the sand – and similarly disposing of the small object that he had picked off the surface.

This rather odd procedure was repeated with the other garments – a fresh sheet of newspaper being used for each – and with the socks, shoes, and cap. The latter he examined minutely, especially as to the inside, from which he picked out two or three small objects, which I could not see, but assumed to be hairs. Even the walking-stick was inspected and measured, and the articles from the pockets scrutinised afresh, particularly the curious pocket-knife, the ivory blade of which he examined on both sides through his lens.

Hallett and Morris glanced in at him from time to time with indulgent smiles, and the former remarked:

"I like the hopeful enthusiasm of the real pukka expert, and the way he refuses to admit the existence of the ordinary and commonplace. I wonder what he has found out from those things. But here he is. Well, doctor, what's the verdict? Was it temporary insanity or misadventure?"

Thorndyke shook his head. "The inquiry is adjourned pending the production of fresh evidence," he replied, adding: "I have folded the clothes up and put all the effects together in a paper parcel, excepting the stick."

When Hallett had deposited the derelicts in the locker, he came out and looked across the links with an air of indecision.

"I suppose," said he, "we ought to notify the police. I'll do that. When do you think the body is likely to wash up, and where?"

"It is impossible to say," replied Thorndyke. "The set of the current is towards the Thames, but the body might wash up anywhere along the coast. A case is recorded of a bather drowned off Brighton whose body came up six weeks later at Walton-on-the-Naze. But that was quite exceptional. I shall send the coroner and the Chief Constable a note with my address, and I should think you had better do the same. And that is all that we can do, until we get the summons for the inquest, if there ever is one."

So this we all agreed; and as the morning was now spent, we walked back together across the links to the town, where we encountered my wife returning homeward with her sketching kit.

This Thorndyke and I took possession of, and having parted from Hallett and Morris opposite the Barbican, we made our way to our lodgings in quest of lunch. Naturally, the events of the morning were related to my wife and discussed by us all, but I noted that Thorndyke made no reference to his inspection of the clothes, and accordingly I said nothing about the matter before my wife; and no opportunity of opening the subject occurred until the evening, when I accompanied him to the station. Then, as we paced the platform while waiting for his train, I put my question:

"By the way, did you extract any information from those garments? I saw you going through them very thoroughly."

"I got a suggestion from them," he replied; "but it is such an odd one that I hardly like to mention it. Taking the appearances at their face value, the suggestion was that the clothes were not all those of the same man. There seemed to be traces of two men, one of whom appeared to belong to this district, while the other would seem to have been associated with the eastern coast of Thanet between Ramsgate and Margate, and by preference, on the scale of probabilities, to Dumpton or Broadstairs."

"How on earth did you arrive at the localities?" I asked.

"Principally," he replied, "by the peculiarities of the sand which fell from the garments and which was not the same in all of them. You see, Anstey," he continued, "sand is analogous to dust. It consists of minute fragments detached from larger masses; and just as, by examining microscopically the dust of a room, you can ascertain the colour and material of the carpets, curtains, furniture coverings, and other textiles, detached articles of which form the dust of that room, so, by examining sand, you can judge of the character of the cliffs, rocks, and other large masses that occur in the locality, fragments of which become ground off by the surf and incorporated in the sand of the beach. Some of the sand from these clothes is very characteristic and will probably be still more so when I examine it under the microscope."

"But," I objected, "isn't there a fallacy in that line of reasoning? Might not one man have worn the different garments at different times and in different places?"

"That is certainly a possibility that has to be borne in mind," he replied. "But here comes my train. We shall have to adjourn this discussion until you come back to the mill."

As a matter of fact, the discussion was never resumed, for, by the time that I came back to "the mill," the affair had faded from my mind, and the accumulations of grist monopolised my attention; and it is probable that it would have passed into complete oblivion but for the circumstance of its being revived in a very singular manner, which was as follows.

One afternoon about the middle of October my old friend, Mr Brodribb, a well-known solicitor, called to give me some verbal instructions. When we had finished our business, he said:

"I've got a client waiting outside, whom I am taking up to introduce to Thorndyke. You'd better come along with us."

"What is the nature of your client's case?" I asked.

"Hanged if I know," chuckled Brodribb. "He won't say. That's why I am taking him to our friend. I've never seen Thorndyke stumped yet, but I think this case will put the lid on him. Are you coming?"

"I am, most emphatically," said I, "if your client doesn't object."

"He's not going to be asked," said Brodribb. "He'll think you are part of the show. Here he is."

In my outer office we found a gentlemanly, middle-aged man to whom Brodribb introduced me, and whom he hustled down the stairs and up King's Bench Walk to Thorndyke's chambers. There we found my colleague earnestly studying a will with the aid of a watchmaker's eye-glass, and Brodribb opened the proceedings without ceremony.

"I've brought a client of mine, Mr Capes, to see you, Thorndyke. He has a little problem that he wants you to solve."

Thorndyke bowed to the client and then asked:

"What is the nature of the problem?"

"Ah!" said Brodribb, with a mischievous twinkle, "that's what you've got to find out. Mr Capes is a somewhat reticent gentleman."

Thorndyke cast a quick look at the client and from him to the solicitor. It was not the first time that old Brodribb's high spirits had overflowed in the form of a "leg-pull," though Thorndyke had no more whole-hearted admirer than the shrewd, facetious old lawyer.

Mr Capes smiled a deprecating smile. "It isn't quite so bad as that," he said. "But I really can't give you much information. It isn't mine to give. I am afraid of telling someone else's secrets, if I say very much."

"Of course you mustn't do that," said Thorndyke. "But I suppose you can indicate in general terms the nature of your difficulty and the kind of help you want from us."

"I think I can," Mr Capes replied. "At any rate, I will try. My difficulty is that a certain person with whom I wish to communicate has disappeared in what appears to me to be a rather remarkable manner. When I last heard from him, he was staying at a certain seaside resort and he stated in his letter that he was returning on the following day to his rooms in London. A few days later, I called at his rooms and found that he had not yet returned. But his luggage, which he had sent on independently, had arrived on the day which he had mentioned. So it is evident that he must have left his seaside lodgings. But from that day to this I have had no communication from him, and he has never returned to his rooms nor written to his landlady."

"About how long ago was this?" Thorndyke asked.

"It is just about two months since I heard from him."

"You don't wish to give the name of the seaside resort where he was staying?"

"I think I had better not," answered Mr Capes. "There are circumstances – they don't concern me, but they do concern him very much – which seem to make it necessary for me to say as little as possible."

"And there is nothing further that you can tell us?"

"I am afraid not, excepting that, if I could get into communication with him, I could tell him of something very much to his advantage and which might prevent him from doing something which it would be much better that he should not do."

Thorndyke cogitated profoundly while Brodribb watched him with undisguised enjoyment. Presently my colleague looked up and addressed our secretive client.

"Did you ever play the game of 'Clumps,' Mr Capes? It is a somewhat legal form of game in which one player asks questions of the others, who are required to answer 'yes' or 'no' in the proper witness-box style."

"I know the game," said Capes, looking a little puzzled, "but…"

"Shall we try a round or two?" asked Thorndyke, with an unmoved countenance. "You don't wish to make any statements, but if I ask you certain specific questions, will you answer 'yes' or 'no'?"

Mr Capes reflected awhile. At length he said:

"I am afraid I can't commit myself to a promise. Still, if you like to ask a question or two, I will answer them if I can."

"Very well," said Thorndyke, "then, as a start, supposing I suggest that the date of the letter that you received was the thirteenth of August? What do you say? Yes or no?"

Mr Capes sat bolt upright and stared at Thorndyke open-mouthed.

"How on earth did you guess that?" he exclaimed in an astonished tone. "It's most extraordinary! But you are right. It was dated the thirteenth."

"Then," said Thorndyke, "as we have fixed the time we will have a try at the place. What do you say if I suggest that the seaside resort was in the neighbourhood of Broadstairs?"

Mr Capes was positively thunderstruck. As he sat gazing at Thorndyke he looked like amazement personified.

"But," he exclaimed, "you can't be guessing! You know! You know that he was at Broadstairs. And yet, how could you? I haven't even hinted at who he is."

"I have a certain man in my mind," said Thorndyke, "who may have disappeared from Broadstairs. Shall I suggest a few personal characteristics?"

Mr Capes nodded eagerly and Thorndyke continued:

"If I suggest, for instance, that he was an artist – a painter in oil" – Capes nodded again – "that he was somewhat fastidious as to his pigments?"

"Yes," said Capes. "Unnecessarily so in my opinion, and I am an artist myself. What else?"

"That he worked with his palette in his right hand and held his brush with his left?"

"Yes, yes," exclaimed Capes, half-rising from his chair; "and what was he like?"

"By gum," murmured Brodribb, "we haven't stumped him after all."

Evidently we had not, for he proceeded:

"As to his physical characteristics, I suggest that he was a shortish man – about five feet seven – rather stout, fair hair, slightly bald and wearing a rather large and ragged moustache."

Mr Capes was astounded – and so was I, for that matter – and for some moments there was a silence, broken only by old Brodribb, who sat chuckling softly and rubbing his hands. At length Mr Capes said:

"You have described him exactly, but I needn't tell you that. What I do not understand at all is how you knew that I was referring to this particular man, seeing that I mentioned no name. By the way, sir, may I ask when you saw him last?"

"I have no reason to suppose," replied Thorndyke, "that I have ever seen him at all;" an answer that reduced Mr Capes to a state of stupefaction and brought our old friend Brodribb to the verge of apoplexy. "This man," Thorndyke continued, "is a purely hypothetical individual whom I have described from certain traces left by him. I have reason to believe that he left Broadstairs on the fourteenth of August and I have certain opinions as to what became of him thereafter. But a few more details would be useful, and I shall continue my interrogation. Now this man sent his luggage on separately. It suggests a possible intention of breaking his journey to London. What do you say?"

"I don't know," replied Capes, "but I think probable."

"I suggest that he broke his journey for the purpose of holding an interview with some other person."

"I cannot say," answered Capes: "but if he did break his journey it would probably be for that purpose."

"And supposing that interview to have taken place, would it be likely to be an amicable interview?"

"I am afraid not. I suspect that my – er – acquaintance might have made certain proposals which would have been unacceptable, but which he might have been able to enforce. However, that is only surmise," Capes added hastily. "I really know nothing more than I have told you, excepting the missing man's name, and that I would rather not mention."

"It is not material," said Thorndyke, "at least, not at present. If it should become essential, I will let you know."

"M—yes," said Mr Capes. "But you were saying that you had certain opinions as to what has become of this person."

"Yes," Thorndyke replied; "speculative opinions. But they will have to be verified. If they turn out to be correct – or incorrect either – I will let you know in the course of a few days. Has Mr Brodribb your address?"

"He has; but you had better have it, too."

He produced his card, and, after an ineffectual effort to extract a statement from Thorndyke, took his departure.

The third act of this singular drama opened in the same setting as the first, for the following Sunday morning found my colleague and me following the path from Sandwich to the sea. But we were not alone this time. At our side marched Major Robertson, the eminent dog-trainer, and behind him trotted one of his superlatively educated fox-hounds.

We came out on the shore at the same point as on the former occasion, and, turning towards Shellness, walked along the smooth sand with a careful eye on the not very distinctive landmarks. At length Thorndyke halted.

"This is the place," said he. "I fixed it in my mind by that distant tree, which coincides with the chimney of that cottage on the marshes. The clothes lay in that hollow between the two big sand-hills."

We advanced to the spot, but, as a hollow is useless as a landmark, Thorndyke ascended the nearest sand-hill and stuck his stick in the summit and tied his handkerchief to the handle.

"That," said he, "will serve as a centre which we can keep in sight, and if we describe a series of gradually widening concentric circles round it, we shall cover the whole ground completely."

"How far do you propose to go?" asked the major.

"We must be guided by the appearance of the ground," replied Thorndyke. "But the circumstances suggest that if there is anything buried, it can't be very far from where the clothes were laid. And it is pretty certain to be in a hollow."

The major nodded; and when he had attached a long leash to the dog's collar, we started, at first skirting the base of the sand-hill, and then, guided by our own footmarks in the loose sand, gradually increasing the distance from the high mound, above which Thorndyke's handkerchief fluttered in the light breeze. Thus we continued, walking slowly, keeping close to the previously made circle of footprints and watching the dog; who certainly did a vast amount of sniffing, but appeared to let his mind run unduly on the subject of rabbits.

In this way half an hour was consumed, and I was beginning to wonder whether we were going after all to draw a blank, when the dog's demeanour underwent a sudden change. At the moment we were crossing a range of high sand-hills, covered with stiff, reedy grass and stunted gorse, and before us lay a deep hollow, naked of vegetation and presenting a bare, smooth surface of the characteristic greyish-yellow sand. On the side of the hill the dog checked, and, with upraised muzzle, began to sniff the air with a curiously suspicious expression, clearly unconnected with the rabbit question. On this, the major unfastened the leash, and the dog, left to his own devices, put his nose to the ground and began rapidly to cast to and fro, zig-zagging down the side of the hill and growing every moment more excited. In the same sinuous manner he proceeded across the hollow until he reached a spot near the middle; and here he came to a sudden stop and began to scratch up the sand with furious eagerness.

"It's a find, sure enough!" exclaimed the major, nearly as excited as his pupil; and, as he spoke, he ran down the hillside, followed me and Thorndyke, who, as he reached the bottom, drew from his "poacher's pocket" a large trowel in a leather sheath. It was not a very efficient digging implement, but it threw up the loose sand faster than the scratchings of the dog.

It was easy ground to excavate. Working the spot that the dog had located, Thorndyke had soon hollowed out a small cavity some eighteen inches deep. Into the bottom of which he thrust the pointed blade of the big trowel. Then he paused and looked round at the major and me, who were craning eagerly over the little pit.

"There is something there," said he. "Feel the handle of the trowel."

I grasped the wooden handle, and, working it gently up and down, was aware of a definite but somewhat soft resistance. The major verified my observation and then Thorndyke resumed his digging, widening the pit and working with increased caution. Ten minutes' more excavation brought into view a recognisable shape – a shoulder and upper arm; and following the lines of this, further diggings disclosed the form of a head and shoulders plainly discernible though still shrouded in sand. Finally, with the point of the trowel and a borrowed handkerchief – mine – the adhering sand was cleared away; then, from the bottom of the deep, funnelled hole, there looked up at us, with a most weird and horrible effect, the discoloured face of a man.

In that face, the passing weeks had wrought inevitable changes, on which I need not dwell. But the features were easily recognisable, and I could see at once that the man corresponded with Thorndyke's description. The cheeks were full; the hair on the temples was a pale, yellowish brown; a straggling, fair moustache covered the mouth; and, when the sand had been sufficiently cleared away, I could see a small, tonsure-like bald patch near the back of the crown. But I could see something more than this. On the left temple, just behind the eyebrow, was a ragged, shapeless wound such as might have been made by a hammer.

"That turns into certainty what we have already surmised," said Thorndyke, gently pressing the scalp around the wound. "It must have killed him instantly. The skull is smashed in like an egg-shell. And this is undoubtedly the weapon," he added, drawing out of the sand beside the body a big, hexagon-headed screw-bolt, "very prudently buried with the body. And that is all that really concerns us. We can leave the police to finish the disinterment; but you notice, Anstey, that the corpse is nude with the exception of the vest and probably the pants. The shirt has disappeared. Which is exactly what we should have expected."

Slowly, but with the feeling of something accomplished, we took our way back to the town, having collected Thorndyke's stick on the way. Presently, the major left us, to look up a friend at the club house on the links. As soon as we were alone, I put in a demand for an elucidation.

"I see the general trend of your investigations," said I, "but I can't imagine how they yielded so much detail; as to the personal appearance of this man, for instance."

"The evidence in this case," he replied, "was analogous to circumstantial evidence. It depended on the cumulative effect of a number of facts, each separately inconclusive, but all pointing to the same conclusion. Shall I run over the data in their order and in accordance with their connections?"

I gave an emphatic affirmative, and he continued:

"We begin, naturally, with the first fact, which is, of course, the most interesting and important; the fact which arrests attention, which shows that something has to be explained and possibly suggests a line of inquiry. You remember that I measured the footprints in the sand for comparison with the other footprints. Then I had the dimensions of the feet of the presumed bather. But as soon as I looked at the shoes which purported to be those of that bather, I felt a conviction that his feet would never go into them.

"Now, that was a very striking fact – if it really was a fact – and it came on top of another fact hardly less striking. That bather had gone into the sea; and at a considerable distance he had unquestionably come out again. There could be no possible doubt. In foot-measurements and length of stride the two sets of tracks were identical; and there were no other tracks. That man had come ashore and he had remained ashore. But yet he had not put on his clothes. He couldn't have gone away naked; but, obviously he was not there. As a criminal lawyer, you must admit that there was prima facie evidence of something very abnormal and probably criminal.

"On our way to the dormy-house, I carried the stick in the same hand as my own and noted that it was very little shorter. Therefore it was a tall man's stick. Apparently, then, the stick did not belong to the shoes, but to the man who had made the footprints. Then, when we came to the dormy-house, another striking fact presented itself. You remember that Hallett commented

174

on the quantity of sand that fell from the clothes on to the table. I am astonished that he did not notice the very peculiar character of that sand. It was perfectly unlike the sand which would fall from his own clothes. The sand on the sand-hills is dune sand – wind-borne sand, or, as the legal term has it, aeolian sand; and it is perfectly characteristic. As it has been carried by the wind, it is necessarily fine. The grains are small; and as the action of the wind sorts them out, they are extremely uniform in size. Moreover, by being continually blown about and rubbed together, they become rounded by mutual attrition. And then dune sand is nearly pure sand, composed of grains of silica unmixed with other substances.

"Beach sand is quite different. Much of it is half-formed, freshly broken down silica and is often very coarse; and, as I pointed out at the time, it is mixed with all sorts of foreign substances derived from masses in the neighbourhood. This particular sand was loaded with black and white particles, of which the white were mostly chalk, and the black particles of coal. Now there is very little chalk in the Shellness sand, as there are no cliffs quite near, and chalk rapidly disappears from sand by reason of its softness; and there is no coal."

"Where does the coal come from?" I asked.

"Principally from the Goodwins," he replied. "It is derived from the cargoes of colliers whose wrecks are embedded in those sands, and from the bunkers of wrecked steamers. This coal sinks down through the seventy-odd feet of sand and at last works out at the bottom, where it drifts slowly across the floor of the sea in a north-westerly direction until some easterly gale throws it up on the Thanet shore between Ramsgate and Foreness Point. Most of it comes up at Dumpton and Broadstairs, where you may see the poor people, in the winter, gathering coal pebbles to feed their fires.

"This sand, then, almost certainly came from the Thanet coast; but the missing man, Roscoff, had been staying in Sandwich, playing golf on the sand-hills. This was another striking discrepancy, and it made me decide to examine the clothes exhaustively, garment by garment. I did so; and this is what I found.

"The jacket, trousers, socks and shoes were those of a shortish, rather stout man, as shown by measurements, and the cap was his, since it was made of the same cloth as the jacket and trousers. The waistcoat, shirt, underclothes and stick were those of a tall man.

"The garments, socks and shoes of the short man were charged with Thanet beach sand, and contained no dune sand, excepting the cap, which might have fallen off on the sand-hills. The waistcoat was saturated with dune sand and contained no beach sand, and a little dune sand was obtained from the shirt and undergarments. That is to say, that the short man's clothes contained beach sand only, while the tall man's clothes contained only dune sand.

"The short man's clothes were all unmarked; the tall man's clothes were either marked or conspicuously recognisable, as the waistcoat and also the stick.

"The garments of the short man which had been left were those that could not have been worn by a tall man without attracting instant attention and the shoes could not have been put on at all; whereas the garments of the short man which had disappeared – the waistcoat, shirt and underclothes – were those that could have been worn by a tall man without attracting attention. The obvious suggestion was that the tall man had gone off in the short man's shirt and waistcoat but otherwise in his own clothes.

"And now as to the personal characteristics of the short man. From the cap I obtained five hairs. They were all blond, and two of them were of the peculiar, atrophic, 'point of exclamation' type that grow at the margin of a bald area. Therefore he was a fair man and partially bald. On the inside of the jacket, clinging to the rough tweed, I found a single long, thin, fair moustache hair, which suggested a long, soft moustache. The edge of the left cuff was thickly marked with oil-paint – not a single smear, but an accumulation such as a painter picks up when he reaches with his brush hand across a loaded palette. The suggestion – not very conclusive – was that he was an oil-painter and left-handed. But there was strong confirmation. There was an artist's pencil – 3B – and a stump of vine charcoal such as an oil-painter might carry. The silver coins in his pocket were blackened with sulphide as they would be if a piece of artist's soft, vulcanised rubber has been in the pocket with them. And there was the pocket-knife. It contained a sharp steel pencil-blade, a charcoal file and an ivory palette-blade; and that palette-blade had been used by a left-handed man."

"How did you arrive at that?" I asked.

"By the bevels worn at the edges," he replied. "An old palette-knife used by a right-handed man shows a bevel of wear on the under side of the left-hand edge and the upper side of the right-hand edge; in the case of a left-handed man the wear shows on the under side of the right-hand edge and the upper side of the left-hand edge. This, being an ivory blade, showed the wear very distinctly and proved conclusively that the user was left-handed; and as an ivory palette-knife is used only by fastidiously careful painters for such pigments as the cadmiums, which might be discoloured by a steel blade, one was justified in assuming that he was somewhat fastidious as to his pigments."

As I listened to Thorndyke's exposition I was profoundly impressed. His conclusions, which had sounded like mere speculative guesses, were, I now realised, based upon an analysis of the evidence as careful and as impartial as the summing up of a judge. And these conclusions he had drawn instantaneously from the appearances of things that had been before my eyes all the time and from which I had learned nothing.

"What do you suppose is the meaning of the affair?" I asked presently. "What was the motive of the murder?"

"We can only guess," he replied. "But, interpreting Capes' hints, I should suspect that our artist friend was a blackmailer; that he had come over here to squeeze Roscoff – perhaps not for the first time

– and that his victim lured him out on the sand-hills for a private talk and then took the only effective means of ridding himself of his persecutor. That is my view of the case; but, of course, it is only surmise."

Surmise as it was, however, it turned out to be literally correct. At the inquest Capes had to tell all that he knew; which was uncommonly little, though no one was able to add to it. The murdered man, Joseph Bertrand, had fastened on Roscoff and made a regular income by blackmailing him. That much Capes knew; and he knew that the victim had been in prison and that that was the secret. But who Roscoff was and what was his real name – for Roscoff was apparently a *nom de guerre* – he had no idea. So he could not help the police. The murderer had got clear away and there was no hint as to where to look for him; and so far as I know, nothing has ever been heard of him since.

CHAPTER EIGHT

The Apparition of Burling Court

Thorndyke seldom took a formal holiday. He did not seem to need one. As he himself put it, "A holiday implies the exchange of a less pleasurable occupation for one more pleasurable. But there is no occupation more pleasurable than the practice of Medical Jurisprudence." Moreover, his work was less affected by terms and vacations than that of an ordinary barrister, and the Long Vacation often found him with his hands full. Even when he did appear to take a holiday the appearance tended to be misleading, and it was apt to turn out that his disappearance from his usual haunts was associated with a case of unusual interest at a distance.

Thus it was on the occasion when our old friend, Mr Brodribb, of Lincoln's Inn, beguiled him into a fortnight's change at St David's-at-Cliffe, a seaside hamlet on the Kentish coast. There was a case in the background, and a very curious case it turned out to be, though at first it appeared to me quite a commonplace affair; and the manner of its introduction was as follows.

One hot afternoon in the early part of the Long Vacation the old solicitor dropped in for a cup of tea and a chat. That, at least, was how he explained his visit; but my experience of Mr Brodribb led me to suspect some ulterior purpose in the call, and as he sat by the open window, teacup in hand, looking, with his fine pink complexion, his silky white hair and his faultless "turn out," the very type of the courtly, old-fashioned lawyer, I waited expectantly for the matter of his visit to transpire. And, presently, out it came.

"I am going to take a little holiday down at St David's," said he. "Just a quiet spell by the sea, you know. Delightful place. So quiet and restful and so breezy and fresh. Ever been there?"

"No," replied Thorndyke. "I only just know the name."

"Well, why shouldn't you come down for a week or so? Both of you. I shall stay at Burling Court, the Lumleys' place. I can't invite you there as I'm only a guest, but I know of some comfortable rooms in the village that I could get for you. I wish you would come down, Thorndyke," he added after a pause. "I'm rather unhappy about young Lumley – I'm the family lawyer, you know, and so was my father and my grandfather, so I feel almost as if the Lumleys were my own kin – and I should like to have your advice and help."

"Why not have it now?" suggested Thorndyke.

"I will," he replied; "but I should like your help on the spot too. I'd like you to see Lumley and have a talk with him and tell me what you think of him."

"What is amiss with him?" Thorndyke asked.

"Well," answered Brodribb, "it looks uncommonly like insanity. He has delusions – sees apparitions and that sort of thing. And there is some insanity in the family. But I had better tell you the facts in their natural order.

"About four months ago Giles Lumley of Burling Court died; and as he was a widower without issue, the estate passed to his nearest relative, my present client, Frank Lumley, who was also the principal beneficiary under the will. At the time of Giles' death Frank was abroad, but a cousin of his, Lewis Price, was staying at the house with his wife as a more or less permanent guest; and as Price's circumstances were not very flourishing, and as he is the next heir to the estate, Frank – who is a bachelor – wrote to him at once telling him to look upon Burling Court as his home for as long as he pleased."

"That was extremely generous of him," I remarked.

"Yes," Brodribb agreed; "Frank is a good fellow; a very high-minded gentleman and a very sweet nature; but a little queer –

very queer just now. Well, Frank came back from abroad and took up his abode at the house; and for a time all went well. Then, one day, Price called on me and gave me some very unpleasant news. It seemed that Frank, who had always been rather neurotic and imaginative, had been interesting himself a good deal in psychical research and – and balderdash of that kind, you know. Well, there was no great harm in that, perhaps. But just lately he had taken to seeing visions and – what was worse – talking about them; so much so that Price got uneasy and privately invited a mental specialist down to lunch; and the specialist, having had a longish talk with Frank, informed Price confidentially that he (Frank) was obviously suffering from insane delusions. Thereupon Price called on me and begged me to see Frank myself and consider what ought to be done; so I made an occasion for him to come and see me at the office."

"And what did you think of him?" asked Thorndyke.

"I was horrified – horrified," said Mr Brodribb. "I assure you, Thorndyke, that that poor young man sat in my office and talked like a stark lunatic. Quite quietly, you know. No excitement, though he was evidently anxious and unhappy. But there he sat gravely talking the damnedest nonsense you ever heard."

"As, for instance?"

"Well, his infernal visions. Luminous birds flying about in the dark, and a human head suspended in mid-air – upside down, too. But I had better give you his story as he told it. I made full shorthand notes as he was talking, and I've brought them with me, though I hardly need them.

"His trouble seems to have begun soon after he took up his quarters at Burling Court. Being a bookish sort of fellow, he started to go through his library systematically; and presently he came across a small manuscript book, which turned out to be a sort of family history, or rather a collection of episodes. It was rather a lurid little book, for it apparently dwelt chiefly on the family crime, the family spectre and the family madness."

"Did you know about these heirlooms?" Thorndyke asked.

"No; it was the first I'd heard of 'em. Price knew there was some sort of family superstition, he didn't know what it was; and Giles knew it too – Price tells me – but didn't care to talk about it. He never mentioned it to me."

"What is the nature of the tradition?"inquired Thorndyke.

"I'll tell you," said Brodribb, taking out his notes. "I've got it all down, and poor Frank reeled the stuff off as if he had learned it by heart.

"The book, which is dated 1819, was apparently written by a Walter Lumley; and the story of the crime and the spook runs thus: About 1720 the property passed to a Gilbert Lumley, a naval officer, who then gave up the sea, married and settled down at Burling Court. A year or two later some trouble arose about his wife and a man named Glynn, a neighbouring squire. With or without cause, Lumley became violently jealous, and the end of it was that he lured Glynn to a large cavern in the cliffs and there murdered him. It was a most ferocious and vindictive crime. The cavern, which was then used by smugglers, had a beam across the roof bearing a tackle for hoisting out boat cargoes, and this tackle Lumley fastened to Glynn's ankles – having first pinioned him – and hoisted him up so that he hung head downwards a foot or so clear of the floor of the cave. And there he left him hanging until the rising tide flowed into the cave and drowned him.

"The very next day the murder was discovered, and as Lumley was the nearest justice of the peace, the discoverers reported to him and took him to the cave to see the body. When he entered the cave the corpse was still hanging as he had left the living man, and a bat was flittering round and round the dead man's head. He had the body taken down and carried to Glynn's house and took the necessary measures for the inquest. Of course, everyone suspected him of the murder, but there was no evidence against him. The verdict was murder by some person unknown, and as Gilbert Lumley was not sensitive, everything seemed to have gone off quite satisfactorily.

"But it hadn't. One night, exactly a month after the murder, Gilbert retired to his bedroom in the dark. He was in the act of feeling along the mantelpiece for the tinder-box, when he became aware of a dim light moving about the room. He turned round quickly and then saw that it was a bat – a most uncanny and abnormal bat that seemed to give out a greenish ghostly light – flitting round and round his bed. On this, remembering the bat in the cavern, he rushed out of the room in the very deuce of a fright. Presently he returned with one of the man-servants and a couple of candles; but the bat had disappeared.

"From that time onward, the luminous bat haunted Gilbert, appearing in dark rooms, on staircases and in passages and corridors, until his nerves were all on edge and he did not dare to move about the house at night without a candle or a lantern. But that was not the worst. Exactly two months after the murder the next stage of the haunting began. He had retired to his bed and was just about to get into bed when he remembered that he had left his watch in the little dressing-room that adjoined his chamber. With a lamp in his hand he went to the dressing-room to open the door. And then he stopped as if turned into stone; for, within a couple of yards of him, suspended in mid-air, was a man's head hanging upside down.

"For some seconds he stood rooted to the spot, unable to move. Then he uttered a cry of horror and rushed back to his room and down to the hall. There was no doubt whose head it was, strange and horrible as it looked in that unnatural, inverted position; for he had seen it twice before in that very position hanging in the cavern. Evidently he had not got rid of Glynn.

"That night, and every night thenceforward, he slept in his wife's room. And all through the night he was conscious of a strange and dreadful impulse to rise and go down to the shore; to steal into the cavern and wait for the flowing tide. He lay awake, fighting against the invisible power that seemed to be drawing him to destruction, and by the morning the horrid impulse began to weaken. But he went about in terror, not daring to go near the shore and afraid to trust himself alone.

"A month passed. The effect of the apparition grew daily weaker and an abundance of lights in the house protected him from the visitation of the bat. Then, exactly three months after the murder, he saw the head again. This time it was in the library, where he had gone to fetch a book. He was standing by the bookshelves and had just taken out a volume, when, as he turned away, there the hideous thing was, hanging in that awful, grotesque posture, chin upwards and the scanty hair dropping down like wet fringe. Gilbert dropped the book that he was holding and fled from the room with a shriek; and all that night invisible hands seemed to be plucking at him to draw him away to where the voices of the waves were reverberating in the cavern.

"This second visitation affected him profoundly. He could not shake off that sinister impulse to steal away to the shore. He was a broken man, the victim of an abiding terror, clinging for protection to the very servants, creeping abroad with shaking limbs and an apprehensive eye towards the sea. And ever in his ears was the murmur of the surf and the hollow echoes of the cavern.

"Already he had sought forgetfulness in drink; and sought it in vain. Now he took refuge in opiates. Every night, before retiring to the dreaded bed, he mingled laudanum with the brandy that brought him stupor if not repose. And brandy and opium began to leave their traces in the tremulous hand, the sallow cheek and the bloodshot eye. And so another month passed.

"As the day approached that would mark the fourth month, his terror of the visitation that he now anticipated reduced him to a state of utter prostration. Sleep – even drugged sleep – appeared that night to be out of the question, and he decided to sit up with his family, hoping by that means to escape the dreaded visitor. But it was a vain hope. Hour after hour he sat in his elbow-chair by the fire, while his wife dozed in her chair opposite, until the clock in the hall struck twelve. He listened and counted the strokes of the bell, leaning back with his eyes dosed. Half the weary night was gone. As the last stroke sounded and a deep silence fell on the house, he opened his eyes and looked into the face of Glynn within a few inches of his own.

"For some moments he sat with dropped jaw and dilated eyes staring in silent horror at this awful thing; then with an agonised screech he slid from his chair into a heap on the floor.

"At noon on the following day he was missed from the house. A search was made in the grounds and in the neighbourhood, but he was nowhere to be found. At last someone thought of the cavern, of which he had spoken in his wild mutterings, and a party of searchers made their way thither. And there they found him when the tide went out, lying on the wet sand with the brown sea-tangle wreathed about his limbs and the laudanum bottle – now full of sea water – by his side.

"With the death of Gilbert Lumley it seemed that the murdered man's spirit was appeased. During the lifetime of Gilbert's son, Thomas, the departed Glynn made no sign. But on his death and the succession of his son Arthur – then a middle-aged man – the visitations began again, and in the same order. At the end of the first month the luminous bat appeared; at the end of the second, the inverted head made its entry, and again at the third and the fourth month; and within twenty-four hours of the last visitation, the body of Arthur Lumley was found in the cavern. And so it has been from that time onward. One generation escapes untouched by the curse; but in the next, Glynn and the sea claim their own."

"Is that true, so far as you know?" asked Thorndyke.

"I can't say," answered Brodribb. "I am now only quoting Walter Lumley's infernal little book. But I remember that, in fact, Giles' father was drowned. I understood that his boat capsized, but that may have been only a story to cover a suicide.

"Well now, I have given you the gruesome history from this book that poor Frank had the misfortune to find. You see that he had it off by heart and had evidently read it again and again. Now I come to his own story, which he told me very quietly but with intense conviction and very evident forebodings.

"He found this damned book a few days after his arrival at Burling Court, and it was clear to him that, if the story was true, he was the next victim, since his predecessor, Giles, had been left in peace. And so it turned out. Exactly a month after his arrival, going up to his bedroom in the dark – no doubt expecting this apparition – as soon as he opened the door he saw a thing like a big glow-worm or firefly flitting round the room. It is evident that he was a good deal upset, for he rushed downstairs in a state of great agitation and fetched Price up to see it. But the strange thing was – though perhaps not so very strange, after all – that, although the thing was still there, flitting about the room, Price could see nothing. However, he pulled up the blind – the window was wide open – and the bat flopped out and disappeared.

"During the next month the bat reappeared at times, in the bedroom, in corridors and in a garret, where it flew out as Frank opened the door."

"What was he doing in the garret?" asked Thorndyke.

"He went up to fetch an ancient coffin-stool that Mrs Price had seen there and was telling him about. Well, this went on until the end of the second month. And then came the second act. It seems that by some infernal stupidity, he was occupying the bedroom that had been used by Gilbert. Now on this night, as soon as he had gone up, he must needs pay a visit to the little dressing-room which is now known as 'Gilbert's cabin' – so he tells me, for I was not aware of it – where Gilbert's cutlass, telescope, quadrant and the old navigator's watch are kept."

"Did he take a light with him?" inquired Thorndyke.

"I think not. There is a gas jet in the corridor and presumably he lit that. Then he opened the door of the cabin; and immediately he saw, a few feet in front of him, a man's head, upside down, apparently hanging in mid-air. It gave him a fearful shock – the more so, perhaps, because he half expected it – and, as before, he ran downstairs, all of a tremble. Price had gone to bed, but Mrs Price came up with him, and he showed her the horrible thing which was still hanging in the middle of the dark room.

"But Mrs Price could see nothing. She assured him that it was all his imagination; and in proof of it, she walked into the room right through the head, as it seemed, and when she had found the matches, she lit the gas. Of course, there was nothing whatever in the room.

"Another month passed. The bat appeared at intervals and kept poor Frank's nerves in a state of constant tension. On the night of the appointed day, as you will anticipate, Frank went again to Gilbert's cabin, drawn there by an attraction that one can quite understand. And there, of course, was the confounded head as before. That was a fortnight ago. So, you see, the affair is getting urgent. Either there is some truth in this weird story – which I don't believe for a moment – or poor old Frank is ripe for the asylum. But in any case something will have to be done."

"You spoke just now," said Thorndyke, "of some insanity in the family. What does it amount to, leaving these apparitions out of the question?"

"Well, a cousin of Frank's committed suicide in an asylum."

"And Frank's parents?"

"They were quite sane. The cousin was the son of Frank's mother's sister; and she was all right, too. But the boy's father had to be put away."

"Then," said Thorndyke, "the insanity doesn't seem to be in Frank's family at all, in a medical sense. Legal inheritance and physiological inheritance do not follow the same lines. If his mother's sister married a lunatic, he might inherit that lunatic's property, but he could not inherit his insanity. There was no blood relationship."

"No, that's true," Brodribb admitted, "though Frank certainly seems as mad as a hatter. But to come back to the holiday question, what do you say to a week or so at St David's?"

Thorndyke looked at me interrogatively. "What says my learned friend?" he asked.

"I say: Let us put up the shutters and leave in Polton in charge," I replied; and Thorndyke assented without a murmur.

Less than a week later, we were installed in the comfortable rooms that Mr Brodribb had found for us in the hamlet of St David's, within five minutes' walk of the steep gap-way that led down to the beach. Thorndyke entered into the holiday with an enthusiasm that would have astonished the denizens of King's Bench Walk. He explored the village, he examined the church, inside and out, he sampled all the footpaths with the aid of the Ordnance map, he foregathered with fishermen on the beach and renewed his acquaintance with boat-craft, and he made a pilgrimage to the historic cavern – it was less than a mile along the shore – and inspected its dark and chilly interior with the most lively curiosity.

We had not been at St David's twenty-four hours before we made the acquaintance of Frank Lumley – Mr Brodribb saw to that. For the old solicitor was profoundly anxious about his client – he took his responsibilities very seriously, did Mr Brodribb. His "family" clients were to him as his own kin, and their interests his own interests – and his confidence in Thorndyke's wisdom was unbounded. We were both very favourably impressed by the quiet, gentle, rather frail young man, and for my part, I found him, for a certifiable lunatic, a singularly reasonable and intelligent person. Indeed, apart from his delusions – or rather hallucinations – he seemed perfectly sane; for a somewhat eager interest in psychical and supernormal phenomena (of which he made no secret) is hardly enough to create a suspicion of a man's sanity.

But he was clearly uneasy about his own mental condition. He realised that the apparitions might possibly be the products of a disordered brain, though that was not his own view of them; and he discussed them with us in the most open and ingenuous manner.

"You don't think," Thorndyke suggested, "that these apparitions may possibly be natural appearances which you have misinterpreted or exaggerated in consequence of having read that very circumstantial story?

Lumley shook his head emphatically. "It is impossible," said he. "How could I? Take the case of the bat. I have seen it on several occasions quite distinctly. It was obviously a bat; but yet it seemed full of a ghostly, greenish light like that of a glow-worm. If it was not what it appeared, what was it? And then the head. There it was, perfectly clear and solid and real, hanging in mid-air within three or four feet of me. I could have touched it if I had dared."

"What size did it appear?" asked Thorndyke.

Lumley reflected. "It was not quite life-size. I should say about two-thirds the size of an ordinary head."

"Should you recognise the face if you saw it?"

"I can't say," replied Lumley. "You see, it's upside down. I haven't a very clear picture – I mean as to what the face would have been the right way up."

"Was the room quite dark on both occasions?" Thorndyke asked.

"Yes, quite. The gas jet in the corridor is just over the door and does not throw any light into room."

"And what is there opposite the door?"

"There is a small window, but that is usually shuttered nowadays. Under the window is a small folding dressing-table that belonged to Lumley. He had it made when he came home from sea."

Lumley was quite lucid and coherent in answers. His manner was perfectly sane; it only the matter that was abnormal. Of the apparitions he had not the slightest doubt, and he never varied in the smallest degree in his description of their appearance. The fact that they had been invisible both to Mr Price and wife he explained by pointing out that the curse applied only to the direct descendants of Lumley, and to those only in alternate generations.

After one of our conversations, Thorndyke expressed a wish to see the little manuscript book that had been the cause of all the trouble – or at least had been the forerunner; and Lumley promised to bring it to our rooms on the following afternoon. But then came an interruption to our holiday, not entirely unexpected; an urgent telegram from one of our solicitor friends asking for a consultation on an important and intricate case that had just been put into his hands, and making it necessary for us to go up to town by an early train on the following morning.

We sent a note to Brodribb, telling him that we should be away from St David's for perhaps a day or two, and on our way to the station he overtook us.

"I am sorry you have had to break your holiday," he said; "but I hope you will be back before Thursday."

"Why Thursday, in particular?" inquired Thorndyke.

"Because Thursday is the day on which that damned head is due to make its third appearance. It will be an anxious time. Frank hasn't said anything, but I know his nerves are strung up to concert pitch."

"You must watch him," said Thorndyke. "Don't let him out of your sight if you can help it."

"That's all very well," said Brodribb, "but he isn't a child, and I am not his keeper. He is the master of the house and I am just his guest. I can't follow him about if he wants to be alone."

"You mustn't stand on politeness, Brodribb," rejoined Thorndyke. "It will be a critical time and you must keep him in sight."

"I shall do my best," Brodribb said anxiously, "but I do hope you will be back by then."

He accompanied us dejectedly to the platform with us until our train came in. Suddenly, just as we were entering our carriage, he put his hand into his pocket.

"God bless me!" he exclaimed, "I had nearly forgotten this book. Frank asked me to give it to you." As he spoke, he drew out a little rusty calf-bound volume and handed it to Thorndyke. "You can look through it at your leisure," said he, "and if you think it best to chuck the infernal thing out of the window, do so. I suspect poor Frank is none the better for conning it over perpetually as he does."

I thought there was a good deal of reason in Brodribb's opinion. If Lumley's illusions were, as I suspected, the result of suggestion produced by reading the narrative, that suggestion would only tend to be reinforced by conning it over and over again. But the old lawyer's proposal was hardly practicable.

As soon as the train had fairly started, Thorndyke proceeded to inspect the little volume; and manner of doing so was highly characteristic. Any ordinary person would have opened the book and looked through the contents, probably seeking out at once the sinister history of Gilbert Lumley.

Not so Thorndyke. His inspection began at the very beginning and proceeded systematically to deal with every fact that the book had to disclose. First he made an exhaustive examination of the cover; scrutinised the corners; inspected the bottom edges and compared them with the top edges; and compared the top and bottom head-caps. Then he brought out his lens and examined the tooling, which was simple in character and worked in "blind" – i.e. not gilt. He also inspected the head-bands through the glass, and then he turned his attention to the interior. He looked carefully at both end-papers, he opened the sections and examined the sewing-thread, he held the leaves up to the light and tested the paper by eye and by touch and he viewed the writing in several places through his lens. Finally he handed the book and the lens to me without remark.

It was a quaint little volume, with a curiously antique air, though it was but a century old. The cover was of rusty calf, a good deal rubbed, but not in bad condition; for the joints were perfectly sound; but then it had probably had comparatively little use. The paper – a laid paper with very distinct wire-lines but no water-mark – had turned with age to a pale, creamy buff; the writing had faded to a warm brown, but was easily legible and very clearly and carefully written. Having noted these points, I turned over the leaves until I came to the story of Gilbert Lumley and the ill-fated

Glynn, which I read through attentively, observing that Mr Brodribb's notes had given the whole substance of the narrative with singular completeness.

"This story," I said, as I handed the book back to Thorndyke, "strikes me as rather unreal and unconvincing. One doesn't see how Walter Lumley got his information."

"No," agreed Thorndyke. "It is on the plane of fiction. The narrator speaks in the manner of a novelist, with complete knowledge of events and actions which were apparently known only to the actors."

"Do you think it possible that Walter Lumley was simply romancing?"

"I think it quite possible, and in fact very probable, that the whole narrative is fictitious," he replied. "We shall have to go into that question later on. For the present, I suppose, we had better give our attention to the case that we have in hand at the moment."

The little volume was accordingly put away, and for the rest of the journey our conversation was occupied with the matter of the consultation that formed our immediate business. As this, however, had no connection with the present history, I need make no further reference to it beyond stating that it kept us both busy for three days and that we finished with it on the evening of the third.

"Do you propose to go down to St David's tonight or tomorrow?" I asked, as we let ourselves into our chambers.

"Tonight," replied Thorndyke. "This is Thursday, you know, and Brodribb was anxious that we should be back some time today. I have sent him a telegram saying that we shall go down by the train that arrives about ten o'clock. So if he wants us, he can meet us at the station or send a message."

"I wonder," said I, "if the apparition of Glynn's head will make its expected visitation tonight."

"It probably will if there is an opportunity," Thorndyke replied. "But I hope that Brodribb will manage to prevent the opportunity from occurring. And, talking of Lumley, as we have an hour to spare, we may as well finish our inspection of his book. I snipped off a corner of one of the leaves and gave it to Polton to boil up in weak caustic soda. It will be ready for examination by now."

"You don't suspect that the book has been faked, do you?" said I.

"I view that book with the deepest suspicion," he replied, opening a drawer and producing the little volume. "Just look at it, Jervis. Look at the cover, for instance."

"Well," I said, turning the book over in my hand, "the cover looks ancient enough to me; typical old, rusty calf with a century's wear on it."

"Oh, there's no doubt that it is old calf," said he; "just the sort of leather that you could skin off the cover of an old quarto or folio. But don't you see that the signs of wear are all in the wrong places? How does a book wear in use? Well, first there are the bottom edges, which rub on the shelf. Then the corners, which are the thinnest leather and the most exposed. Then the top head-cap, which the finger hooks into in pulling the book from the shelf. Then the joint or hinge, which wears through from frequent opening and shutting. The sides get the least wear of all. But in this book, the bottom edges, the corners, the top head-cap and the joints are perfectly sound. They are not more worn than the sides; and the tooling is modern in character, looks quite fresh and the tool-marks are impressed on the marks of wear instead of being themselves worn. The appearances suggest to me a new binding with old leather.

"Then look at the paper. It professes to be discoloured by age. But the discoloration of the leaves of an old book occurs principally at the edges, where the paper has become oxidised by exposure to the air. The leaves of this book are equally discoloured all over. To me they suggest a bath of weak tea rather than old age.

"Again, there is the writing. Its appearance is that of faded writing done with the old-fashioned writing-ink – made with iron sulphate and oak-galls. But it doesn't look quite the right colour. However, we can easily test that. If it is old iron-gall ink, a drop of ammonium sulphide will turn it black. Let us take the book up to the laboratory and try it – and we had better have a 'control' to compare it with."

He ran his eye along the bookshelves and took down a rusty-looking volume of *Humphry Clinker*, the end-paper of which bore several brown and faded signatures. "Here is a signature dated 1803," said he. "That will be near enough"; and with the two books in his hand he led the way upstairs to the laboratory. Here he took down the ammonium sulphide bottle and dipping up a little of the liquid in a fine glass tube, opened the cover of *Humphry Clinker* and carefully deposited a tiny drop on the figure 3 in the date. Almost immediately the ghostly brown began to darken until it at length became jet black. Then, in the same way, he opened Walter Lumley's manuscript book and on the 9 of the date, 1819, he deposited a drop of the solution. But this time there was no darkening of the pale brown writing; on the contrary, it faded rapidly to a faint and muddy violet.

"It is not an iron ink," said Thorndyke, "and it looks suspiciously like an aniline brown. But let us see what the paper is made of. Have you boiled up that fragment, Polton?"

"Yes, sir," answered our laboratory assistant, "and I've washed the soda out of it, so it's all ready."

He produced a labelled test-tube containing a tiny corner of paper floating in water, which he carefully emptied into a large watch-glass. From this Thorndyke transferred the little pulpy fragment to a microscope slide and, with a pair of mounted needles, broke it up into its constituent fibres. Then he dropped on it a drop of aniline stain, removed the surplus with blotting-paper, added a drop of glycerine and put on it a large cover-slip.

"There, Jervis," said he, handing me the slide, "let us have your opinion on Walter Lumley's paper."

I placed the slide on the stage of the microscope and proceeded to inspect the specimen. But no exhaustive examination was necessary. The first glance settled the matter.

"It is nearly all wood," I said. "Mechanical wood fibre, with some esparto, a little cotton and a few linen fibres."

"Then," said Thorndyke, "it is a modern paper. Mechanical wood-pulp – prepared by Keller's process – was first used in paper-making in 1840. 'Chemical wood-pulp' came in later; and esparto was not used until 1860. So we can say with confidence that this paper was not made until more than twenty years after the date that is written on it. Probably it is of quite recent manufacture."

"In that case," said I, "this book is a counterfeit – presumably fraudulent."

"Yes. In effect it is a forgery."

"But that seems to suggest a conspiracy."

"It does," Thorndyke agreed; "especially if it is considered in conjunction with the apparitions. The suggestion is that this book was prepared for the purpose of inducing a state of mind favourable to the acceptance of supernatural appearances. The obvious inference is that the apparitions themselves were an imposture produced for fraudulent purposes. But it is time for us to go."

We shook hands with Polton, and, having collected our suitcases from the sitting-room, set forth for the station.

During the journey down I reflected on the new turn that Frank Lumley's affairs had taken. Apparently, Brodribb had done his client an injustice. Lumley was not so mad as the old lawyer had supposed. He was merely credulous and highly suggestible. The "hallucinations" were real phenomena which he had simply mis-interpreted. But who was behind these sham illusions? And what was it all about? I tried to open the question with Thorndyke; but though he was willing to discuss the sham manuscript book and the technique of its production, he would commit himself to nothing further.

On our arrival at St David's, Thorndyke looked up and down the platform and again up the station approach.

"No sign of Brodribb or any messenger," he remarked, "so we may assume that all is well at Burling Court up to the present. Let us hope that Brodribb's presence has had an inhibitory effect on the apparitions."

Nevertheless, it was evident that he was not quite easy in his mind. During supper he appeared watchful and preoccupied, and when, after the meal, he proposed a stroll down to the beach, he left word with our landlady as to where he was to be found if he should be wanted.

It was about a quarter to eleven when we arrived at the shore, and the tide was beginning to run out. The beach was deserted with the exception of a couple of fishermen who had apparently come in with the tide and who were making their boat secure for the night before going home. Thorndyke approached them, and addressing the older fisherman, remarked: "That is a big, powerful boat. Pretty fast, too, isn't she?"

"Ay, sir," was the reply; "fast and weatherly, she is. What we calls a galley-punt. Built at Deal for the hovelling trade – salvage, you know, sir – but there ain't no hovelling nowadays, not to speak of."

"Are you going out tomorrow?" asked Thorndyke.

"Not as I knows of, sir. Was you thinking of a bit of fishing?"

"If you are free," said Thorndyke, "I should like to charter the boat for tomorrow. I don't know what time I shall be able to start, but if you will stand by ready to put off at once when I come down we can count the waiting as sailing."

"Very well, sir," said the fisherman; "the boat's yours for the day tomorrow. Any time after six, or earlier, if you like, if you come down here you'll find me and my mate standing by with a stock of bait and the boat ready to push off."

"That will do admirably," said Thorndyke; and the morrow's programme being thus settled, we wished the fishermen good night and walked slowly back to our lodgings, where, after a final pipe, we turned in.

On the following morning, just as we were finishing a rather leisurely breakfast, we saw from our window our friend Mr Brodribb hurrying down the street towards our house. I ran out and opened the door, and as he entered I conducted him into our sitting-room. From his anxious and flustered manner it was obvious that something had gone wrong, and his first words confirmed the sinister impression.

"I'm afraid we're in for trouble, Thorndyke," said he. "Frank is missing."

"Since when?" asked Thorndyke.

"Since about eight o'clock this morning. He is nowhere about the house and he hasn't had any breakfast."

"When was he last seen?" Thorndyke asked. "And where?

"About eight o'clock, in the breakfast-room. Apparently he went in there to say 'goodbye' to the Prices – they have gone on a visit for the day to Folkestone and were having an early breakfast so as to catch the eight-thirty train. But he didn't have breakfast with them. He just went in and wished them a pleasant journey and then it appears that he went out for a stroll in the grounds. When I came down to breakfast at half-past eight, the Prices had gone and Frank hadn't come in. The maid sounded the gong, and as Frank still did not appear, she went out into the grounds to look for him; and presently I went out myself. But he wasn't there and he wasn't anywhere in the house. I don't like the look of it at all. He is usually very regular and punctual at meals. What do you think we had better do, Thorndyke?"

My colleague looked at his watch and rang the bell.

"I think, Brodribb," said he, "that we must act on the obvious probabilities and provide against the one great danger that is known to us. Mrs Robinson," he added, addressing the landlady, who had answered the bell in person, "can you let us have a jug of strong coffee at once?"

Mrs Robinson could, and bustled away to prepare it, while Thorndyke produced from a cupboard a large vacuum flask.

"I don't quite follow you, Thorndyke," said Mr Brodribb. "What probabilities and what danger do you mean?"

"I mean that, up to the present, Frank Lumley has exactly reproduced in his experiences and his actions the experiences and actions of Gilbert Lumley as set forth in Walter Lumley's narrative. The overwhelming probability is that he will continue to reproduce the story of Gilbert to the end. He probably saw the apparition for the third time last night, and is even now preparing for the final act."

"Good God!" gasped Brodribb. "What a fool I am. You mean the cave? But we can never get there now. It will be high water in an hour and the beach at St David's Head will be covered already. Unless we can get a boat," he added despairingly.

"We have got a boat," said Thorndyke. "I chartered one last night."

"Thank the Lord!" exclaimed Brodribb. "But you always think of everything – though I don't know what you want that coffee for."

"We may not want it at all," said Thorndyke, as he poured the coffee, which the landlady had just brought, into the vacuum flask, "but on the other hand we may."

He deposited the flask in a handbag, in which I observed a small emergency case, and then turned to Brodribb.

"We had better get down to the beach now," said he.

As we emerged from the bottom of the gap-way we saw our friends of the previous night laying a double line of planks across the beach from the boat to the margin of the surf; for the long galley-punt, with her load of ballast, was too heavy to drag over the shingle. They had just got the last plank laid as we reached the boat, and as they observed us they came running back with a half a dozen of their mates.

"Jump aboard, gentlemen," said our skipper, with a slightly dubious eye on Mr Brodribb – for the boat's gunwale was a good four feet above the beach. "We'll have her afloat in a jiffy."

We climbed in and hauled Mr Brodribb in after us. The tall mast was already stepped – against the middle thwart in the odd fashion of galley-punts – and the great sail was hooked to the traveller and the tack-hook ready for hoisting. The party of boatmen gathered round; and each took a tenacious hold of gunwale or thole. The skipper gave time with a jovial "Yo-ho!" and his mates joined in with a responsive howl and heaved as one man. The great boat moved forward, and gathering way, slid swiftly along the greased planks towards the edge of the surf. Then her nose splashed into the sea; the skipper and his mate sprang in over the transom; the tall lug-sail soared up the mast and filled, and the skipper let the rudder slide down its pintles and grasped the tiller.

"Did you want to go anywheres in particklar?" he inquired.

"We want to make for the big cave round St David's Head," said Thorndyke, "and we want to get there well before high water."

"We'll do that easy enough, sir," said the skipper, "with this breeze. 'Tis but about a mile and we've got three-quarters of an hour to do it in."

He took a pull at the main sheet and putting the helm down, brought the boat on a course parallel to the coast. Quietly but swiftly, the water slipped past, one after another fresh headlands opened out till, in about a quarter of an hour, we were abreast of St David's Head with the sinister black shape of the cavern in full view over the port bow. Shortly afterwards the sail was lowered and our crew, reinforced by Thorndyke and me, took to the oars, pulling straight towards the shore with the cavern directly ahead.

As the boat grounded on the beach Thorndyke, Brodribb and I sprang out and hurried across the sand and shingle to the gloomy and forbidding hole in the white cliff. At first, coming out of the bright sunlight, we seemed to be plunged in absolute darkness, and groped our way insecurely over the heaps of slippery sea-tangle that littered the floor. Presently our eyes grew accustomed to the dim light, and we could trace faintly the narrow, tunnel-like passage with its slimy green walls and the jagged roof nearly black with age. At the farther end it grew higher; and here I could see the small, dark bodies of bats hanging from the roof and clinging to the walls, and one or two fluttering blindly and noiselessly like large moths in the hollows of the vault above. But it was not the bats that engrossed my attention.

Far away, at the extreme end, I could dimly discern the prostrate figure of a man lying motionless on a patch of smooth sand; a dreadful shape that seemed to sound the final note of tragedy to which the darkness, the clammy chill of the cavern and the ghostly forms of the bats had been a fitting prelude.

"My God!" gasped Brodribb, "we're too late!"

He broke into a shambling run and Thorndyke and I darted on ahead. The man was Frank Lumley, of course, and a glance at him gave us at least a ray of hope. He was lying in an easy posture with closed eyes and was still breathing, though his respiration was shallow and slow. Beside him on the sand lay a little bottle and near it a cork. I picked up the former and read on the label "Laudanum: Poison" and a local druggist's name and address. But it was empty save for a few drops, the appearance and smell of which confirmed the label.

Thorndyke, who had been examining the unconscious man's eyes with a little electric lamp, glanced at the bottle.

"Well," said he, "we know the worst. That is a two-drachm phial, so if he took the lot his condition is not hopeless."

As he spoke he opened the handbag, and taking out the emergency case, produced from it a hypodermic syringe and a tiny bottle of atropine solution. I drew up Lumley's sleeve while the syringe was filled and Thorndyke then administered the injection.

"It is opium poisoning, I suppose?" said I.

"Yes," was the answer. "His pupils are like pin-points; but his pulse is not so bad. I think we can safely move him down to the boat."

Thereupon we lifted him, and with Brodribb supporting his feet, we moved in melancholy procession down the cave. Already the waves were lapping the beach at the entrance and even trickling in amongst the seaweed; and the boat, following the rising tide, had her bows within the cavern. The two fishermen, who were steadying the boat with their oars, greeted our appearance, carrying the body, with exclamations of astonishment. But they asked no questions, simply taking the unconscious man from us and laying him gently on the grating in the stern-sheets.

"Why, 'tis Mr Lumley!" exclaimed the skipper.

"Yes," said Thorndyke; and having given them a few words of explanation, he added: "I look to you to keep this affair to yourselves." To this the two men agreed heartily, and the boat having been pushed off and the sail hoisted, the skipper asked:

"Do we sail straight back, sir?"

"Yes," replied Thorndyke, "but we won't land yet. Stand on and off opposite the gap-way."

Already, as a result of the movement, the patient's stupor appeared less profound. And now Thorndyke took definite measures to rouse him, shaking him gently and constantly changing his position. Presently Lumley drew a deep sighing breath, and opened his eyes for a moment. Then Thorndyke sat him up, and producing the vacuum-flask, made him swallow a few teaspoonfuls of coffee. This procedure was continued for over an hour while the boat cruised up and down opposite the landing-place a half a mile or so from the shore. Constantly our patient relapsed into stuporous sleep, only to be roused again and given a sip of coffee.

At length he recovered so far as to be able to sit up – lurching from side to side as the boat rolled – and drowsily answer questions spoken loudly in his ear. A quarter of an hour later, as he still continued to improve, Thorndyke ordered the skipper to bring the boat to the landing-place.

"I think he could walk now," said he, "and the exercise will rouse him more completely."

The boat was accordingly beached and Lumley assisted to climb out; and though at first he staggered as if he would fall, after a few paces he was able to walk fairly steadily, supported on either side by me and Thorndyke. The effort of ascending the steep gap-way revived him further; and by the time we reached the gate of Burling Court – half a mile across the fields – he was almost able to stand alone.

But even when he had arrived home he was not allowed to rest, earnestly as he begged to be left in peace. First Thorndyke insisted on his taking a light meal, and then proceeded to question him as to the events of the previous night.

"I presume, Lumley," said he, "that you saw the apparition of Glynn's head?"

"Yes. After Mr Brodribb had seen me to bed, I got up and went to Gilbert's cabin. Something seemed to draw me to it. And as soon as I opened the door, there was the head hanging in the air within three feet of me. Then I knew that Glynn was calling me, and – well, you know the rest."

"I understand," said Thorndyke. "But now I want you to come to Gilbert's cabin with me and show me exactly where you were and where the head was."

Lumley was profoundly reluctant and tried to postpone the demonstration. But Thorndyke would listen to no refusal, and at last Lumley rose wearily and conducted his tormentor up the stairs, followed by Brodribb and me.

We went first to Lumley's bedroom and from that into a corridor, into which some other bedrooms opened. The corridor was dimly lighted by a single window, and when Thorndyke had drawn the thick curtain over this, the place was almost completely dark. At one end of the corridor was the small, narrow door of the "cabin," over which was a gas bracket. Thorndyke lighted the gas and opened the door and we then saw that the room was in total darkness, its only window being closely shuttered and the curtains drawn. Thorndyke struck a match and lit the gas and we then looked curiously about the little room.

It was a quaint little apartment, to which its antique furniture and contents gave an old-world air. An ancient hanger, quadrant and spy-glass hung on the wall, a large, dropsical-looking watch, inscribed "Thomas Tompion, Londini fecit," reposed on a little velvet cushion in the middle of a small, black mahogany table by the window, and a couple of Cromwellian chairs stood against the wall. Thorndyke looked curiously at the table which was raised on wooden blocks, and Lumley explained:

"That was Gilbert's dressing-table. He had it made for his cabin on board ship."

"Indeed," said Thorndyke. "Then Gilbert was a rather up-to-date gentleman. There wasn't much mahogany furniture before 1720. Let us have a look at the interior arrangements."

He lifted the watch, and having placed it on a chair, raised the lid of the table, disclosing a small wash-hand basin, a little squat ewer and other toilet appliances. The table lid, which was held upright by a brass strut, held a rather large dressing mirror enclosed in a projecting case.

"I wonder," said I, "why the table was stood on those blocks."

"Apparently," said Thorndyke, "for the purpose of bringing the mirror to the eye-level of a person standing up."

The answer gave Brodribb an idea. "I suppose Frank," said he, "it was not your own reflection in the mirror that you saw?"

"How could it be?" demanded Lumley. "The head was upside down, and besides, it was quite near to me."

"No, that's true," said Brodribb; and turning away from the table he picked up the old navigator's watch. "A queer old timepiece, this," he remarked.

"Yes," said Lumley; "but it's beautifully made. Let me show you the inside."

He took off the outer case and opened the inner one, exhibiting the delicate workmanship of the interior to Brodribb and me, while Thorndyke continued to pore over the inner fittings of the table. Suddenly my colleague said:

"Just go outside, you three, and shut the door. I want to try an experiment."

Obediently we all filed out and closed the door, waiting expectantly in the corridor. In a couple of minutes Thorndyke came out and before he shut the door I noticed that the little room was now in darkness. He walked us a short distance down the corridor and then, halting, said:

"Now, Lumley, I want you to go into the cabin and tell us what you see."

Lumley appeared a little reluctant to go in alone, but eventually he walked towards the cabin and opened the door. Instantly he uttered a cry of horror, and closing the door, ran back to us, trembling, agitated, wild-eyed.

"It is there now!" he exclaimed. "I saw it distinctly."

"Very well," said Thorndyke. "Now you go and look, Brodribb."

Mr Brodribb showed no eagerness. With very obvious trepidation he advanced to the door and threw it open with a jerk. Then, with a sharp exclamation, he slammed it to, and came hurrying back, his usually pink complexion paled down to a delicate mauve.

"Horrible! Horrible!" he exclaimed. "What the devil is it, Thorndyke?"

A sudden suspicion flashed into my mind. I strode forward, and turning the handle of the door, pulled it open. And then I was not surprised that Brodribb had been startled. Within a yard of my face, clear, distinct and solid, was an inverted head, floating in mid-air in the pitch-dark room. Of course, being prepared for it, I saw at a glance what it was; recognised my own features, strangely and horribly altered as they were by their inverted position. But even now that I knew what it was, the thing had a most appalling, uncanny aspect.

"Now," said Thorndyke, "let us go in and explode the mystery. Just stand outside the door, Jervis, while I demonstrate."

He produced a sheet of white paper from his pocket, and smoothing it out, led our two friends into the room.

"First," said he, holding the paper out flat at eye-level, "you see on this paper, a picture of Dr Jervis' head, upside down."

"So there is," said Brodribb; "like a magic-lantern picture."

"Exactly like," agreed Thorndyke; "and of exactly the same nature. Now let us see how it is produced."

He struck a match and lit the gas; and instantly all our eyes turned towards the open dressing-table.

"But that is not the same mirror that we saw just now," said Brodribb.

"No," replied Thorndyke. "The frame is reversible on a sliding hinge and I have turned it round. On one side is the ordinary flat looking-glass which you saw before; on the other is this concave shaving-mirror. You observe that, if you stand close to it, you see your face the right way up and magnified; if you go back to the door, you see your head upside down and smaller."

"But," objected Lumley, "the head looked quite solid and seemed to be right out in the room."

"So it was, and is still. But the effect of reality is destroyed by the fact that you can now see the frame of the mirror enclosing the image, so that the head appears to be in the mirror. But in the dark, you could only see the image. The mirror was invisible."

Brodribb reflected on this explanation. Presently he said:

"I don't think I quite understand it now."

Thorndyke took a pencil from his pocket and began to draw a diagram on the sheet of paper that he still held.

"The figure that you see in an ordinary flat looking-glass," he explained, "is what is called a 'virtual image.' It appears behind the

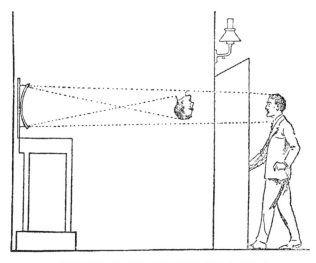

THE APPARITION OF BURLING COURT

mirror, but of course it is not there. It is an optical illusion. But the image from a concave mirror is in front of the mirror and is a real image like that of a magic lantern or a camera, and, like them, inverted. This diagram will explain matters. Here is Lumley standing at the open door of the room. His figure is well lighted by the gas over the door (which, however, throws no light into the room) and is clearly reflected by the mirror, which throws forward a bright inverted image. But, as the room is dark and the mirror invisible, he sees only the image, which looks like – and in fact is – a real object standing in mid-air."

"But why did I see only the head?" asked Lumley.

"Because the head occupied the whole of the mirror. If the mirror had been large enough you would have seen the full-length figure."

Lumley reflected for a moment. "It almost looks as if this had been arranged," he said at length.

"Of course it has been arranged," said Thorndyke; "and very cleverly arranged, too. And now let us go and see if anything else has been arranged. Which is Mr Price's room?"

"He has three rooms, which open out of this corridor," said Lumley; and he conducted us to a door at the farther end, which Thorndyke tried and found locked.

"It is a case for the smoker's companion," said he, producing from his pocket an instrument that went by that name, but which looked suspiciously like a pick-lock. At any rate, after one or two trials – which Mr Brodribb watched with an appreciative smile – the bolt shot back and the door opened.

We entered what was evidently the bedroom, around which Thorndyke cast a rapid glance and then asked:

"What are the other rooms?

"I think he uses them to tinker in," said Lumley, "but I don't quite know what he does in them. All three rooms communicate."

We advanced to the door of communication and finding it unlocked, passed through into the next room. Here, on a large table by the window, was a litter of various tools and appliances.

"What is that thing with the wooden screws?" Brodribb asked.

"A bookbinder's sewing-press," replied Thorndyke. "And here are some boxes of finishing tools. Let us look over them."

He took up the boxes one after the other and inspected the ends of the tools – brass stamps for impressing the ornaments on book covers. Presently he lifted out two, a leaf and a flower. Then he produced from his coat pocket the little manuscript book, and laying it on the table, picked up from the floor a little fragment of leather. Placing this also on the table, he pressed each of the tools on it, leaving a clear impression of a leaf and a flower. Finally he laid the scrap of leather on the book, when it was obvious that the leaf and flower were identical replicas of the leaves and flowers which formed the decoration of the book cover.

"This is very curious," said Lumley. "They seem to be exactly alike."

"They are exactly alike," said Thorndyke. "I affirm that the tooling on that book was done with these tools, and the leaves sewn on that press."

"But the book is a hundred years old," objected Lumley.

Thorndyke shook his head. "The leather is old," said he, "but the book is new. We have tested the paper and found it to be of recent manufacture. But now let us see what is in that little cupboard. There seem to be some bottles there."

He ran his eye along the shelves, crowded with bottles and jars of varnish, glair, oil, cement and other material.

"Here," he said, taking down a small bottle of dark-coloured powder, "is some aniline brown. That probably produced the ancient and faded writing. But this is more illuminating – in more senses than one. He picked out a little, wide-mouthed bottle labelled "Radium Paint for the hands and figures of luminous watches."

"Ha!" exclaimed Brodribb; "a very illuminating discovery, as you say."

"And that," said Thorndyke, looking keenly round the room, "seems to be all there is here. Shall we take a glance at the third room?"

We passed through the communicating doorway and found ourselves in a small apartment, practically unfurnished and littered with trunks, bags and various lumber. As we stood looking about us, Thorndyke sniffed suspiciously.

"I seem to detect a sort of mousy odour," said he, glancing round inquisitively. "Do you notice it, Jervis?"

I did and with the obvious idea in my mind began to prowl round the room in search of the source. Suddenly my eye lighted on a smallish box, in the top of which a number of gimlet holes had been bored. I raised the lid and peered in. The interior was covered with filth and on the bottom lay a dead bat.

We all stood for a few seconds looking in silence at the little corpse. Then Thorndyke closed the box and tucked it under his arm.

"This completes the case, I think," said he. "What time does Price return?"

"He is expected home about seven o'clock," said Lumley. Then he added with a troubled expression : " I don't understand all this. "What does it mean?"

"It is very simple," replied Thorndyke. "You have a sham ancient book containing an evidently fabulous story of supernatural events; and you have a series of appliances and arrangements for producing illusions which seem to repeat those events. The book was planted where it was certain to be found and read, and the illusions began after it was known that it actually had been read. It is a conspiracy."

"But why?" demanded Lumley. "What was the object?"

"My dear Frank," said Brodribb, "you seem to forget that Price is the next of kin and the heir to your estate on your death."

Lumley's eyes filled. He seemed overcome with grief and disgust.

"It is incredible," he murmured huskily. "The baseness of it is beyond belief."

Price and his wife arrived home at about seven o'clock. A meal had been prepared for them, and when they had finished, a servant was sent in to ask Mr Price to speak with Mr Brodribb in the study. There we all awaited him, Lumley being present by his own wish; and on the table were deposited the little book, the scrap of leather, the two finishing tools, the pot of radium paint and the box containing the dead bat. Presently Price entered, accompanied by his wife; and at the sight of the objects on the table they both turned deathly pale. Mr Brodribb placed chairs for them, and when they were seated he began in a dry, stern voice: "I have sent for you, Mr Price, to give you certain information. These two gentlemen, Dr Thorndyke and Dr Jervis, are eminent criminal lawyers whom I have commissioned to make certain investigations and to advise me in this matter. Their investigations have disclosed the existence of a forged manuscript, a dead bat, a pot of luminous paint and a concave mirror. I need not enlarge on those discoveries. My intention is to prosecute you and your wife for conspiracy to procure the suicide of Mr Frank Lumley. But, at Mr Lumley's request, I have consented to delay the proceedings for forty-eight hours. During that period you will be at liberty to act as you think best."

For some seconds there was a tense silence. The two crestfallen conspirators sat with their eyes fixed on the floor, and Mrs Price choked down a half-hysterical sob. Then they rose; and Price, without looking at any of us, said in a low voice:

"Very well. Then I suppose we had better clear out."

"And the best thing, too," remarked Brodribb when they had gone; "for I doubt if we could have carried our bluff into court."

On the wall of our sitting-room in the Temple there hang, to this day, two keys. One is that of the postern gate of Burling Court, and the other belongs to the suite of rooms that were once occupied by Mr Lewis Price; and they hang there, by Frank Lumley's wish, as a token that Burling Court is a country home to which we have access at all hours and seasons as tenants in virtue of an inalienable right.

CHAPTER NINE

The Mysterious Visitor

"So," said Thorndyke, looking at me reflectively, "you are a full-blown medical practitioner with a practice of your own. How the years slip by! It seems but the other day that you were a student, gaping at me from the front bench of the lecture theatre."

"Did I gape?" I asked incredulously.

"I use the word metaphorically," said he, "to denote ostentatious attention. You always took my lectures very seriously. May I ask if you have ever found them of use in your practice?"

"I can't say that I have ever had any very thrilling medico-legal experiences since that extraordinary cremation case that you investigated – the case of Septimus Maddock, you know. But that reminds me that there is a little matter that I meant to speak to you about. It is of no interest, but I just wanted your advice, though it isn't even my business, strictly speaking. It concerns a patient of mine, a man named Crofton, who has disappeared rather unaccountably."

"And do you call that a case of no medico-legal interest?" demanded Thorndyke.

"Oh, there's nothing in it. He just went away for a holiday and he hasn't communicated with his friends very recently. That is all. What makes me a little uneasy is that there is a departure from his usual habits – he is generally a fairly regular correspondent – that seems a little significant in view of his personality. He is markedly ιeurotic and his family history is by no means what one would wish."

"That is an admirable thumb-nail sketch, Jardine," said Thorndyke; "but it lacks detail. Let us have a full-size picture."

"Very well," said I, "but you mustn't let me bore you. To begin with Crofton: he is a nervous, anxious, worrying sort of fellow, everlastingly fussing about money affairs, and latterly this tendency has been getting worse. He fairly got the jumps about his financial position; felt that he was steadily drifting into bankruptcy and couldn't get the subject out of his mind. It was all bunkum. I am more or less a friend of the family, and I know that there was nothing to worry about. Mrs Crofton assured me that, although they were a trifle hard up, they could rub along quite safely.

"As he seemed to be getting the hump worse and worse, I advised him to go away for a change and stay in a boarding-house where he would see some fresh faces. Instead of that, he elected to go down to a bungalow that he has at Seasalter, near Whitstable, and lets out in the season. He proposed to stay by himself and spend his time in sea-bathing and country walks. I wasn't very keen on this, for solitude was the last thing that he wanted. There was a strong family history of melancholia and some unpleasant rumours of suicide. I didn't like his being alone at all. However, another friend of the family, Mrs Crofton's brother, in fact, a chap named Ambrose, offered to go down and spend a weekend with him to give him a start, and afterwards to run down for an afternoon whenever he was able. So off he went with Ambrose on Friday, the sixteenth of June, and for a time all went well. He seemed to be improving in health and spirits and wrote to his wife regularly two or three times a week. Ambrose went down as often as he could to cheer him up, and the last time brought back the news that Crofton thought of moving on to Margate for a further change. So, of course, he didn't go down to the bungalow again.

"Well, in due course, a letter came from Margate; it had been written at the bungalow, but the postmark was Margate and bore the same date – the sixteenth of July – as the letter itself. I have it with me. Mrs Crofton sent it for me to see and I haven't returned it yet. But there is nothing of interest in it beyond the statement that he was going on to Margate by the next train and would write again when he had found rooms there. That was the last that was heard of him. He never wrote and nothing is known of his movements excepting that he left Seasalter and arrived at Margate. This is the letter."

I handed it to Thorndyke, who glanced at the postmark and then laid it on the table for examination later.

"Have any inquiries been made?" he asked.

"Yes. His photograph has been sent to the Margate police, but, of course – well, you know what Margate is like in July. Thousands of strangers coming and going every day. It is hopeless to look for him in that crowd; and it's quite possible that he isn't there now. But his disappearance is most inopportune, for a big legacy has just fallen in, and, naturally, Mrs Crofton is frantically anxious to let him know. It is a matter of about thirty thousand pounds."

"Was this legacy expected?" asked Thorndyke

"No. The Croftons knew nothing about it. They didn't know that the old lady – Miss Shuler – had made a will or that she had very much to leave; and they didn't know that she was likely to die, or even that she was ill. Which is rather odd; for she was ill for a month or two, and, as she suffered from a malignant abdominal tumour, it was known that she couldn't recover."

"When did she die?"

"On the thirteenth of July."

Thorndyke raised his eyebrows. "Just three days before the date of this letter," he remarked; "so that, if he should never reappear, this letter will be the sole evidence that he survived her. It is an important document. It may come to represent a value of thirty thousand pounds."

"It isn't really so important as it looks," said I.

"Miss Shuler's will provides that if Crofton should die before the testatrix, the legacy should go to his wife. So whether he is alive or not, the legacy is quite safe. But we must hope that he is alive, though I must confess to some little anxiety on this account."

Thorndyke reflected awhile on this statement. Presently he asked:

"Do you know if Crofton has made a will?"

"Yes, he has," I replied; "quite recently. I was one of the witnesses and I read it through at Crofton's request. It was full of the usual legal verbiage, but it might have been stated in a dozen words. He leaves practically everything to his wife, but instead of saying so it enumerates the property item by item."

"It was drafted, I suppose, by the solicitor?"

"Yes; another friend of the family named Jobson, and he is the executor and residuary legatee."

Thorndyke nodded and again became deeply reflective. Still meditating, he took up the letter, and as he inspected it, I watched him curiously and not without a certain secret amusement. First he looked over the envelope, back and front. Then he took from his pocket a powerful Coddington lens and with this examined the flap and the postmark. Next, he drew out the letter, held it up to the light, then read it through and finally examined various parts of the writing through his lens.

"Well," I asked, with an irreverent grin, "I should think you have extracted the last grain of meaning from it."

He smiled as he put away his lens and handed the letter back to me.

"As this may have to be produced as proof of survival," said he, "it had better be put in a place of safety. I notice that he speaks of returning later to the bungalow. I take it that it has been ascertained that he did not return there?"

"I don't think so. You see, they have been waiting for him to write. You think that someone ought…"

I paused; for it began to be borne in on me that Thorndyke was taking a somewhat gloomy view of the case.

"My dear Jardine," said he. "I am merely following your own suggestion. Here is a man with an inherited tendency to

214

melancholia and suicide who has suddenly disappeared. He went away from an empty house and announced his intention of returning to it later. As that house is the only known locality in which he could be sought, it is obvious that it ought to have been examined. And even if he never came back there, the house might contain some clues to his present whereabouts."

This last sentence put an idea into my mind which I was a little shy of broaching. What was a clue to Thorndyke might be perfectly meaningless to an ordinary person. I recalled his amazing interpretations of the most commonplace facts in the mysterious Maddock case and the idea took fuller possession. At length I said tentatively:

"I would go down myself if I felt competent. Tomorrow is Saturday and I could get a colleague to look after my practice; there isn't much doing just now. But when you speak of clues, and when I remember what a duffer I was last time – I wish it were possible for you to have a look at the place."

To my surprise, he assented almost with enthusiasm.

"Why not?" said he. "It is a weekend. We could put up at the bungalow, I suppose, and have a little gipsy holiday. And there are undoubtedly points of interest in the case. Let us go down tomorrow. We can lunch in the train and have the afternoon before us. You had better get a key from Mrs Crofton, or, if she hasn't got one, an authority to visit the house. We may want that if we have to enter without a key. And we go alone, of course."

I assented joyfully. Not that I had any expectations as to what we might learn from our inspection. But something in Thorndyke's manner gave me the impression that he had extracted from my account of the case some significance that was not apparent to me.

The bungalow stood on a space of rough ground a little way behind the sea-wall, along which we walked towards it from Whitstable, passing on our way a ship-builder's yard and a slipway, on which a collier brigantine was hauled up for repairs. There were one or two other bungalows adjacent, but a considerable distance apart, and we looked at them as we approached to make out the names painted on the gates.

"That will probably be the one," said Thorndyke, indicating a small building enclosed within a wooden fence and provided, like the others, with a bathing hut, just above high-water mark. Its solitary, deserted aspect and lowered blinds supported his opinion and when we reached the gate, the name "Middlewick" painted on it settled the matter.

"The next question is," said I, "how the deuce are we going to get in? The gate is locked, and there is no bell. Is it worthwhile to hammer at the fence?"

"I wouldn't do that," replied Thorndyke. "The place is pretty certainly empty or the gate wouldn't be locked. We shall have to climb over unless there is a back gate unlocked, so the less noise we make the better."

We walked round the enclosure, but there was no other gate, nor was there any tree or other cover to disguise our rather suspicious proceedings.

"There's no help for it, Jardine," said Thorndyke, "so here goes."

He put his green canvas suitcase on the ground, grasped the top of the fence with both hands and went over like a harlequin. I picked up the case and handed it over to him, and, having taken a quick glance round, followed my leader.

"Well," I said, "here we are. And now, how are we going to get into the house?"

"We shall have to pick a lock if there is no door open, or else go in by a window. Let us take a look round."

We walked round the house to the back door, but found it not only locked but bolted top and bottom, as Thorndyke ascertained with his knife-blade. The windows were all casements and all fastened with their catches.

"The front door will be the best," said Thorndyke. "It can't be bolted unless he got out by the chimney, and I think my 'smoker's companion' will be able to cope with an ordinary door-lock. It looked like a common builder's fitting."

As he spoke, we returned to the front of the house and he produced the "smoker's companion" from his pocket (I don't know what kind of smoker it was designed to accompany). The lock was apparently a simple affair, for the second trial with the "companion" shot back the bolt, and when I turned the handle, the door opened. As a precaution, I called out to inquire if there was anybody within, and then, as there was no answer, we entered, walking straight into the living-room, as there was no hall or lobby.

A couple of paces from the threshold we halted to look round the room, and on me the aspect of the place produced a vague sense of discomfort. Though it was early in a bright afternoon, the room was almost completely dark, for not only were the blinds lowered, but the curtains were drawn as well.

"It looks," said I, peering about the dim and gloomy apartment with sun-dazzled eyes, "as if he had gone away at night. He wouldn't have drawn the curtains in the daytime."

"One would think not," Thorndyke agreed; "but it doesn't follow."

He stepped to the front window and drawing back the curtains pulled up the blind, revealing a half-curtain of green serge over the lower part of the window. As the bright daylight flooded the room, he stood with his back to the window looking about with deep attention, letting his eyes travel slowly over the walls, the furniture, and especially the floor. Presently he stooped to pick up a short match-end which lay just under the table opposite the door, and as he looked at it thoughtfully, he pointed to a couple of spots of candle grease on the linoleum near the table. Then he glanced at the mantelpiece and from that to an ash-bowl on the table.

"These are only trifling discrepancies," said he, "but they are worth noting. You see," he continued in response to my look of inquiry, "that this room is severely trim and orderly. Everything seems to be in its place. The match-box, for instance, has its fixed receptacle above the mantelpiece, and there is a bowl for the burnt matches, regularly used, as its contents show. Yet here is a burnt match thrown on the floor, although the bowl is on the table quite handy. And the match, you notice, is not of the same kind as those in the box over the mantelpiece, which is a large Bryant and May, or as the burnt matches in the bowl which have evidently come from it. But if you look in the bowl," he continued, picking it up, "you will see two burnt matches of this same kind – apparently the small size Bryant and May – one burnt quite short and one only half burnt. The suggestion is fairly obvious, but, as I say, there is a slight discrepancy."

"I don't know," said I, "that either the suggestion or the discrepancy is very obvious to me."

He walked over to the mantelpiece and took the match-box from its case.

"You see," said he, opening it, "that this box is nearly full. It has an appointed place and it was in that place. We find a small match, burnt right out, under the table opposite the door, and two more in the bowl under the hanging lamp. A reasonable inference is that someone came in in the dark and struck a match as he entered. That match must have come from a box that he brought with him in his pocket. It burned out and he struck another, which also burned out while he was raising the chimney of the lamp and he struck a third to light the lamp. But if that person was Crofton, why did he need to strike a match to light the room when the match-box was in its usual place; and why did he throw the match-end on the floor?"

"You mean that the suggestion is that the person was not Crofton; and I think you are right. Crofton doesn't carry matches in his pocket. He uses wax vestas and carries them in a silver case."

"It might possibly have been Ambrose," Thorndyke suggested.

"I don't think so," said I. "Ambrose uses a petrol lighter."

Thorndyke nodded. "There may be nothing in it," said he, "but it offers a suggestion. Shall we look over the rest of the premises?"

He paused for a moment to glance at a key-board on the wall on which one or two keys were hanging, each distinguished by a little ivory label and by the name written underneath the peg; then he opened a door in the corner of the room. As this led into the kitchen, he closed it and opened an adjoining one which gave access to a bedroom.

"This is probably the extra bedroom," he remarked as we entered. "The blinds have not been drawn down and there is a general air of tidiness that suggests a tidy up of an unoccupied room. And the bed looks as if it had been out of use."

After an attentive look round, he returned to the living-room and crossed to the remaining door. As he opened it, we looked into a nearly dark room, both the windows being covered by thick serge curtains.

"Well," he observed, when he had drawn back the curtains and raised the blinds, "there is nothing painfully tidy here. That is a very roughly-made bed, and the blanket is outside the counterpane."

He looked critically about the room and especially at the bedside table.

"Here are some more discrepancies," said he. "There are two candlesticks, in one of which the candle has burned itself right out, leaving a fragment of wick. There are five burnt matches in it, two large ones from the box by its side, and three small ones, of which two are mere stumps. The second candle is very much guttered, and I think" – he lifted it out of the socket – "yes, it has been used out of the candlestick. You see that the grease has run down right to the bottom and there is a distinct impression of a thumb – apparently a left thumb – made while the grease was warm. Then you notice the mark on the table of a tumbler which had contained some liquid that was not water, but there is no tumbler. However, it may be an old mark, though it looks fresh."

"It is hardly like Crofton to leave an old mark on the table," said I. "He is a regular old maid. We had better see if the tumbler is in the kitchen."

"Yes," agreed Thorndyke. "But I wonder what he was doing with that candle. Apparently he took it out of doors, as there is a spot on the floor of the living-room; and you see that there are one or two spots on the floor here." He walked over to a chest of drawers near the door and was looking into a drawer which he had pulled out, and which I could see was full of clothes, when I observed a faint smile spreading, over his face. "Come round here, Jardine," he said in a low voice, "and take a peep through the crack of the door."

I walked round, and, applying my eye to the crack, looked across the living-room at the end window. Above the half-curtain I could distinguish the unmistakable top of a constabulary helmet.

"Listen," said Thorndyke. "They are in force." As he spoke, there came from the neighbourhood of the kitchen a furtive scraping sound, suggestive of a pocket-knife persuading a window-catch. It was followed by the sound of an opening window and then of a stealthy entry. Finally, the kitchen door opened softly, some one tip-toed across the living-room and a burly police-sergeant appeared, framed in the bedroom doorway.

"Good afternoon, Sergeant," said Thorndyke, with a genial smile.

"Yes, that's all very well," was the response, "but the question is, who might you be, and what might you be doing in this house?"

Thorndyke briefly explained our business, and, when we had presented our cards and Mrs Crofton's written authority, the sergeant's professional stiffness vanished like magic.

"It's all right, Tomkins," he sang out to an invisible myrmidon. "You had better shut the window and go out by the front door. You must excuse me, gentlemen," he added; "but the tenant of the next bungalow cycled down and gave us the tip. He watched you through his glasses and saw you pick the front-door lock. It did look a bit queer, you must admit."

Thorndyke admitted it freely with a faint chuckle, and we walked across the living-room to the kitchen. Here, the sergeant's presence seemed to inhibit comments, but I noticed that my colleague cast a significant glance at a frying-pan that rested on a Primus stove. The congealed fat in it presented another "discrepancy"; for I could hardly imagine the fastidious Crofton going away and leaving it in that condition.

Noting that there was no unwashed tumbler in evidence, I followed my friend back to the living-room, where he paused with his eye on the key-board.

"Well," remarked the sergeant, "if he ever did come back here, it's pretty clear that he isn't here now. You've been all over the premises, I think?"

"All excepting the bathing-hut," replied Thorndyke; and, as he spoke, he lifted the key so labelled from its hook.

The sergeant laughed softly. "He's not very likely to have taken up his quarters there," said he. "Still, there's nothing like being thorough. But you notice that the key of the front door and that of the gate have both been taken away, so we can assume that he has taken himself away too."

"That is a reasonable inference," Thorndyke admitted; "but we may as well make our survey complete."

With this he led the way out into the garden and to the gate, where he unblushingly produced the "smoker's companion" and insinuated its prongs into the keyhole.

"Well, I'm sure!" exclaimed the sergeant as the lock clicked and the gate opened. "That's a funny sort of tool; and you seem quite handy with it, too. Might I have a look at it?"

He looked at it so very long and attentively, when Thorndyke handed it to him, that I suspected him of an intention to infringe the patent. By the time he had finished his inspection we were at the bottom of the bank below the sea-wall and Thorndyke had inserted the key into the lock of the bathing-hut. As the sergeant returned the "companion" Thorndyke took it and pocketed it; then he turned the key and pushed the door open; and the officer started back with a shout of amazement.

It was certainly a grim spectacle that we looked in on. The hut was a small building about six feet square, devoid of any furniture or fittings, excepting one or two pegs high up the wall. The single, unglazed window was closely shuttered, and on the bare floor in the farther corner a man was sitting, leaning back into the corner, with his head dropped forward on his breast. The man was undoubtedly Arthur Crofton. That much I could say with certainty, notwithstanding the horrible changes wrought by death and the lapse of time. "But," I added when I had identified the body, "I should have said that he had been dead more than a fortnight. He must have come straight back from Margate and done this. And that will probably be the missing tumbler," I concluded, pointing to one that stood on the floor close to the right hand of the corpse.

"No doubt," replied Thorndyke, somewhat abstractedly. He had been looking critically about the interior of the hut, and now remarked: "I wonder why he did not shoot the bolt instead of locking himself in; and what has become of the key? He must have taken it out of the lock and put it in his pocket."

He looked interrogatively at the sergeant, who having no option but to take the hint, advanced with an expression of horrified disgust and proceeded very gingerly to explore the dead man's clothing.

"Ah!" he exclaimed at length, "here we are." He drew from the waistcoat pocket a key with a small ivory label attached to it. "Yes, this is the one. You see, it is marked 'Bathing Hut.' "

He handed it to Thorndyke, who looked at it attentively, and even with an appearance of surprise, and then, producing an indelible pencil from his pocket, wrote on the label, "Found on body."

"The first thing," said he, "is to ascertain if it fits the lock."

"Why, it must," said the sergeant, "if he locked himself in with it."

"Undoubtedly," Thorndyke agreed, "but that is the point. It doesn't look quite similar to the other one."

He drew out the key which we had brought from the house and gave it to me to hold. Then he tried the key from the dead man's pocket; but it not only did not fit, it would not even enter the keyhole.

The sceptical indifference faded suddenly from the sergeant's face. He took the key from Thorndyke, and having tried it with the same result, stood up and stared, round-eyed, at my colleague.

"Well!" he exclaimed. "This is a facer! It's the wrong key!"

"There may be another key on the body," said Thorndyke. "It isn't likely, but you had better make sure."

The sergeant showed no reluctance this time. He searched the dead man's pockets thoroughly and produced a bunch of keys. But they were all quite small keys, none of them in the least resembling that of the hut door. Nor, I noticed, did they include those of the bungalow door or the garden gate. Once more the officer drew himself up and stared at Thorndyke.

"There's something rather fishy about this affair," said he.

"There is," Thorndyke agreed. "The door was certainly locked; and as it was not locked from within, it must have been locked from without. Then that key – the wrong key – was presumably put in the dead man's pocket by some other person. And there are some other suspicious facts. A tumbler has disappeared from the bedside table, and there is a tumbler here. You notice one or two spots of candle-grease on the floor here, and it looks as if a candle had been stood in that corner near the door. There is no candle here now; but in the bedroom there is a candle which has been carried without a candlestick and which, by the way, bears an excellent impression of a thumb. The first thing to do will be to take the deceased's fingerprints. Would you mind fetching my case from the bedroom, Jardine?"

I ran back to the house (not unobserved by the gentleman in the next bungalow) and, catching up the case, carried it down to the hut. When I arrived there I found Thorndyke holding the tumbler delicately in his gloved left hand while he examined it against the light with the aid of his lens. He handed the latter to me and observed:

"If you look at this carefully, Jardine, you will see a very interesting thing. There are the prints of two different thumbs – both left thumbs, and therefore of different persons. You will remember that the tumbler stood by the right hand of the body and that the table, which bore the mark of a tumbler, was at the left-hand side of the bed."

When I had examined the thumb-prints he placed the tumbler carefully on the floor and opened his "research case," which was fitted as a sort of portable laboratory. From this he took a little brass box containing an ink-tube, a tiny roller and some small cards, and, using the box-lid as an inking-plate, he proceeded methodically to take the dead man's fingerprints, writing the particulars on each card.

"I don't quite see what you want with Crofton's fingerprints," said I. "The other man's would be more to the point."

"Undoubtedly," Thorndyke replied. "But we have to prove that they are another man's – that they are not Crofton's. And there is that print on the candle. That is a very important point to settle; and as we have finished here, we had better go and settle it at once."

He closed his case, and, taking up the tumbler with his gloved hand, led the way back to the house, the sergeant following when he had locked the door. We proceeded direct to the bedroom, where Thorndyke took the candle from its socket and, with the aid of his lens, compared it carefully with the two thumb-prints on the card, and then with the tumbler.

"It is perfectly clear," said he. "This is a mark of a left thumb. It is totally unlike Crofton's and it appears to be identical with the strange thumb-print on the tumbler. From which it seems to follow that the stranger took the candle from this room to the hut and brought it back. But he probably blew it out before leaving the house and lit it again in the hut."

The sergeant and I examined the cards, the candle and the tumbler, and then the former asked:

"I suppose you have no idea whose thumb-print that might be? You don't know, for instance, of anyone who might have had any motive for making away with Mr Crofton?"

"That," replied Thorndyke, "is rather a question for the coroner's jury."

"So it is," the sergeant agreed. "But there won't be much question about their verdict. It is a pretty clear case of wilful murder."

To this Thorndyke made no reply excepting to give some directions as to the safe-keeping of the candle and tumbler; and our proposed "gipsy holiday" being now evidently impossible, we took our leave of the sergeant – who already had our cards – and wended back to the station.

"I suppose," said I, "we shall have to break the news to Mrs Crofton."

"That is hardly our business," he replied. "We can leave that to the solicitor or to Ambrose. If you know the lawyer's address, you might send him a telegram, arranging a meeting at eight o'clock tonight. Give no particulars. Just say, 'Crofton found,' but mark the telegram 'urgent' so that he will keep the appointment."

On reaching the station, I sent off the telegram, and very soon afterwards the London train was signalled. It turned out to be a slow train, which gave us ample time to discuss the case and me ample time for reflection. And, in fact, I reflected a good deal; for there was a rather uncomfortable question in my mind – the very question that the sergeant had raised and that Thorndyke had obviously evaded. Was there anyone who might have had a motive for making away with Crofton? It was an awkward question when one remembered the great legacy that had just fallen in and the terms of Miss Shuler's will; which expressly provided that, if Crofton died before his wife, the legacy should go to her. Now Ambrose was the wife's brother; and Ambrose had been in the bungalow alone with Crofton, and nobody else was known to have been there at all. I meditated on these facts uncomfortably and would have liked to put the case to Thorndyke; but his reticence, his evasion of the sergeant's question and his decision to communicate with the solicitor rather than with the family, showed pretty clearly what was in his mind and that he did not wish to discuss the matter.

Promptly at eight o'clock, having dined at a restaurant, we presented ourselves at the solicitor's house and were shown into the study, where we found Mr Jobson seated at a writing-table. He looked at Thorndyke with some surprise, and when the introductions had been made, said somewhat dryly:

"We may take it that Dr Thorndyke is in some way connected with our rather confidential business?"

"Certainly," I replied "That is why he is here."

Jobson nodded. "And how is Crofton?" he asked, "and where did you dig him up?"

"I am sorry to say," I replied, "that he is dead. It is a dreadful affair. We found his body locked in the bathing-hut. He was sitting in a corner with a tumbler on the floor by his side."

"Horrible ! horrible !" exclaimed the solicitor. "He ought never to have gone there alone. I said so at the time. And it is most unfortunate on account of the insurance, though that is not a large amount. Still the suicide clause, you know – "

"I doubt whether the insurance will be affected," said Thorndyke. "The coroner's finding will almost certainly be wilful murder."

Jobson was thunderstruck. In a moment his face grew livid and he gazed at Thorndyke with an expression of horrified amazement.

"Murder!" he repeated incredulously. "But you said he was locked in the hut. Surely that is clear proof of suicide."

"He hadn't locked himself in, you know. There was no key inside."

"Ah!" The solicitor spoke almost in a tone of relief. "But, perhaps – did you examine his pockets?"

"Yes; and we found a key labelled 'Bathing Hut.' But it was the wrong key. It wouldn't go into the lock. There is no doubt whatever that the door was locked from the outside."

"Good God!" exclaimed Jobson, in a faint voice. "It does look suspicious. But still, I can't believe – it seems quite incredible."

"That may be," said Thorndyke, "but it is all perfectly clear. There is evidence that a stranger entered the bungalow at night and that the affair took place in the bedroom. From thence the stranger carried the body down to the hut and he also took a tumbler and a candle from the bedside table. By the light of the candle – which was stood on the floor of the hut in a corner – he arranged the body, having put into its pocket a key from the board in the living-room. Then he locked the hut, went back to the house, put the key on its peg and the candle in its candlestick. Then he locked up the house and the garden gate and took the keys away with him."

The solicitor listened to this recital in speechless amazement. At length he asked:

"How long ago do you suppose this happened?"

"Apparently on the night of the fifteenth of this month," was the reply.

"But," objected Jobson, "he wrote home on the sixteenth."

"He wrote," said Thorndyke, "on the sixth. Somebody put a one in front of the six and posted the letter at Margate on the sixteenth. I shall give evidence to that effect at the inquest."

I was becoming somewhat mystified. Thorndyke's dry, stern manner – so different from his usual suavity – and the solicitor's uncalled-for agitation, seemed to hint at something more than met the eye. I watched Jobson as he lit a cigarette – with a small Bryant and May match, which he threw on the floor – and listened expectantly for his next question. At length he asked:

"Was there any sort of clue as to who this stranger might be?"

"The man who will be charged with the murder? Oh, yes. The police have the means of identifying him with absolute certainty."

"That is, if they can find him," said Jobson.

"Naturally. But when all the very remarkable facts have transpired at the inquest, that individual will probably come pretty clearly into view."

Jobson continued to smoke furiously with his eyes fixed on the floor as if he were thinking hard. Presently he asked, without looking up:

"Supposing they do find this man. What then? What evidence is there that he murdered Crofton?"

"You mean direct evidence?" said Thorndyke. "I can't say, as I did not examine the body; but the circumstantial evidence that I have given you would be enough to convict unless there were some convincing explanation other than murder. And I may say," he added, "that if the suspected person has a plausible explanation to offer, he would be well advised to produce it before lie is charged. A voluntary statement has a good deal more weight than the same statement made by a prisoner in answer to a charge."

There was an interval of silence, in which I looked in bewilderment from Thorndyke's stern visage to the pale face of the solicitor. At length the latter rose abruptly, and, after one or two quick strides up and down the room, he halted by the fireplace, and, still avoiding Thorndyke's eye, said, somewhat brusquely, though in a low, husky voice:

"I will tell you how it happened. I went down to Seasalter, as you said, on the night of the fifteenth, on the chance of finding Crofton at the bungalow. I wanted to tell him of Miss Shuler's death and of the provisions of her will."

"You had some private information on that subject, I presume?" said Thorndyke.

"Yes. My cousin was her solicitor and he kept me informed about the will."

"And about the state of her health?"

"Yes. Well, when I arrived at the bungalow, it was in darkness. The gate and the front door were unlocked, so I entered, calling out Crofton's name. As no one answered, I struck a match and lit the lamp. Then I went into the bedroom and struck a match there; and by its light I could see Crofton lying on the bed, quite still. I spoke to him, but he did not answer or move. Then I lighted a candle on his table; and now I could see what I had already guessed, that he was dead, and that he had been dead some time-probably more than a week.

"It was an awful shock to find a dead man in this solitary house, and my first impulse was to rush out and give the alarm. But when I went into the living-room, I happened to see a letter lying on the writing-table and noticed that it was in his own handwriting and addressed to his wife. Unfortunately, I had the curiosity to take it out of the unsealed envelope and read it. It was dated the sixth and stated his intention of going to Margate for a time and then coming back to the bungalow.

"Now, the reading of that letter exposed me to an enormous temptation. By simply putting a one in front of the six and thus altering the date from the sixth to the sixteenth and posting the letter at Margate, I stood to gain thirty thousand pounds. I saw that at a glance. But I did not decide immediately to do it. I pulled down all the blinds, drew the curtains and locked up the house while I thought it over. There seemed to be practically no risk, unless some one should come to the bungalow and notice that the state of the body did not agree with the altered date on the letter. I went back and looked at the dead man. There was a burnt-out candle by his side and a tumbler containing the dried-up remains of some brown liquid. He had evidently poisoned himself. Then it occurred to me that, if I put the body and the tumbler in some place where they were not likely to be found for some time, the discrepancy between the condition of the body and the date of the letter would not be noticed.

"For some time I could think of no suitable place, but at last I remembered the bathing-hut. No one would look there for him. If they came to the bungalow and didn't find him there, they would merely conclude that he had not come back from Margate. I took the candle and the key from the key-board and went down to the hut; but there was a key in the door already, so I brought the other key back and put it in Crofton's pocket, never dreaming that it might not be the duplicate. Of course, I ought to have tried it in the door.

"Well, you know the rest. I took the body down, about two in the morning, locked up the hut, brought away the key and hung it on the board, took the counterpane off the bed, as it had some marks on it, and re-made the bed with the blanket outside. In the morning I took the train to Margate, posted the letter, after altering the date, and threw the gate-key and that of the front door into the sea.

"That is what really happened. You may not believe me; but I think you will as you have seen the body and will realise that I had no motive for killing Crofton before the fifteenth, whereas Crofton evidently died before that date."

"I would not say 'evidently,' " said Thorndyke; "but, as the date of his death is the vital point in your defence, you would be wise to notify the coroner of the importance of the issue."

"I don't understand this case," I said, as we walked homewards (I was spending the evening with Thorndyke). "You seemed to smell a rat from the very first. And I don't see how you spotted Jobson. It is a mystery to me."

"It wouldn't be if you were a lawyer," he replied. "The case against Jobson was contained in what you told me at our first interview. You yourself commented on the peculiarity of the will that he drafted for Crofton. The intention of the latter was to leave all his property to his wife. But instead of saying so, the will specified each item of property, and appointed a residuary legatee, which was Jobson himself. This might have appeared like mere legal verbiage; but when Miss Shuler's legacy was announced, the transaction took on a rather different aspect. For this legacy was not among the items specified in the will. Therefore it did not go to Mrs Crofton. It would be included in the residue of the estate and would go to the residuary legatee – Jobson."

"The deuce it would!" I exclaimed.

"Certainly; until Crofton revoked his will or made a fresh one. This was rather suspicious. It suggested that Jobson had private information as to Miss Shuler's will and had drafted Crofton's will in accordance with it; and as she died of malignant disease, her doctor must have known for some time that she was dying and it looked like Jobson had information on that point, too. Now the position of affairs that you described to was this: Crofton, a possible suicide, had disappeared and had made no fresh will.

"Miss Shuler died on the thirteenth, leaving thirty thousand pounds to Crofton, if he survived or if he did not, then to Mrs Crofton. The important question then was whether Crofton was alive or dead; and if he was dead, whether he died before or after the thirteenth. For if he died before the thirteenth the legacy went to Mrs Crofton, but if he died after that date the legacy went to Jobson.

"Then you showed me that extraordinarily opportune letter dated the sixteenth. Now, seeing that date was worth thirty thousand pounds to Jobson, I naturally scrutinised it narrowly. The letter was written with ordinary blue-black ink. This ink, even in the open, takes about a fortnight to blacken completely. In a closed envelope takes considerably longer. On examining this through a lens, the one was very perceptibly bluer than the six. It had therefore been added later. But for what reason? And by whom?

"The only possible reason was that Crofton was dead and had died before the thirteenth. The only person who had any motive for making the alteration was Jobson. Therefore, when we started for Seasalter I already felt sure that Crofton was dead and that the letter had been posted at Margate by Jobson. I had further no doubt that Crofton's body was concealed somewhere on the premises of the bungalow. All that I had to do was to verify those conclusions."

"Then you believe that Jobson has told us the truth?"

"Yes. But I suspect that he went down there with the deliberate intention of making away with Crofton before he could make a fresh will. The finding of Crofton's body must have been a fearful disappointment, but I must admit that he showed considerable resource in dealing with the situation; and he failed only by the merest chance. I think his defence against the murder charge will be admitted; but, of course, it will involve a plea of guilty to the charge of fraud in connection with the legacy."

Thorndyke's forecast turned out to be correct. Jobson was acquitted of the murder of Arthur Crofton, but is at present "doing time" in respect of the forged letter and the rest of his too-ingenious scheme.

R Austin Freeman

The D'Arblay Mystery
A Dr Thorndyke Mystery

When a man is found floating beneath the skin of a green-skimmed pond one morning, Dr Thorndyke becomes embroiled in an astonishing case. This wickedly entertaining detective fiction reveals that the victim was murdered through a lethal injection and someone out there is trying a cover-up.

Dr Thorndyke Intervenes
A Dr Thorndyke Mystery

What would you do if you opened a package to find a man's head? What would you do if the headless corpse had been swapped for a case of bullion? What would you do if you knew a brutal murderer was out there, somewhere, and waiting for you? Some people would run. Dr Thorndyke intervenes.

R Austin Freeman

Felo De Se
A Dr Thorndyke Mystery

John Gillam was a gambler. John Gillam faced financial ruin and was the victim of a sinister blackmail attempt. John Gillam is now dead. In this exceptional mystery, Dr Thorndyke is brought in to untangle the secrecy surrounding the death of John Gillam, a man not known for insanity and thoughts of suicide.

Flighty Phyllis

Chronicling the adventures and misadventures of Phyllis Dudley, Richard Austin Freeman brings to life a charming character always getting into scrapes. From impersonating a man to discovering mysterious trapdoors, *Flighty Phyllis* is an entertaining glimpse at the times and trials of a wayward woman.

R Austin Freeman

Helen Vardon's Confession
A Dr Thorndyke Mystery

Through the open door of a library, Helen Vardon hears an argument that changes her life forever. Helen's father and a man called Otway argue over missing funds in a trust one night. Otway proposes a marriage between him and Helen in exchange for his co-operation and silence. What transpires is a captivating tale of blackmail, fraud and death. Dr Thorndyke is left to piece together the clues in this enticing mystery.

Mr Pottermack's Oversight

Mr Pottermack is a law-abiding, settled homebody who has nothing to hide until the appearance of the shadowy Lewison, a gambler and blackmailer with an incredible story. It appears that Pottermack is in fact a runaway prisoner, convicted of fraud, and Lewison is about to spill the beans unless he receives a large bribe in return for his silence. But Pottermack protests his innocence, and resolves to shut Lewison up once and for all. Will he do it? And if he does, will he get away with it?

Made in the USA
Lexington, KY
11 March 2013